calum lefleur

Goalie

THE
Keeper

dedication

THE FLOWER

There is only one.

1
all kinds of cocky

Cal

Max Terry's office is just about what you'd expect from the owner of a championship-level sports team. Impressive wide windows that look out and down on the world below. Furnishings are crisp and clean. The art lit in a way that communicates it's expensive. It's the kind of space that makes you feel either totally important or completely intimidated, depending on the situation.

I think I'm supposed to feel important.

Leaning forward on an off-white leather couch, elbows on my thighs, hands propping my head up, I might fall asleep.

Dell Richards, my agent, sits to my left, one leg crossed over the other as he scans his phone for emails.

"Fuckin' time difference," he mutters. "Fuckin' asshole put a call on my calendar for six in the morning. I told him I was two hours early out here."

"How long do we wait before I call forfeit and head back to Montreal?" I ask, impatient to get this over with.

Dell cuts me a sideways glance. "They're only five minutes late, Cal. Chill."

"I don't want to be here. Seriously, get me out of this bullshit deal, Dell."

"This *bullshit deal*, as you call it, is worth many millions of dollars. It's not some offload trade, Cal. They needed a goalie in a pinch, and they wanted the best, so they paid for it. That's the way the business works. Grow the fuck up."

Grow up. Not the first time I've heard that statement. What he means is stop complaining. Stop complaining you had to leave your family and your home and your life to come to this unfamiliar place with an unfamiliar team you didn't want to join in the first place. Yeah, I get it, this team is a powerhouse. The best in the business. They have some of the hottest players on the ice right now, and they want one more trophy to add to their case.

"You sticking around long after this?" I ask.

"I've got this god-forsaken morning call and then I head to the airport," he says. "Got to get back to New York for a charity thing."

We're quiet for another minute before I ask, "Did you know Scott Rose represents like a third of this team?"

"Do not utter that name in front of me, Calum Lefleur," he says sharply, putting his phone down to give me a full-on death stare. "You know better."

"Just saying. Perhaps Scott Rose could have kept me where I wanted to be."

"I'm not fucking joking, Cal. Stop saying his name."

Dell Richards and Scott Rose do not get along. They're both high-powered agents with full rosters. I heard there was some beef over a client that left one and went to the other at some point, but I don't know the details. I also don't care all that much. It's more that I find it rather fun to mess with Dell when I'm bored.

Just as I'm about to nudge him again, Max Terry, Coach Brown, and the weird, schlubby-looking GM file in.

Max is all silver hair and white teeth as he extends a hand. "So sorry to keep you waiting up here," he says, smiling as I shake his hand. "You're the boy wonder. Thanks for filling in for us in a pinch."

"Well, I didn't have much of a choice," I say as the three men all find seats around the stainless steel and glass coffee table bearing several magazines with Crush players on the covers.

They all laugh like I've made a joke. It's not a joke. I was told I was being traded. Now I'm here.

"You played a hell of a series last spring," Coach Brown says. "We were damn impressed by you, coaching staff and players alike, so we're glad you're here. We think you'll come to love Las Vegas as much as we all do."

"I can't lie. I've been playing for Montreal since I was eighteen, and I've been happy there. I know I'm good, and the money here proves that. I'll play my best, but it doesn't mean I'm happy to be here." I give each of them direct eye contact, even though it's a conscious effort for me to deliver. Eye contact is not really a strength of mine.

Dell sighs and shakes his head. He's pinching the bridge of his nose between his fingertips. I look back to the three Crush leaders and find the GM's mouth hanging open and Coach sitting back in his chair, arms folded, quizzical expression on his face.

Max Terry chuckles and shakes his head slowly from side to side. "Kid, I've seen all kinds of cocky. All kinds of attitude and prima donna behavior, believe me. Cocky I can handle, but we just dumped a shit-ton of money into your bank account and while I appreciate the honesty, you're about to drop over into an unacceptable level of arrogance."

"He's not being arrogant," Dell offers. "He lacks the ability to be polite just for the sake of being polite."

"I'm being *honest*." And I am. This is unfiltered me. Calum Lefleur, who says whatever's on his mind. I don't know any other way to be. I've always been like this.

Just then, the door to the office suite opens, and Evan Kazmeirowicz, Crush winger and team captain, walks in. He's tall and muscular with an annoying, slick-looking undercut and a boyish smile. He's fit and effective on the ice still, even though he's getting kind of long in the tooth for professional sports, in my opinion.

I'll hand it to him—he reads a room a lot faster than I ever could. His smile dissipates as he looks from

Max to Coach to the GM, whose name I can't even remember.

"Looks like I missed the fun part of the party," he comments, walking over to hold out a hand. As we shake, he adds, "Ready for a tour, new guy?"

New guy. That's me. I'm the new guy. Never in a million years did I believe I'd be the "new guy" somewhere this season, but here I fuckin' am. I stand and nod, ready to just be out of this room. Maybe seeing the ice and the locker room will help me feel a sense of routine. Maybe it will feel real somehow. *Acceptable.*

Dell salutes me as he starts a conversation about my bonus contracts. I should probably say something. Thank them or something. But nothing comes out as I shove my hands in the pockets of my jacket and follow Evan, in all his calm confidence, out the door.

We walk down a dark, administrative hallway, and it's not until we come to an elevator that Evan says, "I take it you weren't expecting a trade?"

"I heard your goalie got hurt or something. But no, I did not want *this* trade."

"Trades happen all the time. It's part of the business," Evan says as we step onto the elevator. "Seven years is a long time at one club."

"No reason to trade me though," I say with a shrug. "I performed well for them. Solid."

"Solid doesn't mean there isn't a reason to trade. Maybe they felt it was time for you to grow and you growing meant someone on the bench could grow, too. Maybe they wanted to make up some space in the salary cap for the development of new talent and the bench was strong enough to lose you to make it happen. Shit happens all the time. None of us are indispensable."

"I was."

"That's arrogant as hell, dude," Evan says, laughing and shaking his head.

"It is what it is. I was performing there. I wanted to be there. No reason to send me packing."

"Well, I'm sorry your feelings got hurt. But we're a good club. We work hard. Some of us play hard. But when we're on the ice we are pros, and we expect you to fall in line with that."

"I mean, yeah, I'll do the work. Doesn't mean I have to like being here."

"So, you're coming in with a massive contract, right? Like, millions?" Evan asks as we walk down a ramp, presumably to the ice.

I don't answer him until we step out onto the ice. "Yeah. It's a good contract."

"Look...what do I call you? Calum?"

"Cal."

"Look, Cal," he says with a soft shake of his head, "there are guys who've been playing their asses off, second string, every damn year, making far, far less than you. Guys who come in with a good attitude, happy to play, happy to suit up even though they know they'll get very little ice time. And they never complain. You need to see the big picture here. You're getting paid millions to do a thing you love and you're good at. You get to do it with a team of guys who've killed it the past few seasons in a city where it's never, ever boring. Do your time. Prove your worth. Then go back in a couple years if that's where you want to retire."

"Retire?" I ask with a disbelieving laugh. "I'm twenty-six. You're the one who looks like you might be past your expiration date."

Evan smirks, unaffected. "That may be true, but I scored on you a few times in the finals, I think. Slap-shot ring a bell for you? Is my old-man memory working right?"

I bite the inside of my lip, not willing to confirm or deny that he scored on me in the finals. He winks and says, "Come on, man, let's go see the weight rooms and PT clinic."

Hmm. Straight shooter.

You're getting paid millions to do a thing you love and you're good at. You get to do it with a team of guys who've killed it the past few seasons. Do your time. Prove your worth. He makes sense. I might like Evan Kazmeirowicz...*a little.* I still don't want to be here, but at least the team captain isn't a total wanker.

2

love scrum

Billie

The last fifteen seconds of the song is all drums as I smash out the outro with a combination of kick drum, rack tom, and ride cymbal that absolutely rocks.

As I finish, the only sound in the space is the last ting from the cymbal. I let it dissipate on its own before looking to the guys to see what they think.

"Wicked," my bandmate Sven says with a nod. "A new combo?"

"Yeah, I thought it had a Killers kind of vibe. What did you think?"

"It was solid," Nikki, our bass player, says.

"Stuart gonna let us get a few extra practices in?" Sven asks, changing the subject. He's scribbling something in his notebook, probably something about the new combo, though who knows. He's our guitarist and singer so scribbling lyrics and changes is standard operating procedure for him.

Love Scrum is our name. I kind of hate it but

whatever. Sven came up with it, and there's some existential, pretentious explanation for it that I don't bother with at all. He's a serious artist and all.

"I don't see why not," I answer, referring to the use of this warehouse space my best friend Stuart lets us use twice a week for practice.

I look around at all of the Las Vegas detritus around us. Big boxes of costume headdresses and glittery bra thingies. There's a whole section of clear bins filled with top hats. It's a crazy place, the kind of crazy place you'd only find in Vegas. And Stuart's job is to manage this beast, assuring each costume item is in its proper home for when the show runners come knocking. Most evenings it's not busy so we can make all the noise we want.

Love Scrum has a big show coming up in a couple of months, opening for a popular alternative rock band at a three-day festival. We're pretty stoked because it's the biggest show we've done yet. Normally we play local clubs, no big deal, but we got this invitation, and now Sven is out of his mind trying to prep for it.

And out of his mind about the implications of it.

Cue his nearly daily questioning.

"So, Billie, when are you planning on telling your family about this little experiment?"

I hit myself in the head with my drumstick.

"I'm surprised he made it this long," Nikki says, tuning her bass.

"Sven, you made it two whole hours before asking me the question. I'm impressed."

"Seriously, Billie."

"What they don't know won't hurt them." I attempt shrugging him off as usual.

"Yeah, but what they don't know might be hurting the band. Your family is super fucking connected. They could probably get us an agent, a deal, a whatever—"

"Sven."

"Billie."

"I left LA to get away from all that bullshit. You know this."

"But we're ready"—his eyes blaze over at me with all the intensity of a laser pointer—"all they'd have to do is snap their fingers and we'd have a record deal."

"And I want us to do this on our own merit. Not because they waved their magic wand and made it happen for us."

"Well, we have worked pretty hard," Nikki chimes in.

"Not you too." I groan. "Guys, we got this gig on our own. We don't need my parents pulling strings. Letting them into the mix is like getting into bed with the devil."

"Don't be dramatic," Sven says. "Poor little Billie, who has parents who would give her the world on a silver platter if only she wasn't so damned stubborn."

"Sven"—my voice comes with a tone of warning—"you didn't spend your whole childhood getting toted around like a commodity. I am not allowing them any level of control over my life now or later, and I'm sorry if that makes you upset."

"I'm just saying—"

"That's enough," Nikki says, scolding him. "She's asking you to stop."

Sven scowls but doesn't say anything else.

"If this thing is meant to happen, it'll happen. And speaking of which, I did get us a couple of hours of studio time so we can record a few more tracks. You just have to let me know when you can make time, like on a Sunday or something." There, I've offered an olive branch.

Nikki pulls her technicolor pink hair up on top of her head and says she's usually working at the restaurant on Sunday afternoons, so either morning or late night would work. Thankfully, recording studios are usually twenty-four-hour joints because artists are weird.

"I'm good with whatever," Sven says, dropping the parental lecture for the moment. "What's our set list for the Smiths and Stones Club?"

"I'm thinking let's lead in with 'Force of Nature,'" Nikki suggests. "Get them dancing right off the bat?"

We hammer out a few more ideas, arguing about changes in tempo and flow of songs until we have a set list we can all live with. We want to have at least two new songs for the festival gig, though, so Sven also wants to run through a basic melody he's been kicking around. There's always too much to do and too little time to do it, with only two practice sessions a week. I see why Sven wants more time, and I promise to call Stuart and ask for another day as we futz around with the new song idea.

It's well into the middle of the night when I lock

up and head to my car, waving to my bandmates as I start the engine. They're obnoxious, but they've become like family to me these past couple of years. He may be an emo wretch, but Sven really is a strong storyteller. His lyrics are sick, and the fact that he can play gonzo guitar and sing in his growly, sexy way makes him a total triple threat. He's tall and lanky, and he moves like a cat. His head is shaved down to a dark stubble that matches his five o'clock shadow. He's pretty hot. If he wasn't pretentious as hell, I might have wanted to sleep with him.

Nikki is a total badass. She's actually older than the two of us but you'd never know it by looking at her. She's calm and easy, where Sven can be emotional and intense. Me? Who knows how I fit in. I play the drums. I've got that going for me, at least.

The band's new melody is stuck in my head as I drive back to my apartment, drumming out a beat on my steering wheel.

Stuart, my bestie and practice space hookup, calls me as I pull into my apartment complex parking lot.

"What's up, big bad Stu?" I ask by way of greeting.

"Did you lock up?"

"Of course," I say. "Can we get a little extra time this week? Big show coming up and all."

"I'll check the schedule, but it should be fine."

"Thanks, bae."

"Barf. Who says bae anymore?"

"I don't know. I was trying to be cute."

"You're always cute, but still. Bae?"

"Sorry. Consider the word banned from my vocabulary."

"Well, I was just making sure you made it home okay. The night is dark and full of scarecrows."

"That's not how the line goes, friend."

"You got me. Speaking of which, are you caught up on *Better Call Saul* yet? Can I talk about it yet?"

"No, man. I'm still only on episode three of the final part. I'm so late to that party."

Stuart groans. "I hate you so much. Please go watch copious amounts of television right now."

I laugh. "Okay. I'll talk to you tomorrow." Not a day goes by that I don't thank my lucky stars for Stuart. Friends since middle school, he's like a second brother to me. Well, more trustworthy perhaps than my real brother. We're tight. Platonic friendship. Loyal. I know I'm lucky.

Always a little wired after playing, I head to the kitchen and make a bowl of cereal before sitting down at my laptop to check email. A note from my mom catches my attention. Or, more accurately, creates a pit of anxiety in my stomach. Don't get me wrong, I love my family, no question. They love me. I love them. But I made a choice to hold them at arm's length a long time ago. Consequently, I always get a little anxious when they reach out.

On its face, the email is nothing remarkable. She mentions a production gig she's been working on, then says my dad did the casting. No big surprise there. They work together all the time. Oh, and there is my brother, magically getting cast in the lead role. One, two, three Hirsch family members all in league on this one movie together. Ugh.

There's a reason I don't want my family to sprinkle

the magical fairy dust and make Sven's dreams come true. They can't stop once they start. They are well-meaning, truly. They just want the people they love to be successful. But it's suffocating. And somehow, even though it often starts out looking like what you might want, it always goes down some other path toward whatever ulterior motive they had. It's never like, *Oh, Billie is a good drummer, and her band wants to get a record deal.* No, it's like, *Billie is now going to be remade into the Ariana Grande of drumming and she'll have a record deal, but some pop-music asshole will be writing her songs, and once she delivers an album, she'll also be in a television show and blah, blah, blah.*

Yeah, it's like that. I speak from years of experience and the resulting therapy sessions to back it up.

Okay, so I read through all the family business garbage before finding the actual point of the email. It's coming up on my father's sixtieth birthday and my mom is throwing a "little party." A loose term indeed because this "little party" will probably be a who's who of Hollywood, including my brother Kit—think Leo DiCaprio-esque to his generation of actors. He's hot shit right now, so everyone who's anyone will want the chance to party with him, even under the guise of celebrating my casting director father's sixtieth trip around the sun.

Fucking wonderful. Sounds just like how I want to spend a Saturday night. *Not.* Reluctantly, and only because I really do love my family, I write back and tell her I'll be there. I block it in my band's calendar so we don't book any gigs for that night.

She replies almost instantly because she's rarely

without access to her email. *Will you be bringing a date? Do you want me to set up hair and makeup for you?*

Oh. My. God.

And people wonder why I don't want to see my family all that often.

3

hot-sh!t goalie from montreal

Cal

We're all lined up on the ice in our practice gear, leaning on our sticks while Coach goes through a long list of housekeeping items. Everything from the parental "Clean up after yourselves in the locker room" to the more motivational "I defy anyone who thinks they can get through our first-line this season."

I'm standing at the edge of the group, and nobody has paid me much attention so far, not even while we were suiting up. Evan gave a nod, but that was about it.

Coach changes all that, though. He says, "You all know Manny is recuperating nicely after his car accident. I think most of you have been over to see him in the rehab facility, and I know he really appreciates that. He's got about three weeks of inpatient time left before he can head home, and then probably twelve weeks of outpatient therapy after that."

"Is he coming back, Coach?" someone asks.

Coach shakes his head, a sad expression on his face. "Unfortunately, I think his hockey days are over, boys. His knee was shattered, and the head injury just added another layer. He can't be crouching down, willing pucks to fly at his head. He may come back to work for us in the front office, and we'd be glad to have him, but not on the ice. It's early retirement for Manny."

Poor fucker. That's depressing shit to be forced out of the game early. There's a chorus of sounds. Some disappointed, some sad. Either way, it's obvious that Emanuel Legace was a beloved goalie among his Crush teammates. He was in a near-fatal car accident over the summer, one he wasn't initially expected to survive. That accident is the reason I'm here, the reason I was abruptly traded.

I'm contemplating how it all went down when I hear my name.

"He nearly stopped us from winning that Cup," Coach says. "His innate ability to predict the angle of a shot so accurately is second to none. I'm sure many of you have been frustrated in the past by his often-impossible stops." Anyone would think Coach is genuinely happy to have me. That the team will share his enthusiasm. *I doubt it.* "Everyone, say hello to Calum Lefleur, hot-shit goalie from Montreal, here to stop all the shots and help us retain our title."

There's a series of grunts and nods. A few guys tap their sticks on the ice. I look at all of them without making eye contact. Well, I make eye contact with Dante Castellano, the dark-haired wall of a second-string goalie who saw all of about thirty minutes of ice time last season. In fact, our eye contact consists pretty much of me smirking at him and him responding with a middle finger shot in my direction. Just about the reception I'd expect from a guy who was probably hoping I'd die in a plane crash on the way here.

Coach gives a few more notes then tells everyone to pair up for skills training. I'm paired with starting left wing Mikhail. I noticed him earlier in the locker room...scowling. "I remember you from the finals," I say.

To which he swears at me in a language I don't recognize. I look around to find Evan laughing and shaking his head. "He's prickly on a good day, new guy. Don't take it personally."

I pull on my mask and take my spot in front of the goal. Mikhail doesn't speak; he just starts lobbing shots like he's firing the pucks from a baseball pitching machine. I've taken his shots in games, and I know how fast and accurate he can be. He's somewhat inconsistent though, which is why he's never taken the top spot among scorers like center forward Boris or right wing Evan. Still, he's riled up today, which means everything is coming straight at me, like he's willingly trying to take my head off.

And maybe he is.

Still, by the end of the skill set, I'm sweating and bruised and feeling a bit like a punching bag. Mikhail gives me a nod, so I guess I did okay against him, but he still doesn't speak to me.

"Does he speak English?" I ask the next guy who comes up to level shots at me.

"Yeah, dumbass," the blond guy says as he drops the puck in front of his stick. I remember him from the conference series. Defenseman who likes to fight. "He's from Detroit."

"Oh." I digest that information. "He swore at me in what I guessed could be Russian."

The guy laughs. "Czech actually. First-generation parents but he's an American hockey player if you can believe it. I have a thing for second-language chirps. My personal favorite is the Russian *mudak*, which just means, like, shithead or something."

"Well, I'm from Canada, so most of the second-language swearing happens in French."

He shoots at me. It's wildly off target and he just sort of shrugs. "I'm Tyler, by the way,"

"Defenseman. I remember you from the finals."

He takes a few more shots and then announces that he needs a water break. I finish out the skills sessions and we move into a scrimmage formation with me at one end and Dante at the other. *That's an impressive stink-eye, Castello.* Not that I give a shit.

Clearly, he's pissed off though, as he follows me straight into the locker room after practice, getting up in my grill before I can even fully turn around to face him.

"This is bullshit, you know," he says, teeth bared, finger pointing into my face. "You just waltz in here and take a spot I've been waiting on for three years? And you get a contract no kid your age should have?"

All I can do is shrug. What can I do about it? "First, I don't want to be here, and I'd gladly have not come if I'd been given a choice. Second, don't you think the contract would've been yours if they thought you were good enough?"

Dante's fist sails past my head and slams into the metal with a satisfying crunch before he turns and stalks off.

The defenseman Tyler snickers. "What a little bitch."

I don't know if he's talking about Dante or me. Well, what the hell ever. I'm not here to make friends. I'm here to do my job. But it certainly wasn't the first day I expected. *Nothing feels right, and probably won't for a long time.*

When I get home, I'm beat and lonely and feeling totally out of sorts. I'm very routine-oriented, and I'm nowhere close to figuring out a routine here in Vegas, which makes me feel comfortable. As a result, it feels a little like I'm wearing skin that doesn't quite fit my bones. I need to talk to someone who knows me, so I call my girlfriend, Emily.

"Hey," she answers.

"Hey, Em. How was today?"

"Mostly spent at the library," she says. "Research day."

"Ah, and how'd that go?"

"Fine. Tedious."

"Sorry to hear that. I had about a thousand shots lobbed at my face in practice."

"That sounds like a normal day in the life of Cal," she says distractedly.

"Half of the guys seem like they genuinely wanted to slice my head off with a puck. Especially the second-string goalie."

"Well, that one makes sense."

"I guess."

"Do you like it there?"

"No," I say sharply. "I hate it. It's too hot."

"And it's unfamiliar. The people. The places. You're not good with change."

"All true. And I miss you."

"Aw. I miss you too."

"Can I fly you in for the weekend?" I ask. "Friday night to Sunday night maybe?"

"Sorry, babe," she says. "This isn't a good week. I've got a hard deadline for Monday afternoon on the first section of my thesis project."

A long silence stretches between us. I can hear her fingers flying over the keyboard of her laptop. She's multi-tasking. I'm used to the sound because she was always working on her laptop, often while we were in bed together at night. She'd be working, I'd be watching video replays. It was familiar, and the sound calms me a little even now when we're so far away, but at the same time annoys me she's working when we have only this small amount of time to talk.

"Maybe I'll make a countdown clock," I say to fill the silence. "Days until you finish your master's degree and can move here to be with me."

She lets out a vacant laugh. "Why would I move to Vegas? You just said you hated it there."

"Okay, then, a countdown clock until this contract is up and I'm a free agent, then, and I can come back home."

She doesn't answer. Obviously, she's focused on

something else. I still hear the click of typing in the background.

"I know we can make this work, Em." I say the words even though she didn't do a thing to indicate otherwise. At least, not in this conversation.

It's something I've been saying since we got the news of the trade. *We can make it work. It's only for a little while. We'll figure it out.*

The truth? Emily wanted to break up immediately. She said it would be too hard to make it work if we lived so far away from each other. Still, I was sure this wouldn't be permanent, that I'd find a way back home again. I told her she was important to me, and I convinced her we should give it a go. Frankly, my travel schedule and her school schedule meant we hardly saw each other during the season anyway. And with my new contract, I'd be making enough to fly either one of us back or forth whenever possible. I assured her it wasn't a forever thing, me being here in Vegas. That she needed me. That I *needed* her.

And I do. She knows me. Knows my routine and my quirks. I feel more comfortable when she's around. More...*whole.*

"We can, Em. I truly believe—"

"You keep saying that, Cal. And I know lots of people do the long-distance thing all the time. I just... don't know if I can do this with you."

"No, Em, you can. *We* can. This is just new. We'll figure it out."

Emily sighs. It's the sigh I most dislike. For some time now, I've heard that sigh regularly. And it's normally followed by an exit, whether it be in person or over the phone. *Am I really the only one in this relationship who thinks we can make it?* "Whatever you say. I've got to run. There's a study group in thirty minutes and I need the feedback on my research methodology homework."

"Okay, cool, I'll call you tomorrow. Same time."

"Okay, Cal."

"I love y—"

The line is dead before I can finish. Panic crawls up my insides as I try to figure out just how the hell my life has become utter shit. How the hell did I go from knowing what's in front of me to being stranded in a city I don't know, away from all the people I care about, with a team that doesn't seem to want me? This is all too...new. Too...different. And my girlfriend? *She's made it clear how much she doesn't want me.* Fuck, surely, I don't have to lose her too.

And it's not just because I'm a creature of habit. I love Emily. We're good together, having spent nearly three years together. How can she want to end things as if I'm so easy to discard? Right now, the *only* comfort I have is the game of hockey.

Times like these, when I'm feeling out of sorts, I'd head to my mom's place. Instead, I have to text her, and thank fuck, she responds quickly. As usual. *Some things never change.*

She knows me, knows when I need attention. She tells me all the right things. I'll find a routine in Vegas, too. It will just take time. This is good for the long-term, as I can save money, and then when I'm a free agent, I can play wherever without worrying about the payday. It's short term. It will be okay.

I wish I had her confidence. But do I want to live my life just waiting for it to be *okay*?

> Mom: Have you been playing your guitar?

I look over and see it sitting in the corner of my living room.

> Cal: No. I haven't played since I've been here. Been busy.

> Mom: Hook it up and play, Cal. It's what you love. It's what soothes you.

She's not wrong. That and Emily are what keep me calm on a normal day.

> Mom: Why don't you find a place that has good live music?

I ponder that for a moment. This *is* Las Vegas. Not everyone will know me here, so I could probably head to a bar and see who's playing.

> Cal: Good idea. Thanks, Mom.

> Mom: How's Emily? Busy with her master's, I bet. When is she coming to see you?

Annnnd there's the kicker. I can't tell my mom the truth that I'm pretty certain Emily won't ever be visiting me.

Cal: You're right. She's pretty busy at the moment with her studies, but I'm sure she'll come out to see me soon.

Mom: There you go. Vegas will feel like home for you in no time. Be patient. I love you.

Cal: Love you too, Mom. Thanks for the chat.

But when we finish our conversation, I sit in silence, knowing two things that I couldn't tell my mom.

I can't see Vegas ever feeling like home.

And things are anything but fine with my girlfriend.

4

crush foundation music workshop

Billie

This kid named Andre is begging me to teach him to play drums. I'm in my office at my day job, where I'm program director for the local boys and girls club at Children's Services Las Vegas, and Andre has somehow found out that I'm a drummer.

"My sister says you're, like, a crazy good drummer, Ms. Hirsch. She saw you light it up at Goldberg's a couple weeks ago."

"I cannot confirm or deny, Andre."

"Well, I'm just sayin' you *gotta* teach me now," he says, bouncing back and forth on his heels. He's tall and skinny with a carefully shaped afro and warm, dark eyes.

"I don't *gotta* do *nothin'*, my guy." I'm grinning so he knows I'm joking.

"Please, Ms. Hirsch," he says, putting his hands together as if in prayer. "I really want to learn."

"How are your summer school classes looking?"

"Good. Two Bs. Please, Ms. Hirsch. *Please.*"

"Oh, since you said please three times *and* you're doing well in your classes, I guess I'll talk to my boss to see if we can get some kind of music thing going."

"Yasss!" Andre pumps his arm in celebration.

"Okay, get gone, I've got work to do." I gesture him away gently.

He bounds off and my heart stays warm for a long time afterward. I really do love my job. I love playing drums in a band, but I also really, really love working with these kids. My parents—practically Hollywood royalty—look way down their noses at my social work degree and my low-paying nonprofit job. Frankly, their disdain is part of the appeal, but only a small part. The kids who come here are kids who might not get dinner otherwise or homework help. Their parents may work several jobs to make ends meet. Some of them are functionally homeless. It can be hard to see kids struggling, but it's also rewarding to see them succeed. It never ceases to amaze me how different a child can be, how well they can do, when there's an adult in their corner. Someone who believes in them, interacts with them, and shows genuine interest in their welfare.

After a quick lunch at my desk, I head in to see my boss, Tara, who runs this place. She's just over forty, I think, with a shoulder-length bob that falls in messy waves. She's pretty. Trendy. Fit. Seems to mostly have it together. She works hard but not in a crazy, workaholic kind of way. I like her.

"What's up?" she asks, not taking her eyes from her computer as I walk in.

"Andre wants me to teach him to play drums."

She laughs and looks up at me. "That kid has big dreams."

"He does. And I could certainly lug my kit in here to teach him, but I'm wondering if there might be other kids who would like to learn an instrument."

"I mean, there probably are. What do you have in mind?"

"I'm thinking we could create a music education program. Maybe start out with basic lessons. Drum kit, bass guitar, electric guitar, keyboard, and whatnot. Then maybe like a rock camp kind of thing where kids can get together and make their own music...maybe?"

"That sounds like quite an endeavor. And expensive," Tara says. "We don't have it in the budget to buy a bunch of instruments."

"There may be a couple of lending libraries in town where kids would check out an instrument for a week or two for home to practice. I can check into that part, but yeah, we'd need a stash for here, too. And you're right, it could be expensive, but not prohibitively so, I don't think. And I was thinking there could be some donors who might be willing to sponsor something like this? I mean, you're the fundraiser, so you tell me, but we have a lot of people interested in music in this town, so..."

"Well, put some ideas down on paper and let me know what your vision is. I like the concept, generally, especially if we could tie it to some minor celebrity or something."

"Speaking of which"—I wiggle a finger back and

forth at her—"why didn't you mention the Crush Foundation called?"

"Indeed, they did." Tara drops her head in mock defeat. "I just got busy with other stuff, but the gist of it is they want to start doing more visible partnership with youth-focused organizations. It's a total PR thing and they picked us as one of the charities. I think they want to engage players and their families where it makes sense but will also allow the guys to engage in ways that are meaningful to them."

"Do we get any money out of it? I mean, it's cool they want to partner but arranging PR events isn't really helping the kids. Not in any tangible way, anyway. Sorry to be crass about it. It just sounds like a lot of work for not a lot of payoff."

She laughs. "Spoken like a person not easily starstruck."

"You don't know the half of it," I mutter.

"I'm hoping we get a nice fat check for programming out of it, and your concern is valid. We can't be putting a bunch of human capital behind something with one-sided value. But hey, maybe there's a way to work in your new music program idea? Instruments cost money, right? The Crush Foundation Music Workshop has a nice ring to it, right?"

"Not bad, I admit."

"Well, why don't you give them a call and set up time to talk? Explore their ideas, pitch yours. See where it goes?"

"Will do, boss." I've seen how sports teams schmooze at elite events over the years. My family plays that particular game well, too. And if the Crush want to start being more visibly involved with youth-focused organizations, what could be better than investing in kids who desperately need to be seen like they do here at CSLV? I've learned how to pitch deals and love the kids here too much not to try. The more I think about it, the more I believe this could work if I pitch it to them the right way. *I want to make a difference.* "Thanks for the go-ahead."

She gives a thumbs-up as she answers an incoming call, and I head out, determined to find the funding necessary to get this music program off the ground.

5

i like music

Cal

"We want the community to get to know you," the redhead Scarlett is saying. "Let them connect with you. As the new guy on the team, we have a unique opportunity to build some excitement around a position that doesn't get as much love as some of the others."

"Perhaps not here, but in Montreal, the goalie position was highly valued," I explain.

"It *is* valued," Scarlett says, "but we have two of the top scorers in the league at center forward and right wing. Evan and Boris are legends, and Georg, Tyler, and Viktor are highly recognizable figures on defense, as well."

"Then Emanuel Legace must not have been very dynamic."

"He was—*is*—a really great guy. Despite the fact he's headed for the Hall of Fame in time—everyone with even half a hockey brain knows that," she says sharply.

I recognize that tone. I can be oblivious, but I do know when someone has had enough of me. "I didn't mean to offend you." Given I'm aware that I come across as being cold, speaking coldly at times, I gentle my voice. It's never my intent to be unnecessarily rude, but according to my mom, I can come off that way.

"You didn't, it's just that Manny almost died in that car accident. It was really hard to see him lose his career on top of it." Sadness has replaced her sharp tone.

I don't have a lot to say about that.

"And furthermore, you seem like a guy who would know the stats of his competitors, so surely you've seen what he did when he was here?"

I shrug. "I didn't say he wasn't effective; I said he wasn't *dynamic*. I meant no offense. Some players are steady but don't have the fan base."

She rolls her eyes and shakes her head. "Trust me, Manny has a loyal fan base in this city. You'll find this out for yourself without any need for me to try and convince you," she says in an annoyed tone that tells me she's done being polite regarding critique of the former goalie for the Crush. Got it.

I can tell Scarlett thinks I'm arguing to argue, and I suppose I am. It's something Emily accuses me of doing all the time. I hold up my hands in mock surrender and give her my attention, ready to move on.

"So, tell me about you, Calum—"

"It's Cal," I correct.

"Cal, then. Tell me about you. What do you do for fun?"

"Playing hockey is fun."

"Well, that's a given. But what about when you're not playing hockey? Surely you have some hobbies that don't require ice skates?"

"I like music. Specifically, I like to listen to live music."

"Oh, cool, any particular type?"

"Rock, mostly. And I play the guitar. Just for fun, not in a band or anything."

"That I can use, sir," Scarlett says with renewed interest. "In fact, the program director for Children's Services Las Vegas was just in to meet with the Crush Foundation team, and she pitched them on the idea of a new music workshop for the kids there. We're working on a plan to get you guys out in the community a bit more, and we want you to make an impact and have fun at the same time. Maybe this one would be a good fit for you?"

"A music program for kids?" I mull the idea over in my head, not sure I'm the best choice for making a good impact on kids, but maybe...

"Yep." She nods her head vigorously, her long red curls bouncing with the movement. "I'm thinking we could give them a check to help pay for new instruments and then you could go in and teach guitar lessons once a week or something?"

I scratch my head and think about it for a second. Community service is very much a part of being a high-profile athlete, and I don't mind getting involved if it's something that is less about the athlete and more about what the kids need. I idolized Mario LeBlanc when I was a young player, not only for his skill on the ice, but also how generously he pledged his support to Montreal Children's Hospital. I remember he made a huge impression on me growing up. *Could I help kids in this way?* I guess it could be kind of fun to teach kids how to play. "Sure. I'll give it a shot. Count me in."

"No argument?"

"Nope. It sounds fun."

"Okay, great!" Scarlett claps her hands together. "I'll set something up so you can go over there and plan things out with them. We'll figure out a time to get some video or photos to use for the PR."

"Fine. Anything else?"

"Yep, I need you to go on down to the photography studio to get some pictures taken for marketing. They'll want you in uniform for most of them."

"Helmet?" I ask.

"For a few maybe, but with a head as pretty as yours, I'd say we'll want that front and center in the bulk of the pics."

She's grinning, but I can't tell if she really likes my looks or if she's joking. I stare at her, trying to figure it out, and she grins even wider.

"I'm serious," she says. "Your appeal to the lady fans is sure to be a thing. Puck bunnies and MILF groups make their feelings known on social media, trust me."

"It's not like that for me," I try to explain. And it hasn't been in the past. While attention from females is pretty much a given for any player in the NHL, some get more attention than others based on the effort they put in. I've never put much effort in or been super involved with fans. It makes me uncomfortable mostly, and I don't know where to put the emotions, so I've only ever done the bare minimum. Just the required pressers and those team events I couldn't get out of have been my mainstay all these years. I have zero public social media and it will likely stay at zero in the future. So, I have no idea if the bunnies like me or not.

"Not in the usual sense of a bad-boy reputation, no, but you've got all the elements going for you. Single, as in not married or engaged yet. You're young and ripped in all the right places, and you're hot. I don't mean that to objectify you, Cal," she says, putting her hand up. "I'm just doing my job as director of social media and community liaison for the Vegas Crush. You're not in Kansas anymore. This is Vegas, baby. You're gonna have plennnnnty of attention from the ladies whether you're wanting it or not. And the color of your hair is great. Dark but sporting some caramel highlights. Do you put those highlights in or are they natural?"

"I don't put highlights in my hair," I answer definitively.

"Lucky. And your eyes? The color is so unusual across the general population. Almost a purply blue. Are those contacts making your striking eyes so very blue, Cal?"

"Um...I do *not* wear colored contacts either." I roll my naturally deep blue eyes right back at her. "I was born with these peepers, and I'm offended you would suggest otherwise, Scarlett." I hope she knows I'm just teasing her because I'm not offended in the least. It takes a helluva lot to offend me. My brain doesn't work that way. Feelings, emotions, sharing, caring are not really in my wheelhouse of skill sets. I've been told my eyes are unusual my whole life, so it's not a newsflash or anything.

"Be prepared for 'Blue Eyes' to be your new nickname from your female fans, then. Oh, that reminds me...every player on the team has an emoji. On game days, we post the lineup in emojis instead of names on our social media. What do you want yours to be?"

"Well, Lefleur means—'the flower' in French, so I guess a flower one will do. I don't really care which one. You can decide."

"Ah...perfect. I detect a bit of a French-Canadian accent. Are you fluent in French, Cal?"

"Functionally." I nod my head. "Not fluent in the truest sense, but I can manage a conversation—due to exposure to the language from my extended family and studying it in school, of course. My grandpa was born and raised in northern Quebec and that's where the French last name comes from. My mom's family emigrated from Scotland so I didn't grow up speaking French in the home, even though I can make out conversations for the most part. I don't love doing a post-game presser in French, but playing in Montreal, it was pretty much a requirement there."

She chuckles. "Gotcha. You won't have to do as many pressers for French media here in Vegas, but there are always requests, as I'm sure you know. I just want to make sure I have your bio correct. The fans are going to want to know little details like that about you. No worries at all. Everything you've shared is great.

Let me walk you down and give some direction for the shoot."

As we walk to the photography studio, Scarlett asks how the transition to the Crush has been.

"It's been okay, but I miss home."

"You grew up in Montreal?"

"Nearby, yes. I played in high school. My parents wanted me to go to MIT because I was really good at math and science, but I got picked up right from high school. Played for Canada in the Olympics at eighteen. I've been in Montreal my whole career."

"So, you miss it?"

"Very much."

"Your family is still there?"

"They are. And my girlfriend. She's in school finishing her master's degree."

"She's not coming here?"

"Oh no."

"Not a fan of Sin City?"

"Not really. But neither am I, and I couldn't ask her to make a commitment to a city I don't want to be in."

"Ah. Yeah, I'd heard that about you, that you were loud about the fact that you didn't want this trade. Pretty much everyone knows you don't want to be here, Cal. But I'll give you some advice. If you don't find a reason to care about being here, it will start to affect your relationship with the team."

"A good team will rally for its keeper."

"That may be true," she says, "but it doesn't mean they'll trust you. And if they don't trust you, the fans will see it play out on the ice. Never a good thing."

I'M STILL THINKING about Scarlett's advice when I'm back in my apartment later that night.

She's right, of course.

I need to find a way to connect, especially with the team, but also with the city. I need to be able to answer questions from the press about what I like about Vegas and how I'm making it my home. And even if I didn't want this, it is my lot now, and I need to get okay with it. I might be loud about my disdain for this trade, but I'll still give everything I've got to perform on the ice for the fans.

I need to find a routine here. My calls with Emily are few and far between, and I feel anxious about not having a regular schedule yet, something I'll need to make me feel grounded here in Vegas.

Thinking about this upcoming music workshop at the boys and girls club at Children's Services Las Vegas, I realize I haven't ventured out to check on the live music scene here. I know there are a lot of dance clubs, and that's not my thing, but there have to be some live music clubs, too.

I find an online resource with a listing of live shows and pick one that sounds like it might be rock-oriented. The club is only a few blocks from my apartment building, so I walk there, arriving early enough to see the band setting up to play. Looks like a three-piece unit named Love Scrum. Interesting name since "scrum" is a hockey term for when players scuffle on the ice over the puck. I wonder if they chose the name because Vegas is a big hockey town these days with a two-time Stanley Cup winning NHL team and a Calder Cup winning AHL team all nice and shiny for the city in the desert.

At the bar, I order a beer and wait for the show to start. When it does, the lead singer comes out with a growling, blues-infused rock sound that I like quite a bit. He's a talented guitarist, too. There's a skinny, pink-haired female playing bass guitar, but it's the drummer that captures my attention. Not a ton of female drummers out there so she's unique already.

But I also have eyes, of course, and she is—*striking*.

She's got long, dark hair that looks like a wave of silk, but halfway down, it changes to a dyed bright electric purple. It's in a side braid that hangs down one shoulder to lie between her breasts. Really beautiful. She's got warm olive skin and wide, expressive eyes. She doesn't wear a lot of makeup that I can see, and she's just in a black tank top and jeans. As simply as she's dressed, I can't take my eyes away. And even more so for how badass she is as a musician. Her drumming is complex, sharp, and powerful.

I watch the whole set, which lasts over an hour with mostly original songs, and then stay to give the band a compliment. As they tear down to make room for the next band, I stand off to the side, eyeing the drummer.

"Hey, Billie," the lead singer says, smirking. "Looks like you've got a groupie."

I shake my head. "Not a groupie. Just wanted to tell you all I really enjoyed the set."

"Thanks, man," the lead singer says. "We're Love

Scrum. Playing the Vegas Music Festival soon. You should come out and watch."

"I may. I just moved here, so I'm just checking out the sounds."

"Specifically, the sounds of our lovely drummer?"

I open my mouth, ready to deny it by the excuse of having a girlfriend, when the drummer walks up and says, "Ignore him. He gets jealous that he'll never get to date me."

"Why?" I blurt out. "I mean, why would he never get to date you?"

"Because he's a pretentious clod, that's why." She laughs and it sends a weird spike of energy down through my stomach and into my toes. "You want to go to an after party, new guy?" *What's with everyone in Vegas calling me 'new guy'?* She hits me with the ask as if we're old friends bantering back and forth instead of total strangers.

I should say no. I do have a girlfriend and should go home and call her. I should not go to an after-party with a woman I find incredibly attractive, not just for her looks but also for her talent. It's been a long time since anyone has caught my eye, and while I am quite sure that this drummer is just being nice and not interested in me that way at all, it still seems an unnecessary risk to take her up on this offer.

"I'm not jealous," the lead singer says. "Just for the record."

"Good to know," I say with a nod. "There's no reason to be."

The lead singer smirks, and the drummer busies herself with her kit, her back turned to me. She mutters something, and the lead singer says, "Snap." I have no idea what he means, so I look over at the pink-haired bassist, puzzled.

"You in or out, new guy? We like dragging groupies along with us. The bigger the entourage the more important we look," the bassist says.

"I'm not a—"

"Come or don't, but we've got to clear out," the drummer says sharply. She starts carrying her gear out toward the back door.

My hands start moving, and suddenly...I'm holding drum parts.

I follow her out into an alley behind the club where a white van is parked. As I help load her equipment into the back of the van, words come out of my mouth that seal the deal for me.

"Okay. I'm in."

6
like blue irises

Billie

Ever had a night when everything seemed to go right? Well, that was tonight. First, I got a call saying the Crush Foundation was going to fund my music program and send a player to help teach. Then I had this killer show with my band in a packed house. Then a hot guy came up to compliment us. He sort of shut me down, but still…

I feel like I can't lose tonight and it's making me feel a teensy, tiny bit reckless.

Okay, a lot reckless, if I'm being honest.

I kind of want to make out with that guy.

We ended up at an apartment just off the Strip. Massive and fancy, I'd bet it belongs to a celebrity, but I don't know who. It's super loud, with the bass thumping so hard I can feel it down through my chest. The hot guy told me his name, but I couldn't hear him. It sounded like he said "Valium" which didn't compute. Val… maybe? It's far too loud for talking, so I'm sort of dancing while he stands awkwardly, beer in hand, mostly staring at me. He looks conflicted, for lack of a better description, like he's left the stove on at home and wonders if he should run out and take care of it.

"It seems like you're not into this party!" I yell to him over a Kanye West song.

He looks confused. Okay, so talking is off the table right now. I put my hands up and then point to his hips, playing charades with the guy to get consent to touch him. He looks down, then at my face, then at my hands, before finally shrugging. I take that as a yes and put my hands on his hips, trying to get him to match my movements.

Gads, this guy is awkward. It's not that he doesn't have rhythm. He does, and from the looks of him, he's got a fit, powerful body. The awkwardness isn't about his body. It's more about the way he looks around the room, like the concept of hanging out with a bunch of strangers makes him feel icky or confused.

I motion for him to focus on me, and he manages to do that, his dark, azure-colored eyes remarkably intense as he works to focus his energy in one place. Those unique and striking eyes of his...Just wow. I've never seen eyes his color or intensity of blue. They remind me of the blue irises my mother has grown in her flower garden all my life.

But somehow, when those blues meet my browns, it does the trick. We move our bodies together to the music, my hands now at his hips, our eyes never leaving each other's as we dance.

He never touches me. One hand grasps a beer, the other hangs at his side. But he also doesn't ask me to move my hands, and I wonder if maybe he's just shy. Or this kind of environment isn't his thing. Especially since he's new to town.

Someone walks by with a tray full of vodka shots, so I grab one and toss it down, then do a second one, just for a little liquid courage. We dance some more, the warmth of the alcohol snaking its way through my veins, my movements becoming more in tune with the music, less worried about the guy in front of me. I move my hands away from his hips to above my head as Arctic Monkeys' "Do I Wanna Know" comes on. Seriously, it's like the sexiest song, and my body moves along with the slow groove all on its own, my eyes closing as I let the words envelop me.

As the song ends, I open my eyes and find the new guy staring at me, a darkness in his eyes that wasn't there before. God, he's hot. I've never met such an intensely sexy man. He's so tall, so strong looking, smells insanely delicious, and is just so...*gorgeous*. And I might never get the chance to do this again, so feeling bold, I lean in and lay a kiss on him.

At first, he's stiff, but after a heartbeat, his lips soften. It's not the hottest kiss I've ever had, and I can't tell if he's into it or not. When I pull away, he looks shocked at first, then his lips pull down in a slight frown. Well, there's my answer. I feel my cheeks heat, embarrassed, and turn away. There's no way I'm staying here after that. I've never had a guy reject me so earnestly. *Weird.*

I should say good night to my bandmates, but I don't want to go back inside once I've reached the door, so I send them both a text before heading out to find a cab.

Just as I slide inside the first one that stops, Blue Eyes slides in next to me.

I look at him, open-mouthed, and he leans in as the cabbie awaits instruction on where to go.

He kisses me.

Soft and tentative, this kiss is only slightly hotter than the last one. But still, he pulls away, that conflicted look back on his face as he says, "I'm sorry, I have to go."

Then he hops back out of the cab, shutting the door, leaving me to squeak out my address to the driver, wondering what in the hell just happened?

As I unlock the door to my apartment, I breathe into my hand, wondering if my breath stinks or something. Why would he follow me out, kiss me again, and then leave? And I still don't have a clue what his name is. *Does it matter, Billie? You'll never cross paths again.* Whatever. It was fun until it wasn't.

I know one thing. I need a shower. I start the water, stripping and stepping into the spray with a sigh. After wetting my hair and lathering up with soap, I find my mind back on the guy with the strange, iris-blue eyes. His hair short but shaggy on the top and sides, and the prettiest colors. I decide he looks a little like a panther in human form but not as confident. What a strange guy.

Without much thought, I find myself rubbing at my nipples, now peaked and hard at the thought of this attractive stranger. My hand moves between my legs, fingertips plucking at my sensitive clit, hot water sluicing over my nipples.

It's been a long time since I've had such a quick physical reaction to someone, and I'm a bit mortified by the way it turned out. I guess I'm out of practice. It was enough, though, to wake my body up. I flip the stream to steady, spreading my lips to expose my sex to the sharp jet of water, my free hand pinching at my hard nipples, electricity shooting to my core, climax coming fast and hard, enough to take my breath away and make my vision go fuzzy. I step out of the shower in a daze, the sexy stranger's face the only thing I can see clearly.

7

a party with strangers?

Cal

*S*hit.

I should not have done that. Her kissing me I could explain. Me following her, getting in the cab, kissing her back? That's on me.

I could blame it on the beer I had, but honestly? I wasn't drunk. Not even close.

I shove my hands in my pockets and slouch down the road in the direction I think my apartment might be. It's probably a mile walk but I need the air. What the heck was I thinking? Seriously. I just told Em we would make this work, and here I am kissing someone else.

Maybe I'm just lonely. Yeah, that's all it is. I don't have anyone here. No friends. I haven't bonded with the team. I don't have family here. It's just loneliness. And she was nice to me. She liked me a little. Enough to dance with me.

And kiss me.

Ugh. I'm an idiot.

You liked it, though.

Cal Lefleur, professional idiot. Also, colossal moron.

I give myself the mental smackdown while I wander around a city I don't know, feeling lost and starting to panic when I realize I don't actually have any idea where I am. Christ. I need a routine. I need to get into a pattern. I need people around me who can help me navigate my life.

This isn't going to work. Being here in Las Vegas with no one.

That's all that kiss was. A moment of weakness because I felt alone. Em and I have been together for almost three years, and although I can sense her pulling away now, it hasn't always been that way. I've never looked or touched another woman. *Never been tempted.*

Moron.

Finally, I give up and hail a cab, giving my address and then feeling stupid when I realize I was only two blocks from my building.

When I fall into bed, the whole night catches up to me instantly. My head hits the pillow and I'm out.

I wake up disoriented, face down on my bed, still in my clothing from the night before. After taking a long, too-hot shower before shuffling to the kitchen to get something to eat. I stare at my cell phone for a long time, contemplating calling my agent. *Will this restlessness ever disappear?*

Still, the money *is* good. The contract is good. And if I can play here for a year or two, I can save a ton, then go back home. I settle on calling Emily instead.

"Good morning, Cal." She sounds sleepy.

"Hello, love. How are you this morning?"

"Tired," she says, yawning for punctuation. "I stayed up way too late last night."

"Doin' what?"

"I had some of my classmates over. We played games and drank wine and ate crappy Chinese food while bitching about our thesis projects."

"Oh? Sounds fun, I guess."

"It was."

I try to push back the bitterness I feel, knowing she was surrounded by friends and having a good time without me. "I went out and saw a band."

"That's good. You love live music. Were they any good?"

"They were, in fact. I went to an after party with them after their set"

"You went to an after party? With strangers?"

"I did."

She laughs lightly. "Well, that's new."

She's not wrong, but it gives me dark satisfaction that she's surprised by it. Still, she doesn't ask for more detail. Doesn't ask anything. She just starts babbling about some story one of her classmates told her about a shared professor. It's meaningless to me since I know none of the people she's talking about. I listen and make noises to show I'm still paying attention, but my mind wanders to the dark-haired drummer. Her hands on my hips. The way her body moved. The feel of her lips against mine.

Billie.

Her bandmate called her Billie.

"Calum?" Em snaps from the other end of the line. "You in la-la land?"

"I guess." An understatement if ever there was one. "Sorry. Listen, Em?"

"Yes, Cal?"

"I really need to see you. Please, please figure out a time? I'll fly you out. This is hard for me, you know. Not having anyone."

She's quiet on the other end for just a heartbeat before answering, "I know. I know it must be hard for you. A whole new routine. New people. New environment. That's probably really hard for you."

"So, you'll find some dates?"

"I'll find some dates."

I let out a breath I didn't even know I was holding. "Good. That's good."

"I'M ALICIA," the tall, dark-skinned woman says. She holds out a hand, which I shake as she says, "I run the Crush Foundation."

"Cal." I give her a nod. "I'm the new goalkeeper."

She laughs, a loud, infectious sound. "I know who you are."

"Oh, sorry."

Alicia explains that she's got a car waiting to take us over to Children's Services Las Vegas, where we're supposed to get a tour and then talk about the new music education program the club is hoping to do with help from the Crush Foundation.

When I was in Canada, we did community things

all the time. Once, they had us do a fashion show, which was really funny, actually. The idea of playing the guitar with some kids seems more up my alley, though, so I'm down with it. And it gives me something to do, which will be helpful.

I follow Alicia, who leads the way in her high heels. She's a very pretty lady, though I've noticed the Crush seems to only hire attractive people. It's kind of weird, actually. Maybe it's a Vegas thing.

When we get to the Club, a blond woman comes out to greet us.

"Tara," she says, offering her hand, "and you must be Cal."

"I am. Nice to meet you."

"You too, Cal. Thanks for doing this."

"Well, it's part of the gig," I say with a shrug.

She cocks her head and laughs. "At least you're honest. Let me show you all around."

We tour the club, Tara pointing out places where donors have given money to help them upgrade the space or enhance the programming. It's Monday morning, so there aren't any kids here. The space seems huge and empty, the large cafeteria echoing as she tells us about the evening meal prepared here by local chefs each night.

"A lot of our kids have parents who work in the service sector on night shifts. They come here after school, have a snack, work on homework, let off steam, and get a hot meal for dinner before heading home. We close at nine each night and there's a bus to get kids home safely. Honestly, many of these kids hardly see their parents at all because of work shifts.

It's likely they might not get much of a meal at all if they didn't come here. And some of them tell us they don't eat anything all day until they get to the club."

"That's really terrible," Alicia says. "They don't eat at home *or* at school?"

Tara makes a face. "The home thing is rough for many of them. If Mom is sleeping or not home from work, they might not have the wherewithal to fix themselves something nutritious before school. The kids are waking themselves up, getting themselves dressed, doing their homework with no help or guidance...you get the picture. It's a miracle some of them actually make it to school each day. Then, if they don't have the money, or their government paperwork for free-and-reduced-lunches isn't filed by their parent, then they don't get lunch at school either, so..." She shrugs and shakes her head. "I mean, there are other factors, too, but suffice it to say we strive to make sure they get nutritious snacks after school and at least one good meal a day. And, most importantly, a safe, supportive place to be."

We keep walking, Tara showing us a huge basketball court, a game room, and a space that looks like a series of standard classrooms with desks and chalkboards.

"We make them do homework or tutoring before they can go do the fun stuff," she explains. "Once the tutors sign off, they can go run around the club and do whatever. We have a program director, whom you'll meet in a minute. She organizes daily programming in addition to the free-play options we have. She runs a gaming club, a theater club, a crafting club...you get the point."

"And, it seems," Alicia says, "a new music education program?"

"She has big vision," Tara says. "Oh, speak of the devil, here she is now."

I turn and almost swallow my tongue, quickly trying to control the shock I feel when I see the drummer from the other night. It's definitely her, though today, her long, purple-tipped hair is pulled up in a messy bun on top of her head. She's in a pair of skinny jeans, a T-shirt, and a blue blazer. I'd know the face anywhere, though, after thinking of almost nothing else for the past day or so.

Her eyes go wide at the sight of me too, a light pink blush coloring her high cheekbones.

"Billie Hirsch," Tara says, "Meet Alicia Borden and Cal Lefleur from the Crush."

Billie reaches out to shake both of our hands. She meets my gaze, but only briefly, before turning to Alicia. "Nice to meet you both. Thanks for coming over to talk about my big idea."

"We like big ideas," Alicia says. "Especially ones that have real impact. The Crush, as you know, have had record-breaking success the past few seasons and it's our goal to really use that to help local organizations."

We all walk into a smallish, empty room. I look around and then back at Billie. "This is where I'd like to run an after-school music education program," she explains. "I know it looks like nothing right now. I mean, it was actually a storage room, which I cleaned out over the past few days, but it's big enough to house a drum kit, a couple of guitar stands, and a keyboard setup. My idea is that we'd do different instrument lessons on different days, and then maybe let the kids come together on Fridays to try to make their own music? Think *School of Rock* if you remember that movie."

"Do other clubs offer programs like this?" Alicia asks. "I mean, is that concept a real thing, or just a movie thing?"

"Actually, there are rock camps all around the country," Billie says with a nod. "Many are just for girls, and they also teach self-defense and empowerment and such. But yes, many communities have programs like this."

"And Billie is uniquely qualified to run a program exactly like this," Tara says. "She's the drummer in a pretty well-known local band."

"Oh?" Alicia raises an eyebrow and grins approvingly.

Billie blushes and scratches the bridge of her nose. "I do play in a band."

And then she looks right at me.

I'm not sure if I'm supposed to admit I've met her and heard her play or keep my mouth shut. I'm not any good at reading these kinds of situations.

"My plan is to teach drumming myself, but I'll be enlisting volunteer help for the other instruments. I've got a pianist from one of the big hotels coming in to do the keyboarding, and the bass player from my band will teach bass."

"Which leaves a spot open for a guitarist," Tara says, smiling in my direction.

All three women stare at me.

"That's me, I suppose. I'm the guitarist."

"Don't sound so excited," Billie mutters under her breath.

"Cal's a shy guy," Alicia says. "I've been assured by our public relations team that this is something he's willing to do. And the Crush Foundation is willing to make a sizable contribution to Children's Services Las Vegas. We're thinking we can provide the funds you need to outfit the space here, and then we can have the kids come and play a bit at the Crush Foundation gala in the spring, where we'll deliver a larger check to support your general operations. The key is to allow us in to do some video of Cal working with the kids that we can use in our promotional materials and at games. We want this to be a win-win."

"I'll have to get media releases signed by parents before we can put them on video," Billie says. "It could take a few weeks."

"That's fine," Alicia says. "We have some time to work with."

Tara and Billie look at each other before Billie turns back to us and says, "Sounds like this could work, then."

Alicia claps her hands together. "Great! We're doing a couple of other fun projects with other players. Cal, here, is new to the team so this will be a super fun way to introduce him to the community. I'll go back and iron out a grant agreement and memorandum of agreement so we can make sure everyone's on the same page, does that sound okay?"

"It sounds great, we really appreciate the support from the Crush Foundation on this," Tara says.

"We're happy to do it," Alicia says. "Tara, why don't we go talk in more detail while Billie meets with Cal about his role in all of this?"

"Sounds good," Tara answers. "Billie, just bring Cal up to my office when you're done chatting?"

"No problem," Billie says, giving a thin smile.

As the two other women leave, Billie turns to me. "Well, this is awkward."

Indeed.

8

i thought you said valium

Billie

"So, new guy, your name is Cal, then?"

"I said 'Calum,' the night we met."

"I thought you said 'Valium' to be honest, but I knew that couldn't be right. It was loud at the party."

"Okay." He looks at me, his profound statement aside.

Well, well, isn't he the charmer. I walked in all excited this morning to have a way of getting this music thing going, and the guy I have to partner with is the same guy I randomly kissed after the show over the weekend. *Oy vey.*

"Look, I'm sorry I kissed you the other night. I'd had a few drinks and I thought you were cute, but obviously you weren't that into it, so..." I give a helpless shrug in his direction.

"This is awkward for me, too. We're adults, though. We can handle it, Billie."

He's not soft about this. It should make me feel

better, right? To have him say we're cool, that we can manage through this weird turn of events and work together? I mean, I guess that's what he's saying, right? It's hard to tell because he's still just as awkward as the other night, kind of standoffish and uncomfortable. His body language is stiff, like he's just totally uncomfortable, even though his words are meant to make me feel more comfortable. It's so weird. I feel weird.

I'm gonna try to shake it off, as the pop juggernaut Taylor Swift would advise.

Not a Taylor Swift fan, though. Just for the record.

"Just so we're on the same page, Cal, you're cool about the awkward stuff from the other night, and we can move past it to do this thing together with the kids and the music?"

He nods once. "It's fine."

I cringe. "Fine isn't really the ringing endorsement of enthusiasm that I'm looking for here."

He just shrugs at me and keeps nailing me with those eyes of his that remind me of the deep blue sea...and other things I shouldn't be romanticizing. Nope. Not at all.

Holy hell.

I throw my head back and sigh. "Okay. Let's start over." I shove my hand out. "My name is Billie Hirsch. I'm the program director here, and I also play drums in a killer three-piece band with the unfortunate hipster name of Love Scrum. We are much better than our shitty name. I love music and hope to help the kids who come here to the club to love it too."

He shakes my hand...and then he speaks.

"I'm Calum Lefleur. I just moved here from Canada and I'm the new goaltender for the Crush now, even though I didn't want the trade. The Crush beat us in the playoffs last season. They're the best overall team. I'm pretty much the best goalie in the league. It makes sense they called me in, but I'm still not thrilled about it."

"That's...arrogant," I say, pushing my lips together in a dubious smirk. "Not sure I'm into the cocky. Dial it back a bit for the kids, okay? They'll be starstruck and think you're great anyway. I just want you to be accessible."

"What does that mean?" he asks, sounding genuinely curious.

"It means that these kids come from all kinds of backgrounds. They weren't born with silver spoons in their mouths, and it will be a treat for them to meet you, let alone learn from you, and I don't want them to be disappointed if you act like an asshole."

This seems to surprise him. He leans back, almost like he's been slapped, and bites his lip, frowning. Or pouting. I think he's pouting.

"I'm sorry. That wasn't a nice thing to say. But I know your type. You're spoiled and rich and you've been the superstar, but now you're just one superstar among many and that feels uncomfortable to you. Frankly, I'm not impressed. I grew up among celebrities and they put their pants on one leg at a time, just like I do. Superstars are overrated."

"That's not really it," Cal says. "I mean, it's not all of it. But whatever. Let's just get this figured out so I can get back to the arena."

I breathe in and out through my nose quickly. It's such a shame when the really hot-looking guys turn out to be spoiled rich boys. *I've seen my fair share over the years, I but had hoped that this one would be different.* Calm, Billie. He's keen to leave, so give him what he wants so he can get out of here. "Okay, well, I'd like to have you here on a consistent basis. Like, the same day and time every single week. Is that doable with your schedule?"

"I'm not sure. As you know, we have a game schedule that will have us on the road. It's likely we can set a schedule based on that, but it's unlikely I can guarantee Tuesdays at four every week or whatever."

"These kids need someone they can count on," I tell him plainly. He needs to know this is not just some photo op for his image.

"I understand, but I have hockey responsibilities, and while the team is supportive of this, they also pay me to play hockey. So, we just need to look at the calendar and work something out."

I feel my face twisting. Maybe I'm being unfair. Maybe the events of the other night are coloring my opinion of this guy. And really, that's uncool since I'm the one who kissed him in the first place. And he's right, of course, that hockey is a long season with a lot of games and practices and training sessions.

Calum Lefleur is a very attractive guy. As pretty in the daylight as he was the other night in the dim light of the evening. His hair has gorgeous golden highlights throughout and enough of a natural curl to look artfully messy. Great lips, not too full, not too thin.

And his eyes—yeah, well, suffice it to say I've dreamt about those sea-blue, Van Gogh iris-colored eyes of his more than I should've since we met the other night. He'll look fantastic on those larger-than-life posters the Crush likes to hang outside the arena every season.

"Okay, sure," I finally say. "I just want you to be clear on this one point, okay? These kids need role models. They need people who show up consistently. They need people who care about them in authentic ways. If you're just going to phone this in, I'd rather not do it."

"I've been asked to do this by our public relations team," he answers, shoving his hands in his pockets. "I'll do what is expected of me."

My nostrils flare as I grit my teeth, biting back the response I'd really like to give him. I need to stay civil, though. "Okay. Well, let's go up to one of the homework rooms. There are a couple of home-school kids up there doing some work. They'll be happy to meet you and it's on the way to Tara's office."

I walk off, assuming he'll follow me. I don't look back. I'm not going to hold this guy's hand. *He's going to do what's expected of him?* What a joke.

He does follow, at a meandering distance, and I spend the whole five minutes being angry at myself for kissing a guy who is clearly an arrogant asshat. Or if not arrogant, at least aloof enough to be annoying. Boy, do I know how to pick 'em.

Inside the homework room, the ten kids who do homeschool work here look up as we walk in.

"Hi, Miss Hirsch," they all say.

"Hey, guys. Thought you might like to meet Calum Lefleur. He's the new goalie for the Crush."

"Whoa!" one of the kids yelps, jumping up and running over.

Pretty soon, the excitement spreads, the kids asking Cal questions about being a professional hockey player. He answers but seems kind of overwhelmed. I get the impression he hasn't been around a lot of kids before. Still, he's not unkind, so I think he'll do okay, especially in the small-group lessons. Kids are so perceptive and know when adults are ingenuine. *Please be kind to these kids, hockey hero.*

Man, I hope he can play guitar. I hope he has the people skills to *actually teach it.*

After a few minutes, Cal announces that he needs to get to a team meeting, and I walk him back to Tara's office, where the head of the Crush Foundation whisks him away with a promise to be back in touch soon to firm things up.

"How was it?" Tara asks after they walk out.

"I'm not sure, honestly. He's a strange dude."

"Great," she says, rolling her eyes. "Just what we need."

"Let's hope for the best," I say, puffing out my cheeks and blowing out a breath. "We need this money."

"Yes, we do."

God, please don't let this be a colossal disaster.

9
who's nick?

Cal

Em is one of the last people to come down the escalator to baggage claim. It's been a month since I've seen her in person. As she approaches, I hold out the bouquet of flowers I brought for her. She takes them, and when I lean in for a kiss, she turns her head so that my kiss lands on her cheek.

She mutters something about the flight being bumpy and then wanders off toward the baggage claim station. I follow along, standing next to her while she checks her phone.

"I had a draft paper due yesterday," she explains. "I was hoping for quick feedback."

"Well, I'm hoping to make you forget your master's program and papers and thesis arguments for about forty-eight hours."

She looks up at me. I was hoping for the playful smile I love, but all I get is a look of exasperation.

Emily is traditionally pretty in a lot of ways with her honey-blond hair, bright hazel eyes, and a cute, upturned nose. She's in a white T-shirt, jeans, and a navy blazer, looking like she could go horseback riding or teach a college class. Either way, she'd look good even in spite of the downward tilt of her pink mouth. I reach out and trace my thumb along her lips.

"Your face is gonna freeze like that," I say, leaning in for a kiss.

She allows it but turns away as soon as the baggage claim buzzer goes off.

As Emily makes her way closer to the carousel, I shove my hands in my pockets and blow out a sigh. I've been feeling so guilty about kissing Billie. It won't happen again, especially now that I know we have to work together on this project at the boys and girls club. Still, I wonder if I should tell Emily about it. Although, at this moment, I doubt she'd care.

When she spots her bag, I jog over to grab it for her. She thanks me, and I pull it along behind me as we make our way out to grab a taxi.

"So, what do you want to do this weekend?" I ask. "I made us a reservation for dinner tonight but thought I'd see what you were up for."

"Have you done any sightseeing?" She stares out the window at the sights as they pass.

"Not really. I mean, I walk around a little, but I don't do too much besides work stuff."

"Why doesn't that surprise me?" she mutters to herself.

"Well," I say, feeling affronted, "I mean, I did go out to see some live music one night."

She turns and appraises me. "Cal, I know you pretty well. You like routine and you're way out of yours."

I'm not sure how to take the statement. It could be that she's saying she understands why I haven't seen a lot yet. Her tone makes it seem otherwise, but I'm bad at reading people most of the time, even people I know well. I can read one thing, though. Em hasn't smiled once since she got here. She keeps looking at her phone. I guess she's just distracted by her school stuff, but still.

When we get to my apartment, Em dumps her things in the bedroom and then disappears into the bathroom. A moment later, I hear the bath water running. I knock lightly on the door.

"Want some company in there?" I ask through the door.

"No, I'm good," she answers back.

I frown and sit on the couch to watch sports highlights while she does her thing. When she finally comes out, she's in a fluffy white robe, her blond hair piled on top of her head in a dancer's bun, tight and perfect. I pat the couch, and she sits, leaning into me as I put my arm around her.

"Feel better?" I press a kiss to the crown of her head.

"I guess. I hate flying, I've realized."

"Oh. Sorry to hear that."

"It just makes me feel crowded and dirty. Nick says the air doesn't just circulate and recirculate, but I can't help but feel planes are just germ factories."

"Who is Nick?" *Don't like the sound of him.*

"He's a guy in my master's cohort. We work on a lot of projects together."

"How does he know how air circulates in a plane?"

She shrugs. "When is dinner?"

I look at my phone. "An hour."

"Okay. I'll go get dressed."

She starts to get up, but I pull her back, leaning in to kiss her neck. "We have time," I say against her skin.

She swats me away and mumbles something about needing to send an email before we leave. I follow her into the bedroom, watch as she pulls her laptop from her bag, opens it up, and crawls onto the bed with it on her lap.

"Really, Em?"

She looks up and her eyebrows knit in the center of her forehead. "What?"

"I haven't seen you in weeks. I've missed you. I'm trying to kiss on you and you're sending an *email*?"

"Sorry." She doesn't sound sorry at all. "Nick's expecting my feedback on this project. I'll be able to focus on your needs more thoroughly if you let me get this off my plate."

I grit my teeth. "Em, I flew you all the way here. I want to see you. Talk to you."

"Fuck me?" she asks, not looking up from the screen. Her fingers fly over the keys.

"Well, yeah. Maybe that, too."

"Pardon me if I don't rip my clothes off so you can take me like some animal."

"That wasn't how I..."

"Whatever. Fine. Let's get it over with." She puts

the laptop down and lies back on the bed like a cold, dead fish.

"Wow, that's certainly hot, but I think I'll wait until you're actually interested."

Emily sits back up and rolls her eyes, grabbing her laptop, her attention back on her email.

An hour later, she's in a little black dress, her hair still up in that fussy bun. I compliment her for about the tenth time, telling her how beautiful she looks and how much I've missed her as we're led to our seats at the restaurant. It's on the sixtieth floor of a hotel, looking out at the Strip, lights twinkling around and below us.

"Nice view," she says flatly.

"I mean..."

She gives me a half smile as she sips her water. "There are views like this in Montreal."

"Of course, there are."

"Nick and I went to Trillium Park not too long ago," she says as the waiter comes to take our drink order. Em orders iced tea. I encourage her to share a bottle of wine with me, and she says primly, "No, thank you. You know how you get when you drink."

"Excuse me?"

The waiter shifts from one foot to the other, face pinched. "Shall I come back?"

"No. I'll have a Stella. The lady just wants iced tea."

I stare at Emily as the waiter walks off. "Really?"

She shrugs. "You have very little filter even when you're sober, Calum. I'm not in the mood to babysit you if you get drunk."

There is no part of me that wants to have an

argument with my girlfriend when she's only just arrived. I have missed her, missed the comfort of having someone around who knows me well.

"So why did you go to Trillium Park?" I ask, trying to change the mood.

Emily is looking at her phone again. "Hmm?"

"You said you and somebody went to Trillium Park, but the waiter came, and you didn't finish your thought."

She looks up. "Oh. Nick. The guy in my cohort? We went one day a week or two ago. The weather was as amazing as that view of the skyline. I love Montreal; it's just the best."

This feels like a dig. We're looking down on an iconic view of the Strip in Las Vegas. There are lights of all colors, fountains, and every kind of structure imaginable. It's not like the skyline of Montreal, that's true, but it is special in its way. A view I've started to value in a different way. The thought of my hometown's cityscape hurts my heart a little, though. I miss home and she knows it. To remind me of a place I can't be right now seems cruel. Still, I'm less interested in picking a fight about that than I am in finding out why she was with some other guy in the park.

So, I go for it and ask, "Why go to the park, though? How can you get research done in a park?"

"We were actually just reading case studies," she says, tight-lipped. "I don't need to justify it to you."

The waiter returns with our drinks. Emily glares at my bottle of beer as if it has caused her a great disrespect. She manages a thin smile as she orders a salad for dinner.

"You could have anything on the menu and you're getting a salad?"

"I'm not very hungry," she says, looking out the window.

My nostrils flare as I breathe in and breathe out. "I'll have the sirloin medium, and a baked potato," I tell the waiter, handing him my menu.

After he leaves, Emily hits me with what's really on her mind. "Why do you have to make everything so uncomfortable?"

"I'm not trying to make things uncomfortable."

"I mean, even now, you're acting like a child."

I hold her stare until she shakes her head and looks back out the window.

We sit in silence for at least five minutes; the time straining between us. Finally, I attempt to make peace for a third time or maybe the fourth at this point. "What are you working on for your thesis right now?"

Emily brightens a bit at this. She is a true academic, and she's likely to go on to her Ph.D. next. She never passes up an opportunity to talk about her work and she doesn't disappoint now.

"Well, remember before you left, and I was working with the local school systems to survey kids regarding their interest in and access to counseling and psychological services?"

"Vaguely." Now, less than enthused.

"Well, the responses were pretty wild, especially when I compared them to the same survey to their parents, regarding how they felt about mental health care when they were their children's ages."

"What is your plan with all of this research?"

"Really?" Emily folds her arms across her chest. "I've only explained my goals like six billion times, Cal."

"I mean, I know you want to get this degree so you can go on to the next one, and then you want to teach at the college level."

"But the research is important. I'm trying to correlate the changing attitude toward mental health care to the too-slow growth of the counseling and psychological services industry."

"And how will that help anyone? I mean, it's not like you're going to take your Ph.D. in social work and then go help people with it. You're going to study it, write a paper, and then go teach people about something you've never once done in practice. It's weird."

"Cal," she says, her jaw tense with warning, "you don't need to say every little thing that pops into your head."

"What? We're talking about your studies. I'm just trying to understand. What is the point of all of this?"

"See? This is why I hang around with people like Nick, who understand what this work is all about and why it's important."

"Nick again. Nick's a real hero, I suppose."

"Don't be an ass."

"I'm the ass? Emily, you keep talking about this guy like he's a god or something. I'm starting to feel like maybe I should be worried. What's going on between you and this guy?"

"Nothing's going on," she snaps. "He's in my cohort. We share similar research interests. I find him interesting."

"More interesting than your boyfriend, the professional hockey player who flew you in for the weekend because he misses you?"

"You miss your routine more than you miss me," Emily says.

"No, I miss *you*." *How many times do I have to fuckin' say it!* "I'm the one calling you all the time, not the other way around."

"To complain and tell me how much you hate Las Vegas."

"You're my *partner*, Emily. You're the person I'm supposed to be able to talk to about these things."

"And yet, you never allow me the same opportunity. You can't even tell me what my career goals are, even though it's tantamount to every important thing in my life right now."

"Well, it sounds like this Nick guy is pretty high on that list right now, too. And I need you to focus on me and not some other guy, especially when I've just spent the money to bring you here."

"A plane ticket is a drop in the bucket for you, Cal. You make millions-per-season money, and you hardly spend any of it. So don't lord the expense over my head. I came here at your request when I have other things I could be working on, and you're picking a fight with me."

"Well, you don't act like you want to be here at all."

"I don't, Cal. Every time you call, I tell you how busy I am. There's a lot to do, and taking a weekend away puts my timeline behind schedule."

"And it keeps you away from Nick." The name sounds acidic in my mouth. I know it sounds that way when it comes out, too.

"Don't be a jealous asshole."

I sit back in my chair as the waiter approaches with our meals. Emily musters a weak smile and thanks him when he places her salad on the table. When he leaves, I apologize, playing peacemaker for the fifth?—*I've lost fuckin' count*—time. "I'm sorry. You're right. I am being a jealous asshole. But can you blame me? This is hard for me. I'm in a town I don't know. I have no one here. My team seems to hate me. I have to do some dumbass public relations thing with a bunch of poor kids. Everything is so random, and I need you right now."

"Some *dumbass thing with a bunch of poor kids*?" Emily asks, eyebrow raised. "You're in rare form tonight, Calum Lefleur."

"What's that mean?"

"It means you're being a total dick."

"I'm just trying to talk to you."

"Well, you sound like a poor little rich boy to me. *Wah*, I make a truckload of money to play a game. *Wah*, I have to slum it with the poor kids to make myself look like a good guy. It's no wonder you don't have any friends here, giving off a vibe like that."

I spear my steak and shove a bite into my mouth, glaring at her. A few minutes of thought, though, makes me realize she's right. And I didn't mean it that way. The public relations thing is whatever, but I'm not judgmental about poverty. And I like kids, usually, so I'm just projecting my frustration in the wrong direction. I much prefer interacting with kids at games than the press. I make sure to pass off pucks and the occasional stick, *always* to a little kid. It feels good seeing their happy faces light up when they're handed a prize from a player on the ice.

"Okay, okay. Okay. You're right. That didn't come out right. The volunteer gig with the kids is not a problem. I'm just frustrated."

"Look, you're right, too, you know? I came here in the wrong mood. I'm anxious about school stuff. My program is stressing me out and you're kind of stressing me out, and it's not making for a very nice reunion, I agree."

I reach across the table and take her hand. "I'm sorry. I don't want to stress you out. I just wanted to show you Las Vegas and spend some time with you."

She squeezes my hand. "I'm sorry, too. Let's start over?"

I nod and squeeze back before focusing on my now-cold dinner. We don't talk much for the rest of the meal, but it's better than fighting, and I'm just glad to have someone familiar here with me.

We take a long walk after dinner, exploring the Strip before going back to my apartment. As we step inside, I pull her in for a kiss. She's stiff at first but then softens slightly. Shuffling as we kiss, we end up in my bedroom, where I pull her dress over her head and loosen her hair from that tight bun. She looks more like my Emily now in the soft light of the bedside lamp. I kiss her cheek, then her ear, then her neck, but when I try to guide her onto the bed, she pushes me away, shaking her head.

"I'm sorry, Cal. I'm just not in the mood."

"Oh," I say, rubbing my thumb along my bottom lip.

"It's not...I'm just tired. And I'm having a hard time not thinking about the work I need to get done for class. Can I just...let me just get some things done and then I can focus on you, okay?"

My jaw clenches, but I put my hands up and step back, giving her a curt nod before wandering out into the living room to plop onto the sofa. I watch sports highlights for a long time, hearing the click-click of Emily's typing on her laptop in the bedroom.

I try to focus on the television, but my mind is full of questions. Can this thing between us still work? Maybe I'm not a good boyfriend. Maybe she's seeing someone else. Does it matter if she is? I kissed someone else, too. It's the distance, right? *Has to be.*

My stomach twists with anxiety because these are all the things I can't control. Nothing seems within my control right now, and that is very, very hard for me. In Montreal, I had routine. I had stability. I knew my place. Here? Everything is new and untested and unsure, and those are not places where I like to live.

A couple of hours after sitting down, I get up to check on Emily and find her asleep on the bed, her laptop still open next to her. As I go to move it, the screen lights up, and where I expect to find something school related, I see a Facebook Messenger pop-up, a whole slew of direct messages from Nick.

I think about reading them, but in the end, I just shut the laptop and put it in her bag. What's the point, anyway?

I turn off the light and head down the hall to sleep in the second bedroom.

10
garbage guitars

Billie

"This is like Christmas!" Stuart exclaims as we wander up and down the aisles at Guitar Center.

"You realize that saying something is like Christmas to a Jew doesn't have the same impact, right?" I elbow him in the ribs to give my teasing a little extra effect. Stu and I are easy friends like that.

He grins. "Well, let's just say that for those of us raised in loosely Christian households, having a day a year to wake up to a bunch of presents for no good reason is pretty fuckin' awesome. And it feels like this. We get to go spend other people's money on awesome musical equipment."

"For the club, Stu. It's not like we're padding our own stash with hockey money."

"Still, it's fun to shop for cool stuff."

"Okay, I'll give you that."

"How much do we have to spend?"

"A lot. They gave us enough to build a lending

library so that the kids can borrow the instruments overnight if they want to practice at home."

"What could possibly go wrong with that?" he asks sarcastically, not expecting an answer, of course.

My best friend, long and lanky with curling, dark hair that falls past his shoulders, wanders off to look at a wall of bass guitars. I follow along and only half-listen as he quizzes the salesperson about the different guitars, asking which ones would be good for beginners and which ones are lighter and with shorter stems.

The Crush will have us come and accept an oversized check at a charity gala this fall. In the meantime, they sent us the real check so we could get started right away. Enough to get a cool instrument library stocked while leaving money to soundproof a small music room and pay part of my salary. It's a good gift, and it'll be put to good use.

"This one might be good, yeah?" Stuart's long arms reach up to pluck a navy-blue bass from its place on the wall. He plucks at the strings and bounces it up and down a bit. "Nice and light. Not too big."

I peer at the price tag. "Yeah, it looks good. I want to get two or three of different colors and sizes. Instruments are personal. They have to feel right when you play them."

"Spoken like a true musician, Bill. But what a cool way to mix your day job with your talent, yeah?"

"It is pretty cool, I agree." I can't hold back my sigh, however. "But for the idiot hockey player I got stuck babysitting because of it."

"Oh, you got a hockey player to go with the hockey money?"

"Of course. Big public relations thing. The money comes with strings."

"Most money does." He cocks his head to the side and winks.

"Well, these strings are called Calum Lefleur."

"Calum Lefleur?" Stuart's voice cracks as he fans himself with his hands. "I have such a sports crush on that dude. Holy smokes, he's like the best goalie in the league."

"Well, that's what he said about himself, too. Cocky jerk-wagon that he is."

Stuart shrugs. "When you've got it, you've got it."

"Puke. Whatever. I assume he'll get bored of it after a while, so I'll just entertain him until then, in the name of putting together this awesome program for the kids."

"Well, a little cocky can't hurt when you're out there getting a hard hockey puck winged at your head every few minutes."

I make a "meh" noise as we play around with the bass guitars some more. Once I've made my decisions, we move on to electric, acoustic, and bass guitars, grab a drum kit, then two keyboards. I talk to the manager once we get everything picked out, explaining what we're doing, and he gives us a nice discount so that we can use more of our budget. This enables us to buy guitar leads, straps, music stands, and sheet music, but also the amps for the guitars. A portable mixer is added to the mix with complementary speakers. If we ever get a "band" up and running, we'll add in more speakers, maybe some mics. It's just so exciting.

As we load everything into the back of Stuart's work van, he says, "You look very smug right now. Proud of your negotiation skills?"

"Proud of my begging skills, more like. Maybe I should be a fundraiser instead of a program director."

"Maybe you should be a rock star instead of a program director."

"Did Sven put you up to that comment?" I give him the side-eye.

He shrugs. "You guys are good enough—"

"Ugh, not you, too. Dude, I have told them time and time again that it will happen if and when it's meant to happen."

"It could happen faster if—"

"Don't you dare. Stuart Robertson, I swear if you say one word about my parents, I will cut you."

He laughs and holds his hands up in surrender.

As we load the last box, he pulls me into a side-hug and kisses my temple. "You are a badass Billie Hirsch. The kids are going to love these."

He slams the van doors, and I wander to the passenger side, feeling good about what we're doing for the kids while also overthinking the kiss my best friend just placed on the side of my head. It's not like Stuart hasn't been cuddly with me before. He has, and while I usually allow it, I've had more and more concern over how he views it. Does he think we're headed toward something beyond friendship? Would I want that if we were?

He's important to me and he has been for a long time. We met when I came to live in Las Vegas with my grandmother, we were inseparable all through high school. He knows my crazy parents, knows the reason I came to Vegas, knows how much I love music and how much I don't love the idea of asking my parents to get us an "in" in the industry. I tell him everything, and if we tried something and it didn't work, I'd be devastated to lose him. I know he likes me as more than a friend. I can feel it. He would never push it. He would only do something if I initiated it, and I appreciate that so much.

"Are we taking these to the club?" he asks, starting the engine and pulling me from my thoughts.

"Uh, yeah. If you could help me unload, then take me to band practice, I would be very appreciative."

"That's all I am to you? Muscle? And a car?" His grin tells me he's not that upset about it.

"Well, I'll have to make you dinner one night soon to thank you for being muscle and car and best friend ever. Also, this isn't your car anyway."

"Yes, I'm using my work van to assist you. Breaking the rules just to show you how much I care about your program."

I narrow my eyes at him, and he just laughs it off.

THE NEXT AFTERNOON, I've unboxed all of the equipment and am in the process of tuning a drum kit when goalie boy wonder walks in.

He does not say hello.

He does not ask me how things are going.

No, he stands with his hands on his hips, surveying the instruments with a scowl on his face.

And *I* simply refuse to respond to whatever game he's playing at.

So, I ignore him completely. I bang on the drums, adjust the heads, and make sure everything is nice and tuned while he pokes around. He peers at the guitars for a while before picking one up, strapping it on, plugging it into an amp. He plucks out a few notes, messing with the tuning as he does so. Systematically, he does this with every guitar, electric and acoustic. He doesn't skip a single one.

Finally, he looks up, a bright red guitar still strapped across his shoulder. "These guitars are garbage. I hate them all."

"Well, hello to you, too." I peer over at him from the drum dial I've set on top of my snare and narrow my eyes.

"Why did you get such cheap instruments?"

"Because these kids are just starting to learn and we're a nonprofit, so I wanted to stretch the budget. And some of these will be part of a lending library and I don't want a reason to freak out if they don't come back in a timely manner."

"I think they should learn on good equipment, so they can hear what these instruments *should* sound like."

"This isn't music appreciation class, Cal. The kids want to learn the basics of how to play. They need a creative outlet. These instruments will work fine. Most of these kids don't have families who can afford stuff like this, so it will be really exciting for them, even without the most expensive equipment."

"I just think—"

I put up a hand to stop him from saying anything else. "Look, I need you to just chill out and teach the guitar. Do the little PR thing and then move on. Can you do that? Do you even know *how* to teach someone to play the guitar?"

He glares at me for a second but then sort of tunes me out, going back to the red guitar and tuning it a bit more before plucking out a familiar tune. I think it's a White Stripes song, and I listen in, adding in a drumbeat to confirm. Well, hell...

Calum Lefleur is a decent guitarist.

He's clearly very technical in his approach, but good, nonetheless. At one point, I catch him looking at me as I drum, the same look of rapt fascination on his face as when he watched us play at the bar. He appreciates music and musicians—that much is obvious. Which will be the tie that binds, the thing to make this partnership work, I think. I hope...

We riff off each other for a few minutes, and when he stops playing, I give him my full attention, and while it's not exactly a ringing endorsement, it's the best I can do for him at the moment.

"Okay, you're not fired. *Yet.* See you next week for your first lesson with the kids."

The handsome bastard stares at me for a second and then gives me a sharp nod.

A nod.

No words, no gesture, no smile or readable facial

expression, just a firm nod. A firm nod that just might melt my panties away if I must define it.

It'd be a lot easier to work around him if I didn't have to look at him.

Calum Lefleur may need charm school, but damn, he's a beautiful man.

11

let loose, try new things

Cal

"How's it going?" Evan asks as we huddle up for practice instructions.

I lift a shoulder. "It is what it is."

He huffs a laugh and rubs his bearded chin. "I see you've not yet gotten comfortable in your new home."

"This isn't home to me. Montreal is home."

"I get that. It's hard to assimilate somewhere new, with a bunch of people you don't know. And this is your first trade, so it's doubly hard. Maybe we can grab a beer one night, talk it out? I want you to feel welcome here. I want you to be part of the team. I, for one, am happy to have a goalie like you on the squad."

Evan has always been nice. He's the team captain and it's his job, I guess, but his words do give me some comfort. No one really talks to me here. People are pleasant, I suppose, but I see their relationships and their bonds, and I feel very out of place. I just don't know how to fit in.

"I'd like that. To grab a beer sometime."

"Great," he says with a sharp clap on my back. "Let's make it happen. Now, I think, fundamentally, our team totally gets how good you are. They saw you in action in the finals. But *knowing* a thing is different than integrating it into a team environment. They loved Manny, not just the goalie but the man and their very good friend. It's hard to let go of someone you love, and they're possibly in mourning right now. It was not just a season-ending injury for Manny, it was the end of a twenty-year career for a guy who's a shoo-in for the Hall of Fame one day. But, having said all that, they can love you too, when they see what you can do for the team."

"I don't need to be loved." As soon as I say the words, I wish I'd not said them.

"Then respect. Whatever. They'll step up and protect you as best they can, but you want more than that. You want to feel a sense of place with this team." He puts up a gloved hand as soon as I open my mouth. "I know, I know. You're going to say you don't care about this team, that you didn't want to be here in the first place. I get it. You want to go back to Montreal. But you can't. You're under contract here, dude, and you're serious enough about the game to make the best of it, even if it's just on the ice. Thing is, that won't be good enough to sustain you here, not for the duration of the contract."

I bite back the automatic argument that buds in my throat. He's just trying to help, I remind myself. I nod, and he claps me on the back one more time just as the coaching staff lays out our next drill.

It's a simple shot-on-goal exercise. The team splits up into two lines as I take my place at one goal and Dante Castellano takes his place at the other end of the ice. He stares me down like he wants to tear my head off. He probably does want to tear my head off. What he doesn't realize is that he should be directing all that energy to the drill, to stopping goals. He could outshine me here, prove his worth.

Tugging down my goaltender's mask, I crouch in front of the goal, hyper-focused as the first in line skates forward with the puck.

The players have been instructed to come in hard, fast, and from different angles. This exercise is partially about their ability to pivot and shoot from various positions, but partially about my ability to see the shots and react quickly.

Each time a player scores on one of us, the buzzer goes off, loud and obnoxious in an empty arena. The team wings shot after shot, and I get into a game-based mindset. Stop the puck. Don't worry about anything else. What angle is it coming from? Where do I position myself? Should I come out or pack in tight?

Vaguely, I hear the buzzer go off a few times. Only one am I certain is for me.

When the coaching staff calls time, I'm sweaty and out of breath as I look up and see that I only let in one goal, while Dante let in eight.

He stares, open-mouthed, at the scoreboard before pulling his mask off, letting it dangle from his fingertips as he processes the reality presented. He looks at me, and his expression turns from disbelief to frustration or anger before he turns and skates toward the edge of the ice, letting himself out, slipping on some blade covers, and disappearing down the tunnel.

As the other guys get their next instructions, I skate off, following Dante, finding him standing in the tunnel, forehead against the wall.

"Castellano," I say on the approach.

"Fuck off, Lefleur."

"Why do you let shit get into your head? It's a drill and you acted like it was an Olympic trial."

"Look, Manny got hurt and I thought it was my turn. I've been here, drilling, working, waiting. I stopped almost every shot in college but since I've been here, I can't get the consistency I need to make first string and now some fucking whiz-kid comes in and there's no hope at all for any real playing time. Again. I'd prefer they fucking trade me down to the AHL at this point. At least I'd get to play."

"I don't know how that feels because I've never been second string." Castellano bares his teeth at me, which I interpret to mean I've said something stupid, as usual. Still, I continue, "But I do know how it feels to want something so badly. I want to go back to Montreal. I'm trying to convince them to take me back. If I leave, there's an opening. You just need to get focused and be ready for when it happens."

"Why the fuck are you so focused on getting back to Montreal?" He throws up his hands. "Trades are part of the deal in pro hockey. You got a platinum package coming here and this is a platinum team."

"My life is there. My girlfriend is there. And I think she's cheating on me. I need to get back to my life and my routine."

Castellano chuckles. "If she's cheating on you, you probably fucking deserve it."

I shrug and chew on my bottom lip. "Maybe so. Listen, I'm not your enemy. I came here because I got traded but I'd leave in a heartbeat if it meant I could go home. I'm going to do my job here, but you have a job, too, which is to be ready for anything."

He takes a breath and nods curtly, heading back out on the ice to finish practice. I follow, unsure if I've made things better or worse for myself.

EVAN MAKES good on his offer, asking me to grab a beer after practice. He can't stay out long, as his wife and kids are waiting on him at home, but he doesn't seem rushed as we grab a pint in the restaurant that's attached to the arena. He asks me all about Montreal, says he's never been there except for games. He tells me about how he met his wife, who worked for the Crush before starting her own public relations firm.

"I wish she'd come back. Scarlett is making me teach guitar to kids at Children's Services Las Vegas as part of some stunt with the foundation."

"Well, I can't say I feel badly for you on that one," Evan answers. "Even when I was my worst self, I still gave to charity."

"What was your worst self?"

Evan runs a hand through his hair as he considers. "I guess I thought I was hot-shit. I treated women like garbage. I drank a lot."

"Sounds like about fifty percent of the guys in hockey."

"Unfortunately, it can be," he answers with a slow nod, tapping fingertips against his glass. "All it takes is the right person to turn you around, I've found."

"Mmm. Well, I thought I found that person, but it seems like she's slipping away."

"Tell me about her."

"She's blond. Petite. Pretty. Smart."

Evan shakes his head. "No, I didn't ask what she looks like. I wanted to know what drives the relationship. Why do you care about her? What do you love about her?"

I open my mouth, then close it. "Honestly? I need stability in my life. I need structure and routine. Less so, maybe, as I'm getting older, but I still need it. It's part of my DNA."

"You didn't answer the question at all, man."

I take a swig of my beer and can't deny it. I suck at explaining my emotions.

My team captain then starts waxing poetic about his wife, and all the things he loves about her. I listen, but I'm not a big romantic, so it doesn't sway me in any particular way. Still, I can see he truly loves her and his kids.

"She didn't fall for me right away. Didn't throw herself at me just because I was a pro athlete. I'm sure you've had that before, right? Women who want to sleep with you just so they can say they made it with a hockey star?"

"I have. It doesn't impress me."

"Well, Holly wasn't like that. She was driven and

smart and she wanted to keep her job. But there was this...chemistry. Something. It drew us to each other and while I maybe started out thinking of it as a challenge or a conquest, it quickly turned into something more. More meaningful. I saw the puzzle pieces fitting together. I wanted to be better because of her, for her. I wanted her to know I was worth something. Worth her love."

"I'm not really into the love stories, though." I shrug. It's the God's honest truth.

Evan frowns at his beer, but only for a moment. When he looks up, he says, "Then maybe that's what's wrong with your relationship."

Touché. He's got me there, so I change the subject. "Are you going to retire at some point?"

Evan's eyebrows shoot up into his hairline. "That's bold. Looking to get rid of me?"

"No. Sorry. It just seems like you're a happy homebody. Ready to get home and do dad stuff."

"Well, I won't lie, I miss them when I have to travel. But I still love playing. I'm still good at it. Body's still holding up and I'm not *that* old..."

I can't help but grin at this. Evan is probably ten years older than me. It's not ancient for hockey, but a lot of guys go to the front office once they settle down.

Evan pays the bar tab and says he'll see me later.

Dissatisfaction.

That's what I'm feeling right now. It's not just about being here in Vegas. It's about life in general. Evan's got me thinking. What *do* I love about Emily? I felt like we barely connected when she was in town. It could be blamed on her hyper-focus on schoolwork, but really, I think we don't have that much in common. And if her negative, somewhat patronizing comments were anything to go by, I think she feels that way too. There was a constant, uncomfortable strain between us that I'd never noticed before. I slept in the spare bedroom and Emily didn't even comment about it. There was no kissing, no cuddling, no...*connecting*. The first real smile I saw was when she was texting someone just as she got to the airport to return to Montreal. Am I a fool for trying when she's probably already left our relationship? Am I simply coldhearted that I can't see clearly what I love about her?

It's as I'm pondering this that I receive three texts from Emily. Ones I should have been expecting if I'm honest.

Emily: I think we need some space.

Emily: This weekend was weird, and I think the distance is hard.

Emily: I'm sorry. I just need a break.

I have no idea how to respond to them, so I walk out into the evening and look for a bar with live music. It's what I need right now. Music. When I find one worth listening to, I step in and take a seat at the bar, ordering another beer.

The music is good. Not as good as Billie's band, if I'm comparing. Thinking back on our impromptu jam session, she really is an amazing drummer. Expressive about music in a way I could never be. I feel a little badly about how I reacted to the low-cost musical equipment she purchased for the program. In hindsight, I was still smarting from the weekend with Emily, which did not go as I envisioned. I think I took it out on Billie, who was totally valid in her point about buying cheaper equipment for kids who are just starting to learn the instruments.

I'm two beers in when someone sits next to me. A woman, with dark hair. At first, I pay her no attention as I watch the band. The crowd is picking up, and the music is growing on me.

When I turn, though, I realize it's Billie. She smirks at me. "Hello, Cal."

"Hello."

"Wondered when you'd realize I was sitting here."

"Just here to listen to some music," I say, taking a sip of my beer.

"Well, don't let me stop you. I just wanted to say hi since I saw you sitting here."

"Okay."

Billie's nose and mouth do a crinkly thing that's cute but makes me think I didn't answer the way she wanted me to. I don't know. I'm not good at reading people, I guess.

"Can I buy you a beer or drink of choice?" I ask after a moment.

She shrugs. She's dressed simply, in a white T-shirt, jeans, and tall boots. Her hair is piled up big on top of her head in a wild way. It's pretty though, the purple ends falling down, making me want to touch it. I like how she looks. Real and approachable. Sexy, but in an understated way that I like very much.

"You look nice," I say before signaling the bartender, who comes over and gets her drink order.

"Thanks. You look tired."

"I am. I had a strange weekend and a strange practice today. I'm having a hard time settling in here."

"I gathered that. Sorry it hasn't been an easy transition for you. I read about you. You got a crazy-good deal when you came here. Most pro players would be thrilled."

"Most pro players would, you're right."

Her beer arrives, and she clinks it against mine before taking a swig. "Do you like this band?"

"They're okay. The energy is better now than when they started."

"That happens sometimes. Bands get energy from the crowd, for better or worse. This crowd seems good."

"Do you know them?"

"No." She shakes her head. "As much as we play out, you'd think I'd see more live music, but I really don't. This is the first time I've come out in a long while."

"By yourself?"

She looks around and gestures. "Me and all my friends," she jokes with a laugh.

"You surely have friends, Billie."

"I do, but no one wanted to come out tonight, and I was in the mood for a drink and a listen, so here I am. And here you are. Small world."

"Small world," I repeat for lack of an original thought of my own.

Things feel awkward as we sit next to each other,

drinking our beers, listening to the band. It's not a bad feeling, so much as I don't know what to say to her. I'm glad for her company, though.

We have a few more drinks, commenting on certain songs or funny things people in the crowd are doing. As the night goes on, it becomes more comfortable between us, and I enjoy her company, the conversation, the music vibe of the club. It's a good time with her. Even more than that, if I'm truthful. I'm fixated on her lips, remembering the kisses we shared on that first night we met.

I try to shake it off. I am still, technically, with Emily. I am still, technically, committed to trying to make our relationship work. And Emily is still, technically, with me, though her actions over the weekend certainly gave a different impression.

When one particularly good song comes on, Billie jumps up and claps her hands over her head, her hips swaying. She crooks her finger to get me to dance with her, but I shake my head, unable to stop myself from grinning. She rolls her eyes and dances in front of me for at least three songs, shaking her butt and being silly before grabbing my hands and saying, "I'm hungry!"

"Want to go get food?"

"Yes, sir, that's why I said it!"

I stand, tossing money on the bar to close out our tab as she tows me out the door.

"I want chicken and waffles," Billie announces, holding my hand and pulling me down the street to a small take-out place.

"Chicken and waffles?" I frown at her. "That just sounds weird."

"You're gonna love it, I promise."

"I'm not so sure…"

Twenty minutes later, I've devoured my portion, a whole fried chicken breast, and a crispy waffle, both slathered in maple syrup.

"I stand corrected." I rub my stomach. "That was tasty."

"See? You need to let loose and try new things."

"What makes you say that?"

"I can tell you're a little uptight. You like your life to be tidy and predictable. Which is why I have a hard time figuring out why you play hockey. How you play hockey. It seems like the inability to control the outcome would drive you crazy."

"I don't worry about anything other than my own job. I can control my own outcomes."

"Spoken like a man who likes to be in control."

"It's not a control thing really," I try to explain it to her. "It's a routine thing. I like routine."

"So, you had your routine in Montreal and now you're figuring out what your routine will look like in Vegas?"

"I suppose I must because it looks like I'm going to be here for a while."

"Hmm." She puts her lips together as she makes the sound. Billie has very pretty lips.

"Can I get you a cab to take you home, Billie?"

"Will you share the ride with me, Cal?"

"I don't know where you live. Does it make sense to share a ride?"

"We'll figure it out," she says with a smile.

She goes to hail a cab. I can't help but think about Emily's text messages earlier. *I think we need some space. I'm sorry.* Should I be texting Emily back, agreeing with her? Should I be telling her that *while we have space* and *while she needs a break* I'm going to sleep with another woman? Would. She. Care?

I look up as a cab pulls up and Billie hops in, leaving the door open. "You okay there, Cal?"

Seeing her beautiful, eager face, I make my decision. I nod, sliding in next to her. "I'm fine."

"Where to?" the driver asks.

"Just drive for a minute," Billie tells him. "We're figuring it out."

The cab starts moving, and I'm confused. Just as I'm about to ask what she has in mind, she crawls onto my lap, puts her hands on my cheeks, and kisses me hard on the mouth. She bites softly at my bottom lip, and I open my mouth, our tongues mingling, our mouths a mix of beer and chicken and the sweetness of maple syrup. It's weird and hot at the same time. As our kissing intensifies, she grinds her hips against me. I'm getting hard when I find my hands have moved to her hips, holding her against me. A firm yank pulls her even closer. She feels too good to resist.

I break from her mouth to kiss her neck, her hair tickling my face. She sighs and then rolls away, taking her seat next to me, fanning her face with her hand as she giggles slightly.

"I'm not drunk," she says breathlessly. "I just want you to know that."

"Okay?" It comes out as a question, because I feel I

should ask her what she wants here. I think I know, but then I'm worse than bad at reading interactions with people I barely know.

"What's your address?" Billie asks abruptly, breaking through my spiraling thoughts.

I don't know if I should do this...if we should do this. But then I think of Emily's texts...

She wants her "space" and needs "a break."

Well, she's had both, hasn't she? I'm far away, in another country even. And I'm all alone. She's got Nick, whoever that is. The guy she can't stop messaging when she's spending what little time I made for us to be together.

Billie is real. She's here, and she's warm, and her mouth feels good on mine. She doesn't seem to care that I'm awkward, that I'm strange. She doesn't care that I'm a hockey player. She seems, at this moment, to simply want me. And I think I want her too. It's a hard pill to swallow, to believe you're in it for the long haul with someone, only to see it fall apart at the first challenge.

But then, a bright light appears in the form of a woman who can beat the hell out of a drum kit, a woman who shows up right when I seem to need her the most.

I look over, and she's obviously awaiting a response. What's my address? She asks again, more insistent this time.

I tell the driver my address.

12

pretend it didn't happen

Billie

I want to fuck him so badly.

Such a very crass thought to be crashing around inside my head right now, but it's exactly how I feel.

It's been a long time since I've been in a relationship, a long time since I've had sex with anyone other than battery-powered devices. Because I am not a one-night stand kind of girl. This is not random, of course, because it's Calum Lefleur, a well-known goalie in the NHL. Also, the guy I have to work with once a week on a music program at my job.

This is stupid. Of course, it's stupid. I can't have hookup sex with a guy I have to see every week for the next few months. It'll be terribly awkward and weird, and he's already terribly awkward and weird. And I don't even know if I like him that much. He doesn't think before he speaks. He's judgmental. He's aloof. He's infuriating as hell to me, more often than not.

He's also a gorgeous guy who doesn't at all act like he even knows it.

Which is a very rare quality for a man who looks like he does. Cal is such a conundrum in so many ways.

"I'm sorry," I blurt. "Maybe I shouldn't have—"

"Did you change your mind?" His intense blue eyes swing over to me, holding me in place, keeping me from telling the cabbie to pull over so I can get out and run fast in the opposite direction.

"No, I..." Big breath in, big breath out. "If we do this, can we pretend it didn't happen afterward? Like, when we work together at the center, can we pretend it didn't happen so things don't get weird?"

"Yes, we can pretend it didn't happen. If that's what you want, Billie."

"It is."

The cab stops at what I assume is his building, and we tumble out, Cal paying the driver before shutting the door. Then he stands on the curb, hands in pockets, chewing on his bottom lip. The look on his face is definitely one I'd describe as pensive, but as usual, he doesn't give anything away.

Neither of us say a word. We just stare at each other.

I want to give him all the time he needs because I get it—I'm not a hookup person, and maybe he isn't either. It's hard to decide if this is a step we should take or a huge, messy misstep that'll land us both in a big pile of something unpleasant.

This feels crazy and complicated, but also exciting.

There's definitely something drawing me to this man, at least sexually, and I do want to be with him. I tell myself there's always tomorrow. Tomorrow...I can go back to finding Calum Lefleur strange and annoying if this doesn't work out.

Finally, after what feels like ages, he nods to himself, his decision made apparently. There is a subtle movement of his hand as he starts walking ahead of me. Just a quick reach in my direction—an offering of a sort.

So, I put my hand into his much bigger one. His grip, firm and warm, envelops mine as he leads me inside the building.

My heart is pumping heavily inside my chest, but yet, I know I won't change my mind.

His sixth-floor apartment is a compact two-bedroom, sparsely decorated. The things that are visible are neatly organized, folded, and put in their places. The colors are beige and gray, navy blue. Everything feels controlled and impermanent. It's a nice space, but it doesn't feel like a home. It doesn't feel like he plans to invest any time in it because he doesn't plan to stay long at all, but he's invested enough in his own comfort to ensure that things don't feel untidy or unmanaged. It's so contained...much like the man himself. Strangely, I like the quietness of it, which is very unlike me.

"Ah..." he says, putting his keys on the kitchen counter.

I let out a bubble of a laugh that sounds stupid—far girlier than I think I come off on a normal day. It makes my cheeks heat with a blush that I'm hoping he can't see in this dim space lit only by a standing lamp near the door. I clear my throat nervously. "They say you can tell a lot about a person from the way they arrange their private space."

"I'm not that complicated. And nothing in here is *arranged.*"

"We're all complicated. Humans are complicated beings."

Cal chews on that for a minute as I take in the look of him. He's tall, a robust six foot three. I know this because I've read his official NHL bio. Yeah, ya got me. I'm guilty of googling Calum Lefleur and searching the Internet for details about how tall, broad-shouldered, and long-legged he is. How he has really good hair the ladies are just dying to drag their fingers through. How he has eyes the color of the deep blue sea they could drown in. Yeah, I might have read some stuff like that about him. And none of it is untrue. Opinions are individual, but I agree with what the writer said about Calum Lefleur. He does have good hair—a sun-streaked brown artfully mussed into place. It suits him. His clothes work similarly in their suitability: a long-sleeved, navy T-shirt, dark jeans, and navy Adidas shoes. Understated and simple on their face, but once attached to his sculpted form become something arresting that catches the eye. I suspect the rest of the clothes in his closet transform in a similar way once he puts them on his body.

He takes the few steps back so that we're facing each other. "I'm not, ah..."

"You're not what? Not sure what to do next? Not sure this was a good decision?"

"Maybe both?"

"I'll take the lead if you can relinquish control?"

He nods, just once. He still looks like he's thinking on something.

"Don't overthink this," I tell him. "We'll get this… whatever this is…out of our systems. We'll move on from it after. Deal?"

"Deal," he says softly.

I put my hands on his biceps. God, they are muscular. Exploring with clothes still on, I feel the corded muscle of his forearms, the bulge of pectorals, the ripple of abdominals. Yep. All the right things are there. An ache blooms in my lower belly, an ache I haven't felt since the night I met him, the night I kissed him so carelessly.

"You are…very fit." The words come out of my mouth breathlessly, making me flush hotter.

"Athlete," he says, his eyes closing as I cup his cock through his jeans. He's semi-hard, for sure, like he was when I straddled him in the cab. He wants me—that much is totally clear.

I help divest him of his shirt and am rewarded with maybe the most perfect upper body I have ever seen in person. I actually sigh, much to my chagrin. It makes him smirk. Not a smile. I don't know if I've ever seen him truly smile. He always looks slightly uncomfortable, even when I know he's having a decent time. It's good to see him make a face resembling happiness or enjoyment or amusement.

Taking my time, I repeat the exploration, hand on

skin, gooseflesh erupting all over his arms as I run my fingertips and palms over every muscle, savoring the feel of his warm skin.

Calum Lefleur is a work of art with his slightly golden skin. He looks like he belongs on the pages of a California surf magazine more than a far-northern Montreal ice hockey rink. He is, quite simply, delicious from head to toe.

He does not stop me as I reach for his belt. So, I move on to unbuckling him, then working the button free, and then unzipping, the sound of the zipper practically screaming into the silence.

The sound triggers something in Cal, and he starts helping to free himself from the jeans and the socks until he's standing before me in nothing but thin gray boxers.

"I want to see you." Oh, how I want to see him. I've never been this bold with a partner before, and it shocks me to hear myself saying the words at this moment. But I don't have time to ponder my boldness for long.

Because he ditches the boxers and tosses them away before straightening again to his full height— every naked inch of him on display for my eyes to devour.

Holy Moses. Inches indeed. A lot of inches.

As I assess the loooong, hard length of his cock, I take a pass around him, touching his ass, which is sculpted and perfect. His quads are insane. He just gets better and better the more I look.

While admiring the very naked and spectacular Cal, I start to feel a little nervous he might not like my body. I haven't been naked with a man in a long time. I decide my approach will be to make him want me so badly that he won't care about anything other than being inside of me.

I fall to my knees, stroking his cock with my hand, cupping the twin weights with the other. I take a taste, first, just a quick swirl of my tongue around his head. His hips jut forward, lust taking over as he stares at me, his intense eyes darkening with desire.

Encouraged, I slip my mouth around him like a sheath, taking in as much of his length as I can. Back and forth, a slow torture, I work his cock, my tongue licking, my mouth sucking, unabashed noises of desire building in the back of my throat as his hands find my hair and his hips pump. He fucks my mouth with his hands gripped firmly in my hair. It's erotic overload to the millionth power as I let myself awash in the sensation of sex and fucking and the forbidden. All of it...

A trickle of salty precum tells me to back off before this party ends too quickly. I give a last lick, and he helps me to my feet, tearing my shirt up over my head to get it off me quickly. His lips crush against mine as he pulls me toward him, my breasts smash against the hardness of his chest, our skin so warm together.

Cal picks me up easily; those beautiful muscles of his more than just for show. My legs wrap around his waist as he carries me to the bedroom and deposits me onto his bed. Making quick work of my boots, jeans, and socks, he leaves me in nothing but my bra and panties. As he looms above me, I can see how his carved chest moves along with each breath, appearing more intense than I've ever seen him. A wildness has set into Cal, and it makes me want him even more.

He stares down at me, and then, with no hesitation whatsoever, he takes ahold of each of my thighs with his hands and parts them. He does pause then, another offering of consent, perhaps? The communication between us flows with a knowledge of where this will go. I nod once up at him, letting him know my answer.

Then he buries his face between my legs.

I cannot hold back the gasp that slips out of me as his hot breath burns through the black satin of my panties. Rubbing myself shamelessly against his face, and nearly out of my mind from the sexual heat of his lips against my clit, separated only by a thin wisp of satin, I bury my hands in his hair—hair I've wanted to touch since the day I first laid eyes on him. *Soft—so much softer than I thought it'd be.*

I lose all conscious thought once he pulls my panties to one side and slips a finger inside me while keeping up with what his clever mouth was doing already. I won't last long at this rate. I can't stop what's coming. Literally. Coming.

Incoherent words bubble out of me. "Oh, God, yes. Please. More of that." When a second long finger penetrates me, I feel the wave of pleasure start its fatal roll. My head thrown back against his bed, I try to encompass everything I'm feeling with him. *Yes. Yes. This is what I needed. What I craved. Yes. Yes. So much, yes.*

Doing this with him *was* worth it.

When he interprets my signals of impending

orgasm (thank the Lord) he rips my panties off fully, grabs a condom from his nightstand, and sheaths himself.

"Is this okay?" More intense staring out of those deep blues of his. "Billie?"

I love the way he says my name, his Canadian accent working as a sort of beacon, forcing me out of my head and back into this moment with him. "Yes. Yes. Please. Please." I'm begging him now, panting, half-crazed, wanting to come so badly, I don't care about the hurt that's coming—the good hurt I'll feel when he stretches me wide with that huge cock he's sporting.

Calum slides inside me without hesitation, then. He holds still for a moment while I get used to the fullness. "Tight," he breathes, his forehead on my forehead.

"Been a long while," I say, widening my legs, allowing him fuller entrance.

When he starts to move, I come. No buildup. No preamble. I just come, tightening and pulsing around him as he sucks in a surprised breath. My hands on his perfect ass, I encourage him to move faster, to go harder. He does, and it seems my orgasm goes on forever and ever until I can't breathe. I think I forget how to say real words. It's just me and him and the intensity of my body's reaction to him.

"Harder, Calum."

He fucks me, then. Hard. His every muscle straining as he pushes in and out of me, the headboard banging against the wall. His eyes are on mine, teeth bared like an animal until he climaxes, when his face relaxes into a state of ecstasy. It's gorgeous, really, to see him like this. Totally abandoned.

He slows a bit, his cock throbbing inside of me, and when it finally settles, he stops, falling to the side of me, breathing heavily.

"That was—"

"Intense?" I ask.

"Yes."

"Good intense?"

He considers my face for a moment. He looks a bit dreamy, heavy-lidded, lips slightly parted. Relaxed looks really fantastic on him.

"It was more than good, at least for me." There's a bit of a question in the statement.

"Good. I liked it, too." I put a hand on his smooth cheek and lean in, softly kissing his lips.

Calum kisses me back, softly, sweetly. Not a kiss I would call forgettable. Not a kiss I would give or receive from someone who should be forgotten.

My eyes are heavy, and while I know I should leave, should thank him for the massive orgasm and head home, never to speak of this again, I don't.

I don't do any of that.

I don't leave.

Instead, I let my eyes close, drifting in and out as I struggle to stay awake.

But staying awake is an impossibility.

Impossible once I feel the gentle weight of a soft blanket being tucked around me, my naked body still tingling from what he just did to it.

Impossible with the way he lies next to me—close but not making it feel too intimate, too soon.

Impossible because everything feels too wonderful to do anything *but* give in to the call of glorious, superb, intoxicating sleep.

So, I do.

I let myself fall asleep next to a man I *know* I should not be falling asleep next to.

13
it's...complicated

Cal

I wake up feeling oddly groggy. Not hung over because I wasn't drunk, but definitely...fuzzy. As I roll onto my back, my brain comes fully online. I remember.

I remember what Billie Hirsch and I did in my bed last night.

My bed that she later fell asleep in.

After the best sex I've ever had.

In my life.

Full stop.

What the fuck did you do?

Billie's gone now, of course. I guess I shouldn't be surprised. She did say she wanted to forget about it afterward. But when she fell asleep so peacefully, a part of me thought maybe she would stay. Maybe she wouldn't run.

But then, it's probably best that she did take off before I woke up. What was I even thinking? Yeah, I realize there's been this instant chemistry thing happening between us for a while. And maybe not consciously, but I *was* about to get in that cab last night, even without the direct invite from Billie.

When Em texted, asking for a break, something just snapped. My decision was made even easier when Billie asked if we could just forget it ever happened afterward and just leave the experience behind us. *Why yes, Billie. Yes, we can certainly do that.* Like passing GO and getting the two hundred dollars, plus a Get-Out-of-Jail-Free card, all on the same roll.

And I never texted Em back.

Emily Marshall and I have been together for more than two years. We met at a college party. I was the interloper, as always, not a college student. Already playing in the NHL, but there with a high school friend, sticking to the sidelines. I was watching the fun, as per usual, nursing my beer and saying every wrong thing to every young woman who came up to talk to me.

Emily had just graduated college and moved to Montreal to start her master's program. She was pretty and petite, and she seemed just as uncomfortable at the party as I was, so we took a walk outside, sat on a deck bench, and started to talk. She didn't seem bothered by my awkwardness, by the directness of my communication style. I relaxed a little more each time we hung out, and suddenly we were a thing, a couple. We had melted into a routine that had her staying at my place several nights a week.

She's never been much of a hockey fan, though she would come out periodically to watch me play. Our relationship wasn't built on what I do for a living or what she studies. For me, it was built on a sense of comfort. I felt comfortable with her.

Lately, I'm not sure what she saw in me. When Evan asked me what I loved about her, I found it hard to find the words to answer.

Still, I don't feel great about what I just did. I slept with another woman. And I liked it. A lot. I like Billie a lot, to be honest. She has a wild spirit about her that she keeps mostly contained, even though it's still clearly visible. Like the wild strands of her purple-tipped hair, slipping free of their braid here and there in a kind of defiance. Intriguing…

I chew on this, these new realizations, as I stare at my phone. I should call Emily.

It takes me maybe fifteen minutes to psych myself up to make the call, and when I do, she answers, "Yes, Cal," as if I'm annoying her.

"Hey, I wanted to call and talk. I got your texts last night."

She's quiet on the other end of the line. "This isn't really a good time."

"Why?"

"Just…because. I'm researching."

"Do you miss me at all?" *You shouldn't have to ask her that.*

"I just saw you last weekend."

"That's not an answer, Em."

"Look, I'm just really busy. It's a weird time. School is busy. You're in another city. It's hard right now, and that's why I suggested a break."

"A breakup you mean."

"I mean…I guess…it is technically, but you don't

have to classify it like that if you don't want to. Just... let's back off. You try to settle into Vegas. Make more of an effort. Stop clinging to me. I can't help you there, Cal, because I have to attend to my life in Montreal."

"I'm not clinging." A rising tide of anxiety fills my head with fuzz. "We're a couple. We're in a relationship. You're supposed to be my partner and I'm far from home. Expecting a little of your attention doesn't seem like that much to ask."

"My attention isn't going to fix this. You want what you had before. You want routine surroundings, routine schedules. My paying attention to you on the phone or whatever isn't going to make that happen."

"But you have to put *some* effort into trying to make it work, Em. I was willing to try because you understand me and that's hard to find."

Emily laughs, and it's a bitter sound. "Well, I imagine it is hard to find a partner who can live with your undiagnosed Asperger's."

My stomach sinks. "I don't have Asperger's."

She laughs again. "Okay. Whatever you say."

A heartbeat passes. Two. I can't be on this call anymore. "I'm gonna go. Call me if you want to talk later. Maybe. Whenever."

She doesn't even bother to reply before the call disconnects.

So, I guess this makes it official. Dumped by Emily Marshall a little over a month in to our new reality.

I stare stupidly at my phone like it might light up with Em calling me back, saying she didn't mean it, but I know that's not happening. The situation with her hasn't been good for a while, if I'm honest...

obviously…based on what I was doing last night with Billie, break or no break. It hasn't felt right because everything was fucked the minute I got traded. *Did I do this? Am I to blame for the failure of our relationship?* Replaying our conversation—the way Em spoke down to me, her insinuations—makes my skin crawl, so much so, I want to scratch it all off.

This is not good for me.

I need to blow off some steam.

So, I dress quickly and head to the gym at the practice arena. One of the physical trainers, a guy named Dale, is there when I walk in. He's got a weightlifter's build and an affable personality, personified by the upbeat welcome I get as I walk in.

"Hey there," he says as I toss my bag on the floor. "Thought it might just be me and the ghosts in here this morning. You're up early, big guy."

I head to the treadmill and start my run as a warmup without saying anything. He wanders over and analyzes my gait for a minute.

"Try to get that knee up a bit on your stride. And pitch forward just a hair. You'll be able to get more power out of your stride that way."

"I didn't ask for your advice," I growl, yet still trying to do what he advises.

He chuckles. "So, this is a mood-enhancing workout, then?"

"I guess."

Dale pushes the tempo of the run up a notch and gives some more instruction. I have to admit I do feel better as I run, implementing his slight adjustments to my posture and gait. I run about two miles before he tells me to hop off. I let him lead me through a workout as he talks and gossips the whole time.

"You're new here, so you probably don't know all the stories. It's so crazy. So, Evan Kazmeirowicz was a total ladies' man a few years back. He was a strong player, no issues there, but not the leader he is today. He met his wife, and there was a non-fraternization policy designed to prevent players and staff from intermingling. But he fell hard for her, and management made an exception, which was good because it really straightened him up. He made all-stars and got team captain. Super solid now, two kids, kick-ass record."

"He's a good captain," I admit as I test out the weight on a deadlift. This is not what I came here for. I don't care about Evan's relationship woes. It's all white noise to me. As long as he's a skillful captain, that's okay.

"And Georg?" Dale whistles through his teeth and rolls his eyes. "What a hot-ass mess. Seriously. He was a total drunk, only sober to play. He'd come in here and practically throw up, sweating out last night's alcohol. Shitty contract. He was not in good shape, but then he met Pam, and it was like he turned into a new man."

I open my mouth to say I haven't properly met Georg Kolochev yet. I mean, I've seen him at practice, and I know he's good from seeing him play in the finals, but we haven't had a real conversation. Dale coaches me through the deadlifts, though, and the thought is forgotten as we switch out the weights for back squats.

"Then Viktor came and got with Scarlett and now they have a baby," Dale continues chattering. "Next, the new guy, Boris comes in and, *bam*, he's in love and settled down, too. Meanwhile, holy shit, Tyler? Have you met that guy? Most obnoxious dude I've ever met. Total hound dog behavior with the females. And who does he end up with? Friggin' Kolochev's little sister. And I mean little. She's barely an adult, seriously. But he's all moony and on the straight and narrow. It's like the old men's club around here now. Hey, you got a girl?"

I finish the reps on these squats and wipe the sweat from my forehead with the sleeve of my shirt. I've tolerated the team gossip, as it's pointed me away from thoughts of Emily and my situation with Billie. I mean, I guess there isn't a situation with Billie, per se. We agreed it was a one-time thing and we wouldn't make it weird. Still, I feel weird, because even though Emily said we're no longer together—even though I know in my heart she's probably cheating with her study partner Nick—I still feel like it was me who did the bad thing.

Now, though, here is the question. Do I have a girl?

"It's complicated."

"That's a Facebook answer if I've ever heard one. What do you mean, *it's complicated*?"

"I thought I had a girl, but she's been distant since I moved here. She's doing her master's degree in Montreal, so she claims it's just because she's busy, but I'm sure it's more than that. It's been strained between us. She lacks her usual…tolerance. And she's talking about this other guy—"

"Wait, she's talking about another guy? To you?"

"Some guy in her program. He was DM'ing her while she was here to visit recently."

"Did you read through the DMs?"

"No." I shake my head. Dale has me do a series of sit-ups where he throws me a medicine ball and I throw it back each time I sit up.

"What the hell? Why not?"

"I guess I didn't really want to know. I just want things to get back to normal. I'm a routine-oriented guy. I like things where they belong and nothing feels like it's where it belongs right now, including me."

"Well, moving to a new place and a new team can't be easy. And as for your girl? If you really want her, maybe you should do some big, grand gesture to reignite the romance or whatever. Those seem to be popular around here, too. Georg's lady came out in a playboy bunny outfit to propose to him, so..."

I cringe at the thought. I'd be so uncomfortable doing some big thing in front of a bunch of people. I'm fine just being the guy at the net, no eyes on me until a puck comes my way. Still, I find myself lost in thought about the idea of romance as Dale continues to talk his way through my workout. He says he keeps waiting for lightning to strike him, too, but that he has bad luck with women. The ones he likes are always taken.

I only half hear him as I contemplate the idea of romance. Have Emily and I ever really had what would be considered a romance? Certainly, during the best times, there was comfort and companionship. But romance? Not really.

Even the sex...I shake it from my head. Billie and I

have real chemistry, that much is obvious. I've never felt freer in the bedroom or more confident. Billie Hirsch and I fit together in that way. The sex with Emily was always sort of prescriptive and lukewarm.

My thoughts are a jumble. Maybe this break with Emily is a good thing. Maybe we should just end it, and maybe I should put more effort into making a new life here in Las Vegas?

As I'm finishing up the workout, other players start to arrive. Many of them give a nod or short hello, better than the cold reception I received when I first arrived. At the end of the day, I know the team will protect and support me—which is how good sports franchises work. The team works together, and this one definitely does.

At least there is that. The possibility of feeling like I am part of this team after all.

If nothing else, I am still a damn good goalie.

14

mr. great goalie

Billie

I'm just finishing our first drumming lesson, and the kids want me to do a solo to close things out. I start by giving them a simple quarter note beat to follow, and we play together for about sixty seconds before I take off with a solo from one of my band's songs. It's one of my favorites, mainly because it features some broken beats that aren't common in a lot of songs today.

I finish with a big fill and the crash of cymbals, to which the kids all clap and cheer. Scrambling to talk over each other, they excitedly tell me they can't wait to learn more licks.

Cal has come in at some point, I realize as I have the kids help pull the kits along the wall and clean up random sticks and drum keys laying about. He's leaning against the closed door, arms folded over his broad chest, looking far too distractingly handsome for me to ignore. Cal doesn't smile a lot, I've realized, but his expression isn't cold, either. It's more along the lines of amused, like he thinks what I just did was cute.

I push back the thoughts of the night we shared, the way our bodies fit together, the way he made me feel. I've been pushing those thoughts back since I woke up at dawn, naked in the bed next to him as he slept. He looked so young, boyish, free of whatever wicked thing controlled him during the sex we had the night before. His lips were slightly parted, his arm thrown up over his head on the pillow. I wanted to kiss him awake, to have him inside me again, but instead, I left. I found my clothing, put it on, and left, ready to make good on the promise it was a one-time thing, something to be put behind us.

Our eyes meet and I blush. Clearly, I've got some work to do on the "putting-it-behind-us" part.

As my drummers leave, thanking me for a fun lesson, the group of guitarists come in. I have them all sit on the carpet for a minute.

"Kids, this is Calum Lefleur—"

"Cal," he corrects.

"Cal," I say with a nod. "He's the new goalie for the Vegas Crush hockey team. Any hockey fans among us?"

A couple of hands go up. One kid says, "He's supposed to be the best goalie in the game."

"I *am* the best goalie in the game." His French-Canadian accent comes out stronger than I've noticed before today. Probably because he doesn't talk all that much. Still, it's incredibly sexy and makes my lady parts tingle in a way that's far from appropriate for a community center music lesson with a bunch of bright-eyed kiddos in the room watching *everything*.

Hello? Supposed to be working here. Damn Calum Lefleur and his hotness.

I try to shake off the weird changeling effect he seems to have on me, clearing my throat for impact. "Well, being a great goalie has absolutely *bupkus* to do with teaching the guitar. And that's what Cal is here to do. Thanks to the Crush Foundation, we have all these awesome new instruments, and we have Mr. Great Goalie here to teach you guitar. Have at it."

I head for the door but hang out as Cal peruses the row of guitars and chooses one. He straps it on and plucks out a few notes before announcing everyone needs to learn how to properly tune a guitar before anything else. He has them all choose a guitar, and then they all work on tuning. He talks about the frets and the notes each string makes. He has a clip-on tuner with him, and he talks about the different types of tuners guitarists can use, especially when they are just learning.

It's impressive, really. He's less awkward than usual. He's even...engaging. Sweet. Patient. He talks about taking care of the instrument, what to do if a string breaks, and how to tune by ear if you don't have a tuner.

Once the guitars are tuned, he teaches basic notes. Everyone seems to be fine and happy, so I step out, heading for my office to check email and give myself a break from whatever this crush is I've developed for Calum Lefleur. It's not made any easier by how good he is with those kids. I expected him to be standoffish and possibly rude to them, but he's not, and it both confuses and delights me.

About forty-five minutes later, I head back to find him playing a song on one of the acoustic guitars. It's pretty, and I don't recognize it, but I doubt he's a songwriter, so I make a mental note to ask what it was later.

"Okay," I say from the doorway as he finishes, clapping my hands. "That was awesome. Can you all thank Cal for coming out today?"

The kids thank him and ask when he'll come back.

"Next week, for sure," he says, nodding, "but not the same day of the week. We start traveling for pre-season games, so I'll have to check my hockey schedule and then set some times with Ms. Hirsch."

"Oooh, can we come to the big hockey arena and skate?" one of the girls asks.

A chorus of "yeah" and "please" follows, and Cal holds up his hands, looking a little overwhelmed.

"I will see what I can do," he says, which seems to appease the horde.

We clean up and send the kids off to their next activity before Cal follows me to my office to figure out when he can come again.

"You did well," I say as I sit at my computer, pulling up the club's activity schedule.

"I told you I knew how to do this."

"Your overconfidence makes me want to gag sometimes, buddy, not gonna lie."

"Well, I know what I can do well and what I cannot. There is no reason to feign humility."

I laugh out loud at this and find him smirking

slightly, a wicked glint in his eye. "Well, I guess that's why you're so good in bed, then." It slips out, and though I blush, I hold his gaze, trying to come off as confident and sexy rather than embarrassed and awkward. "Oops. I talked about the thing we weren't supposed to talk about."

"It is what it is. The sex was really, really good. I'm not sorry about it."

It feels like the energy between us is supercharged all of a sudden. He licks his bottom lip. I think it's an unconscious action, but it's delicious, nonetheless. I stand up, practically panting.

"Is it hot in here?" My attempt at a joke.

Cal kicks the door shut and steps forward, pulling me to him and kissing me hard on the mouth. "What are you doing to me?" he muses to himself in between kisses.

"What am *I* doing to *you*? I'm not even sure I even *like* you all that much," I tell him on a shaky laugh.

"That's fine. I'm used to people not liking me."

That stops me. I put a hand on his chest and back away. "Really? That's...kind of sad."

"Don't pity me." He shakes his head as if shaking away the dreamy desire of a moment ago in a return to reality. "I'm fine with it. It takes me a long time to get to know people, to figure out how they fit into my life. It's hard for me to make connections and people are not patient, so they often move on."

For whatever reason, this levels me. It hurts my heart. I understand what it means to not fit a mold. I'm a Hirsch, right? A daughter of Hollywood. And yet, I've never felt less than others. Cal is a rich, famous hockey player, but I think the rich and famous doesn't matter to him at all. I'm just realizing this now, and I feel stupid for not recognizing it sooner.

"Well, Cal, maybe we should just be friends, then. Take the time to get to know each other?"

"How would we do that, Billie?"

"We both like music. We can go to some shows together. Enjoy some music?"

He presses his lips together, considering.

"We can get to know each other. I'll take the time, Cal. I'll be patient."

He stares me straight in the eyes for so long it begins to feel uncomfortable. Finally, he nods. "Okay. Actually, one of my favorite bands is playing in LA in a couple of weeks. The show is on an off night in between games in LA and Oakland. I was going to try to make it when I'm in town. Maybe we could see the show together if you're up for a trip?"

I check the date and realize it's the same weekend as my dad's party. "That's, uh, the same week as this family thing. My dad's turning sixty and my mom's throwing a big thing for him."

"Oh." Cal is frowning at me and still manages to look hot.

"I mean, it's not the same night as the show. I could still go. But if I'm in LA, then I have no excuse to skip the party, and my family stresses me out." I'm babbling because thoughts of my family make me panic. I go to this stupid party and my mom will try to fix me up with some dumbass Hollywood type, and my father will compare me to my A-list actor of a brother, and I'll feel like jumping off the balcony to an early grave by the end of the night. But then, I think of a way that things might not go that way at all as I turn to Cal, the hot hockey player. "So, I just got an idea. You could stay in town for the weekend after the Oakland game and go to this party with me and pretend to be my boyfriend?"

Cal's face opens up and he laughs; he actually laughs. "Why on earth would you ever need to have a fake boyfriend?"

"It's complicated. My family's complicated. And it would only be for a night. I can fill you in when we go to the concert. Deal? Do this thing for me?"

"Well, Billie, I guess I can understand when you say 'it's complicated,' so I'll do it." He says all of this with a very non-complicated shrug of his shoulders. Typical Cal behavior paired with that signature subtle smirk he's perfected plastered on his handsome face.

His response makes me happy for some reason.

So happy, in fact, I jump up and kiss him on the cheek. "Yay. We can figure out our plans next week. Now, let's get your next lesson scheduled."

15

i would allow it

Cal

Emily's got her phone propped up, and she's working on her computer as we FaceTime. I was surprised when she suggested it because I was *not* expecting to hear from her so soon after our last conversation.

"Pre-season is starting next week. We start in LA and then play Oakland."

"Well, good luck. How's the team treating you?"

"Fine. They really loved their old goalie, but they understand how important it is to protect their assets."

"Is that what you are? An asset?" Something about her tone sounds intentionally snarky and provocative.

"I'd like to think so, yes." I decide not to rise to the bait.

"Hmm," she answers, smirking to herself as if I can't see her. She doesn't look at me at all, only at her computer.

"Em, what is this? Are we done?" I ask with a sigh.

"Done? We just got on the phone."

"I *mean*, is our relationship done?"

"No," she says, finally looking at me through the screen. "I just said we needed space. A break. Time to focus on other things. I'm busy with school; you're trying to settle in there. We just need some time."

"That's not how I read into it when you suggested a break."

"Well, I'm sorry if that's the case."

"Are you? I mean, you talk about this Nick guy all the time. I just wonder if—"

"If what, Cal?" She's now officially irritated. Her mouth puckers.

"If you're seeing him. Nick. Are you?"

"That's stupid, Cal. Get out of your own head."

To me, her tone sounds defensive, and she's turned away again, back to her computer screen, dismissing me.

"But is it stupid?" I challenge.

"Yes. I'm not seeing Nick. He's in my cohort. We spend a lot of time together. Doing work. That's all."

A part of me, I think, wanted her to admit to it. To tell me she's seeing him. It would make my raging guilt a little less...I wonder if, maybe, if I told her the truth, she would tell me the truth as well. We could work it out from there. This break. A breakup. I still feel a little in the dark about what this break really is.

"Do you still love me?" *I shouldn't have to ask.*

"Oh my *God*, Cal," she heaves, exasperated. "I feel like I'm dating a middle schooler. You need more pats on the head than a golden retriever. It's exhausting."

"Well, the last time you were in town, you barely touched me, even to hold my hand. You certainly didn't want to be intimate. Is it any wonder I'm feeling a little unclear about your feelings for me these days?"

She sighs dramatically and faces me through the camera again. "Calum. We've hit a lull. A low point. It's to be expected, I think. We're in two different places, going through two different points in our careers. We need different things right now. Which is why I called a halt."

"To our relationship."

"Yes."

"And this halt—it's a breakup, right?"

"I mean, I guess? But the kind where you know you'll eventually get back together. We just need time to get through this. I need to focus on my work here. You need to settle into your new team. We need to see where the wind blows us. Maybe it will bring us closer together. Maybe further apart. But for now? I just need to focus. I still care for you, but I just need space."

Well, that's about as clear as mud. In my mind, it's all systems go for moving on. At least for now. Still, I need to know for sure. "So, in a break, are we seeing other people?"

She laughs. "Well, I suppose you can try."

The fuck? I can try? "What's that supposed to mean?"

"It means you're not exactly a lady killer."

"I'm a professional hockey player, Emily. I don't have to be a lady killer. The ladies come to us."

She scoffs at me. "Calum Lefleur, you're not talking about sleeping with one of those hockey hoes, are you?"

I raise a shoulder and make a noise, just to spite her.

She laughs out loud. "Well, good luck with that."

I've already had sex with another woman, Emily, and no luck was needed. Just incredible chemistry.

Of course, I can't say that. I'm not that disrespectful. I am still trying to process her words though. *"We need to see where the wind blows us. Maybe it will bring us closer together. Maybe further apart."* She didn't say whether or not she still loves me. She wants to live her life without me until *the wind blows* and we possibly end up together. And what it also boils down to is that she doesn't believe anyone else would want me. As if she's the only woman who would want to be with me.

It's as if she thinks of me as this puppy, this little dog to be petted, sitting patiently, awaiting her attention. Well, I'm not.

"I was going to ask if you wanted to have phone sex."

"Only you would be oblivious enough to ask for phone sex after talking about a breakup," Emily says, shaking her head.

"I said I was *going* to ask. Just trying to reconnect is all, to see if we still have something there. Remember how we did phone sex when I was on the road that one time?"

"Cal, phone sex is not the way to reconnect."

"Well, Em, neither is actually reconnecting, I guess. Romantic dinner? Weekend in a fun city? No, and no."

Emily is quiet for a minute, and then she says,

"Things change, you know?" It's probably the most honest thing she's said to me in a long while. At least she finally sounds sincere, and her tone isn't bitter.

"They do," I agree. I blow out a loud breath and add, "I'm sorry, Em. If a break is what you need, then let's take a break. I want you to be happy."

"I know you do, Cal, but right now I've got to go. We'll talk in a few weeks, okay?"

She hangs up before I can even respond.

WE'VE JUST WON our first pre-season game, three to one. I'm in awe, really, of the precision of our starting lineup. I guess I shouldn't be since I played them in last season's divisional finals.

Of thirty shots on goal by LA, only about eighteen came close enough to need a save. Only one went in, which I consider good odds. Not great. I hate letting anything in, but the score was fair and sharp, and I can't fault someone with good aim. The LA team was ready for us, and they put up a good fight.

Now we're in the hotel bar, where a raucous country band is playing. The guys with wives and girlfriends are sitting around a few tables, shoved together haphazardly, various empty beer bottles and soda glasses strewn about.

Some of the rowdier guys have gone out for the night, but a few others sit at the bar with me. It's nice to be included, and I'm getting a lot of claps on the back, but I feel like a fish out of water just sitting there, not understanding their inside jokes or knowing which puck bunny they're referring to with their bedroom bragging.

I've never been into one-night stands or sleeping with groupies like some of my teammates have. It's not that I judge them. I understand, I guess, the allure of it, of the party scene, of living fast and free. It's just… I'm not built for that. I'm too reserved, too set in my ways, too reliant on structure.

"You look miserable, dude," a voice says to my left. It's Evan. "You stopped a shit-ton of shots tonight. You should be happy."

"Well, I didn't stop all of them."

Evan lifts a shoulder and takes a swig from his beer bottle. "Enough to give us a win in our first preseason."

"A win is a win."

"Exactly. You looked good out there; did you feel good?"

I nod. "Once I'm on ice, other things go away."

"I understand that feeling. Guys being nice?"

"They're fine."

"And off ice? How are things with your girl?"

I shake my head and work on peeling the label from my beer bottle. "Taking a break."

"Your call or hers?"

"Hers, but it's fine. I thought a lot about what you said, and it was hard to pinpoint why we were together. A break is probably the best thing for us right now."

"Plenty of fish in the sea," Evan says, though it's lukewarm. I know he's a changed man now that he's married with kids. Dating random women isn't part of his lifestyle anymore.

"I did make a new friend," I offer.

"A female friend?"

I hold back a grin at the thought of Billie. *Yes, she is very, very female.* I have to physically stop myself from drifting off into the thoughts I've had about her ever since our night together.

"Okay, so I'm going to assume yes," Evan says. "Who is she?"

"Billie. We met doing the PR thing with the Crush Foundation Music Workshop at the boys and girls club I told you about before."

"Oh? You're teaching kids how to play guitar, right?"

"Right. It's actually a lot of fun. I'm really liking it."

He makes a surprised face.

"What?"

"Well, now, Cal," he says while taking another pull from his beer, "I just haven't seen you get excited about much since you got to Vegas. And here you are grinning over a girl and telling me you're having fun with a volunteer gig."

My mouth pops open. I'm not sure how to respond, but he's right.

Evan Kazmeirowicz gives me a wide grin and claps me a hard one on the back. "Be careful, young keeper; someone might think you're happy here in Las Vegas."

I MEET BILLIE AT A TINY, dimly lit LA restaurant that looks like a whole lot of nothing compared to some of the flashy places I've seen in Vegas. She's already there when I arrive, looking amazing in black jeans, tall boots, and a black and white plaid shirt. Her hair is in a long braid. There's something wild about the way she looks. She's really put together, but she still looks like she'll fit right in at a rock concert. Maybe it's the gleam in her dark eyes or the mischievous way her mouth curves. Whatever it is, I have to hold myself back from kissing her right here in front of the hostess.

"Hey," she says with a little wave and a big smile. "Glad you found me here okay." *I could find you in a crowd with no problem at all.*

I look around at the simple environment. "I thought I had the wrong place when the cab pulled up here."

"I know it doesn't look like much, but it's delicious. Your belly will be happy after you eat here."

"Okay. I trust you."

She grins and gives the hostess a thumbs-up. We follow, heading back to a two-top table in a secluded alcove. I pull out her chair, and she sits, thanking me.

She chooses the wine, and then we look over the menu for a few minutes. I find my eyes sliding frequently to take in the fullness of her lips, the prominence of her nose. She's such a unique woman, beautiful in a way I can barely process. I want desperately to unclothe her again, to take in every inch of her body. I want to hear her crying out when she's coming like she did during our night together. It's all I can think about.

She asks what I'm having, and I force my mind back to the menu. I rattle off the first thing I see. "Good choice," she tells me.

After our order is in, she focuses her attention on me. "I'm getting the feeling your mind is somewhere else tonight, Cal. Would you rather not go to the show?"

I recoil, surprised by the question. "What? No."

"You just seem…distracted. If you don't want to go out, I understand."

"No, I want to go out," I say quickly. "I'm sorry, I—"

"You what?"

"I'm finding myself distracted, that's true. By you. By how you look tonight. I think you're really beautiful, Billie."

Her cheeks alight with color as she grins and swats at me like she's swatting away the compliment. "Oh. Well, then."

"Let's talk about something," I suggest. "Music? Since we're going to a show?"

"Well, I like rock and alternative primarily, but I'll listen to anything that's musically or lyrically interesting," she offers, the blush in her cheeks still clearly visible. *Compliments make Billie blush.* Duly noted—as I make plans to give her more compliments throughout our evening. Seeing Billie blush really works for me. A. Whole. Fucking. Lot.

"Do you find yourself listening for the drumbeats in songs since you're a drummer?"

"I used to." She twirls her braid in her hand and I'm fascinated. "It was all I could hear when I was first learning, and I'd put on my headphones and try to match beats. I taught myself to play that way. Now, though, unless something is particularly interesting or complex, I try to let go of the layers and hear the whole song. What about you? Are you a guitar-riff kind of guy when you listen to music?"

"No. I just enjoy music. Playing the guitar was something I did just to see if I could do it. I found that I had an aptitude for it so I kept playing, but I'm not very creative, so I can't write. I can only repeat what I hear or play from sheet music."

"Interesting," she says with another rotation of her braid, the electric purple of the last two inches or so of her braided hair flashing as it whips through her fingers.

She rattles off a long list of bands she loves. Some I've heard of, and others are more obscure. We have plenty in common, though, and I find that I enjoy just talking with her. I'm loosening up in Billie's presence in a way I don't usually loosen up with people. She does most of the talking because, let's be honest, I'm not the best conversationalist. Either way, it feels comfortable and good to me in a way I can't recall because I've never experienced it before. I would know if I had. I might suck at sharing my feelings and emotions, but I am crystal fucking clear on when I'm feeling relaxed and comfortable *and good* all together at the same time.

The room is warm and candlelit, and Billie's cheeks are flushed as she pours herself a second glass of wine from the bottle we ordered. I'm still sipping my first and she offers me a pour, but I decline.

"Not a wine guy?" she asks.

One side of my face scrunches up ruefully. "Not really, no. More of a beer guy."

"That seems right to me. Well, order a beer then."

I shake my head. "I'm good with this wine you picked."

Our salads come and I ask her about her family, to which she makes a face, rolling her eyes and sticking out her tongue.

"My parents are both in the entertainment business here in Los Angeles. You'll meet them this weekend if you're still up for the role of fake boyfriend?"

"I'm still up for it, though I don't really know why anyone like you would ever need a fake boyfriend. I'm sure you can get a real one on your own."

"Oh, the sweet things you say," she says with a laugh. "It's not that I can't get a boyfriend. It's that I don't have one at the moment and my mother does not need to be meddling in my love life."

"She's a meddler, your mother?"

Billie barks a loud laugh, then slaps her hand over her mouth, peering around to make sure she didn't call too much attention to herself. When she uncovers her mouth, she says, "My mother is a meddler to the thousandth degree, yes."

"And she wants you to have a boyfriend?"

"Oh, my dear darling Cal, she wants lots of things for me and so far, I've been one disappointment after another. You see, my mother toted me around to be in commercials and television shows and on talent shows for the first ten years of my life. I lived, ate, and breathed child stardom, and I hated every minute of it. So, in retaliation, I went to live with my grandmother in Vegas when I started middle school. Spent middle and high school living a normal life like a normal kid. Got a normal college education and a normal job. My mother is beside herself over the wasted talent."

"What about the band?" I ask as she sits back to sip her wine, her spiel finished, and I suspect finished talking about her "complicated" family relationships as well.

"What about it?" She lets out a bitter laugh and takes another drink of her wine.

"Well, you hated all the show business stuff, but you're in a band. You don't totally hate performing, then."

"True. But I'm no actress. And I'm no performer or dancer. The band is for me. It's on my terms, though my band mates certainly hate that I won't use my parents' clout to get us a record deal."

"They don't know you're in a band, your family?"

She shakes her head. "Nope. It's none of their business."

"That still doesn't explain why you need a fake boyfriend."

"Oh, well, my mom has her heart set on me marrying a celebrity or studio executive. It makes me want to puke, just thinking about the terrible men she could hoist on me. I'd rather her think I'm involved than have to spend the evening being forced to chat with men I'm not interested in, you know what I mean? Plus, fake boyfriend or not, I like hanging with you. Your presence will make the whole night more bearable."

Interesting. "Well, I'm happy to play fake boyfriend, and I'm really enjoying hanging with you, also."

She grins and tips her wine glass to clink against my own. "What about you? You have family back in Montreal?"

I nod, biting the inside of my lip a little as I think about Montreal. Strangely, I haven't thought about going back over the last few days. Funny the effect Billie Hirsch has on me. *And perhaps I am finding my groove in Vegas.* But I do still miss my family. "I'm an only child but I have lots of cousins and other family there. My grandparents were the ones who really supported my interest in hockey growing up, more so than my parents. So, I do understand how family can put pressure on. My parents are both academics. Professors in math and science at Bishop's University in Sherbrooke where I grew up. It's about an hours' drive from Montreal, so everyone is a Habs fan from birth by default. I was good at math and science, so I was supposed to go to MIT and follow in their footsteps but here I am, playing a game for a living."

"Oh, the horror! A professional athlete in the family—what will we tell the neighbors?" Billie teases. Her ability to make jokes as easy as breathing. They're funny too.

I grin and she stares at my mouth as if she's never seen me smile before. "What?"

"It's just, you don't smile that much. I've seen you do it several times tonight and I've decided it's going to be my daily mission this weekend to make it happen again because you have the freaking cutest dimples I've ever seen when you smile."

"Dimples?"

"Yes, sir. So cute. I want to kiss them."

"I would allow it." *And so much more, beautiful Billie.*

"Would you now?" She tilts her head at me and licks her bottom lip but then goes the extra step of biting down on it in a wicked sexy way that shoots a whole lotta heat straight south.

The waiter delivers our main entrees, breaking the chemistry that's built up between us as I gulp down some more wine.

I need a minute to return to focus now that my cock is *wide awake* at the thought of her tongue and her lips...and what she might do to my dimples.

16

sexual frustration is a crazy thing

Billie

ood lord, I am having fun with Calum Lefleur. He's less awkward tonight, for the most part. I feel like he's opening up a bit and I like it. A lot, which is probably not a good thing. We do still have to work together on the music lessons for the kids.

Still, the way he looks at me? I don't think a man has ever looked at me that way and I can't say I hate it. It's dark and sexy and intense. And yet, he's also smiling. Well, grinning, at least, which is an upgrade. He's so sexy with those dimples.

We finish dinner and head to the show, arriving just as the opening band finishes, which bums me out but seems to please Cal. He says he hates sitting through "shitty no-names," and then I explain that, technically, Love Scrum is also a "shitty no-name."

"Always putting my foot in my mouth," he answers as we stand in line for beer.

"Yeah, I'm learning that about you, Cal," I say with a wink.

"I really like your band. And I'm not just saying that to make up for my stupid comment."

"I know you do…but it's only because you want to fuck the drummer."

Cal's mouth drops open at the forwardness of my statement. I raise an eyebrow flirtatiously, but he composes himself quickly. "Well, I already fucked the drummer. And I still like the band."

This makes me laugh out loud, hard, and I look up and find Calum smiling at me, sea-blue eyes and everything. Like, really smiling for the first time ever that I've seen.

"Damn, you're handsome when you smile." I lean in without even a thought and lay a kiss on him.

He hesitates, and I panic, thinking maybe PDA isn't his thing, but then he puts his hand at my waist and pulls me firmly against him. He slides his tongue into my mouth for a hot kiss that has people in line telling us to "get a room."

We break apart, Cal blushing and me trying to catch my breath enough to order our beers before we head down onto the floor for the show.

The Lumineers are a lighter fare than I usually play or listen to, but I do love them. They open with "Ophelia," which we both sing at the top of our lungs. We pretty much sing every song after, and I find myself lost in the good vibes of the crowd. It's an easy, light atmosphere, and I'm having a great time.

As we leave the venue at the end of the show, I don't miss that Cal is holding my hand. I love the way we fit together, and I'm about to say it as we step out into the evening air. Cal beats me to a comment, though.

"Thanks, Billie," he says with a squeeze of my hand. "You're my only friend in Vegas, and you're making the transition bearable for me."

"Oh," I say, pulling my hand away. *Friend. He said friend.*

"What? Did I say something stupid again?"

"No, it's just...you said friend. You called me your *friend.*"

"Well, what was I supposed to call you?"

"I don't...I guess I don't know." I laugh lightly. "Sorry. It's just that—"

"That friends don't do what we did, Billie? What I'd like to do again?" His blue stare, so intense and sexy, has me remembering our night together (not for the first time) because I've logged some serious minutes remembering our night together. While doing the quarterly reports for CSLV, for example. Or when working out the kinks on a song at band practice. But I digress. Back to Cal's pseudo-questions I have no answer for.

Cal seems to accept my silence, and I decide I like the way he says my name. Very much.

Also, that fizzy crackle of energy between us is back, big-time.

That crackle of energy that never really left, I mean. The sexual tension's been bouncing all night, making heat bloom between my legs. I run my fingertips over my forehead and blow out a long breath. Sexual frustration is a crazy thing.

"Where are you staying?" Cal asks.

"With my parents. In my childhood bedroom, which is a riot. But any minute away is a minute well spent. So, thank you. I've had fun tonight."

"I'd invite you to stay with me, but we leave early in the morning for Oakland. I'd hate to kick you out."

"Yeah, I need my beauty sleep," I tell him, shrugging off the sense of rejection I'm feeling. "And so do you. You have to play hockey tomorrow. So, I'm gonna go home and you'll go to your hotel, and we'll avoid this getting any more awkward than it already is."

"Is it awkward?" Cal looks genuinely perplexed. "I thought I was doing better than usual."

"You're perfect. It's me. I'm being awkward. I'll call you Saturday morning and we'll figure out the party plans, okay? We need to get our story straight. My mom can spot a lie a million miles away."

"And you said you're a bad actress." He gives me another shot of dimple that should be illegal.

"No, I said I hated acting, not that I was a bad actress. It's you I worry about."

"You should. I am not a good actor."

"That's truly shocking, Cal."

He narrows his eyes and leans in, kissing me on the cheek, the hint of beard stubble pressing into my skin in a way that makes me want to shiver. "Take this next cab, Billie. I'll talk to you Saturday."

I blow a kiss as I hop into the back of the cab, giving the driver my family's Malibu address.

He stands on the sidewalk as my cab pulls away,

watching with all the intensity I've grown to recognize as classic Calum Lefleur.

I MANAGE to get in the house and up to my room without being seen, but my mom pops her head in as I'm slipping on my pajamas after a shower.

"Where have you been all night?" It's not a curious question or a light one. She expected me to be here, helping with party planning or something. Dorothea (aka Ditta) Hirsch never asks a question that doesn't demand an answer.

"Out with my boyfriend."

"Your boyfriend." Not a question. Rather, a lead balloon hitting the ground with a loud thunk.

"Yep. I met him through work in Vegas. He's a hockey player for the Crush."

"Right."

"He is," I lie as easily as if it's the truth. "He's my plus-one tomorrow."

"Billie," my mother warns with a cock of her head and a widening of her eyes.

"Ditta," I respond with as little emotion as I can muster.

"So, you never come home. Never visit the family. We know nothing about your life these days and yet you can just waltz in here with some man we don't know? You have a boyfriend and you can't be bothered to tell us that?"

"It's new with him," I say, raising a shoulder. "No big thing."

"Big enough that you're bringing him to your father's birthday party."

"No, I'm bringing him to Dad's party because he's in the area for a game and I wanted to actually have a good time."

"What does that mean?"

"You know what it means."

"Billie, so help me…"

"So help you what? I don't want to be dragged around meeting douchebag studio sons with appropriate backgrounds. I don't want to be pimped out to Kit's celebrity crowd either. I just want to have fun with my boyfriend."

"Your hockey player boyfriend." Again, not a question. She raises a judgmental eyebrow. "Who probably doesn't have three brain cells in his empty jock head."

"Actually, Cal could have gone to MIT. He's super smart."

My mother purses her lips. She looks like she ate a lemon. Just as she raises her index finger to start pointing or jabbing or whatever thing she's about to do while informing me of all the reasons I should have told her I was bringing my "dumb jock of a boyfriend" to her fancy party, my father walks in.

"What's all this ruckus?" he asks. "My baby girl is home for two minutes and already you two are bickering. It's my birthday; can I call a ceasefire?"

"You certainly can, Dad." I give him an air-kiss.

"We will have this discussion," my mom warns as she leaves the room.

My dad winks as I mouth *thank you* when he shuts

my door, leaving me to slump onto my bed, exhausted from the exchange.

It's well after one in the morning, and I'm totally beat, but when FaceTime pops up with Stuart's face, I answer.

"Yo, Stu. What up?"

"Well, I was going to see if you wanted to go get pancakes at an all-night diner like we used to do in high school."

"That's...really random." High school feels like such a long time ago now, and these random requests are becoming a little more regular. Which is concerning.

"Is that a yes?

"Unfortunately, it is not. I'm not in Vegas. I'm at the Hirsch compound under strict house arrest."

"What? Why?"

"It's my dad's big birthday bonanza weekend. Ditta has *big plans*. Huge."

"Wow, and you didn't call me in for backup? I'm wounded."

I don't have the heart to tell him I invited Cal as backup. Stuart is always my plus-one, which never freaks my mom out because she knows it's not like that between Stuart and me.

"Are you wounded?" I ask, grinning. "Really?"

"No, not really," he says. "Well, actually, a little. I thought I was your go-to man for awkward family events?"

"Don't take it personally. I wasn't even sure I was going to come."

"That's a line if I've ever heard one. You may be oil

and water with your mom, but there is no way that you're missing David Hirsch's birthday."

"There's no getting anything past you, Stu."

"Because I know you. What are you not telling me?"

"Nothing!" I laugh to try to prove the point.

He makes a dubious face, lips pushed to one side, one eyebrow raised, and says, "Well, either way, I've got something I want to tell you when you get back."

"Tell me now."

"No, it's a face-to-face thing."

"You're pregnant?"

"Har, har," he answers, rolling his eyes.

"Okay, well, I'll try to keep my raging curiosity at bay. We'll hang out when I get back."

"Deal. Have a fun party that you didn't invite me to."

"Have fun planning out the thing that's so important you can't say it on the phone to my face, which you can see just like you could see it in person."

"Have fun annoying your mother all weekend at the party you didn't invite me to."

"Have fun being a jealous little bitch that I'm hanging out with the great Kit Hirsch at the party I don't want to go to except for the fact that I love my dad."

"Okay, hang up."

"You hang up."

Finally, grinning, I hang up. But as I do, I think about Stuart's jealousy at not being invited, about his desire to talk in person when I get back. It makes my stomach flip with anxiety, wondering what's on his mind.

And then, of course, my thoughts jump to Cal, to the way he made me feel tonight. Like I could really talk to him, really share. He listened, and that meant something. He couldn't have cared less that I was born to Hollywood royalty. He didn't push me to use them to get access for my band. He just listened. And he understood, because his family expected him to follow a line of legacy as well, but he went his own way.

There is something between us, so it won't be a hardship on my end to pretend he's my fake boyfriend this weekend. And then I think about his kiss in the line earlier...delicious.

The heat between my legs is back as I think about the different kinds of smiles I got from him tonight. Several grins, which would have been a coup, except I got a joke from him. An actual joke and a real smile. It was glorious and turned me on.

If I hadn't already slept with him, hadn't already had him inside me, I might have been able to calm down. But no. I know what we can do together. I know how our bodies fit and how he can make me feel. And I want more. Once wasn't enough.

I think about calling him and about asking him to stroke himself while I watch through the screen. I think about showing him as I touch myself, strumming my clit like a guitar, making myself come with him on my mind. And before long, that's exactly what I'm doing—stroking myself alone, in the dark of my childhood bedroom, willing myself up the mountain, feeling the precipice looming. I slide my fingers over my tingling clit, desire so painful I have to use two fingers, then three, to fill myself. I stroke in and out, my pussy slick with arousal, pulsing as I inch closer, frustration starting to set in.

My mind on Calum, on his smile, his hand holding on to mine, his eyes dark and intense as he watched me drive away in the cab.

Fuck it. I make the call.

Calum's face is sleepy as he answers. "Billie? Everything okay?"

"Sorry to wake you," I apologize.

"What's wrong?"

I'm almost too shy to say it. I almost lie and tell him I couldn't sleep. "I need to come," I blurt the words out before I can change my mind.

"Oh," he says, then his eyes go wide. "Oh!"

"Yes. Will you stroke yourself? Will you let me see you? I need to see you." I *know* I sound desperate, half-crazed with desire and frustration, but I can't seem to help myself.

He's quiet for a moment, and I think, for a moment, he might say no. He might even turn me down.

But he doesn't.

Calum shuffles around for a second, then holds out the phone. I can see his hand is on his cock. His big, long, beautiful cock.

"I wish I could put that in my mouth," I tell him.

"I wish you could, too." He's stroking his fist up and down the stiff length.

"It felt good, when I did that for you?"

"So good," he moans.

"And when you put your mouth on me?"

"I loved the taste of you," he says on a heavy breath. "I loved it. I loved being in control like that. Loved losing control."

"Me too. I'm touching myself, Cal. Do you want to see?"

"Fuck yeah," he moans in the affirmative, so I move the phone so he can see me. We both touch ourselves, watching, and when I see the slick tip of his cock, wet with precum, I tell him I'm close.

"I want to see your face when you come," I say.

He moves the phone so I can see him, his teeth bared as the phone shakes a bit. He's pumping his cock hard now, and it's really helping me along.

"I'm there, Cal. So close. I'm there."

"Let me see you," he grounds out harshly.

I position my screen so he can see me as we finish, both spectacularly.

He groans out a loud "ahhhhh" while I forget all about breathing, arching my back, pushing through the glorious, spectacular orgasm.

It's not enough, not by half. I know what it feels like to come with him inside of me now. But it will do.

"Thank you," I whisper.

"I should be thanking you, I'd say." He gives me a little breathless laugh.

"Well, I woke you up, so maybe not."

"Worth it."

"Good night, Cal."

"Good night, Billie." He blows a kiss through the phone as I give a sleepy smile and hit the *End* button.

I hang up and throw my phone on the carpet

beside my bed. I don't know what is going on with me. Truly, I haven't felt like this about someone in a long, long time. And to think, I kind of hated Calum Lefleur when I first met him.

Now, though, he's all I can think of...

I want him.

And I can't shake the feeling that this might be a recipe for disaster.

17
a nice shiner

Cal

Game two of our pre-season is a harsh, ultra-physical, back-and-forth with a lot of shots on goal, but only one score by Boris in the third period. A win is a win, and I feel good about the fact that I let nothing get by.

In the locker room, I get tons of slaps on the back, guys telling me what a killer I am at goal. After about the tenth compliment, I feel compelled to respond to all the praise. "This is why I get paid the big bucks—"

Dante Castellano gets in my face, his finger nearly poking me in the eye as he growls, "You arrogant *prick*."

As soon as the words were out of my mouth, I realized I'd fucked up with my social commentary. Again. Wrong thing to say at the wrong time to the wrong people. Happens frequently.

I raise an eyebrow in response to Castellano's hostility and move to turn away from him, but he steps into my space again and says, "One of these days, you're going to end up with a broken arm or a concussion and you're gonna fuckin' deserve that shit."

"Oh, I recognize you, *Dan*. You're the schoolyard bully who threatened to beat me up when he realized I was smarter than him."

Defenseman Tyler snickers over by his locker, but Dan is not laughing. "Yes, I realize you think you're better and smarter than all of us here. Go take that shit to college. We don't need it here."

"That's literally the dumbest thing I've ever heard." I roll my eyes. "Being better and smarter is literally the job. You need to stop being such an entitled little bitch. Go work on your goalkeeping skills and maybe you'd land a first-string deal."

"You came in and *stole* my first-string deal."

"I didn't steal anything. I was told to come here, so I came. It's not my fault they didn't bump you up, man." He pushes me against the locker, and I shove him right back. "Get *out* of my face, dude. I'm serious."

"Or what?" he taunts, a weird smile on his face. "You're gonna beat me up?"

"Why would I beat you up? I've got no issue with you. You're the one all up in my face, because your fragile ego got hurt. I thought we were past this."

"Stop mocking me," he says, slamming me against the locker again. "You arrogant fucking prick."

"Literally not mocking you." I look out to see who's going to have my back. Evan steps toward me, ready to grab Dante. Tyler and Georg seem to be lining up to help, as well.

"Castellano," Evan warns.

I push him away, hoping the tone of our captain and a sharp shove will get him to come to his senses, but it only pisses him off and he throws a punch. It lands at the side of my nose with a crack and my vision goes white for a second.

I'm not a big fighter, but damn. I grab Castellano and put him in a headlock. He battles to get loose, but I train every day, and my guess is that he does not, so he's got nothing on me for brute strength. I disable him long enough for Tyler and Evan to grab him, dragging him toward the door and out into the hallway.

Tyler comes back almost immediately to check on me. "You all right, man? That's gonna be a nice shiner. Hope it doesn't block your view from goal."

"Go see the team doc," Georg says, peering at me. Then he grins and says, "I'm channeling Kazmeirowicz. Pretend I'm the team captain now."

I shake my head and wander off, finding a facility person outside who ushers me toward the medical office, where I get checked for concussion and have a bag of ice thrown at me. I sit with it on my face for a while, and when I get back, the locker room is empty. I sit in the quiet and just breathe. I know I'm a good player, a great one, even. It makes sense that this goon would be upset about not getting the chance to move up, but I find it hard to believe he's even worth the payroll he's on now. I might have to talk to the coaching staff about him. Physical violence toward a teammate isn't totally out of the realm of possibility. I mean, it's a physical sport, but usually, it's not tolerated.

When I get back to my hotel room, my mind is still buzzing about the tussle with Castellano. I order room service and flop on the bed, flipping on the television to try to get my mind on something else.

Billie texts me just as my food arrives.

Billie: Good win tonight. You're a beast.

Cal: You watched?

Billie: God help me, I did.

Cal: Was it a sacrifice for you?

Billie: Surprisingly, no.

Cal: LOL

Billie: Whatcha doin'?

Cal: Eating room service and overthinking a locker room brawl.

Billie: Brawl?

Cal: Well, more like me getting punched in the eye.

Billie: Yikes.

Cal: Second-string goalie has issues.

Cal: Should I still come to your dad's party tomorrow?

Cal: Black eyes probably aren't black tie material.

Billie: No, it'll make you look tough and intimidating.

Cal: I'm pretty sure nothing makes me look tough or intimidating.

Billie: LMAO

Billie: Well, a black eye will. And it's probably kinda hot. Send me a pic?

Cal: Scandalous

Cal: *sends pic*

Cal: Your parents will think I'm a brute.

Billie: Meh, you're a hockey player. Goes with the territory.

Billie: Plus, you're my fake boyfriend, so you don't actually have to care what they think.

Cal: True, true.

We text and flirt for about an hour before I hit the post-game wall and need to sleep. I get all the party details and tell her I'll see her tomorrow night. I go to bed smiling, thinking about how she watched the game tonight.

Billie Hirsch watched the game to see *me* play.

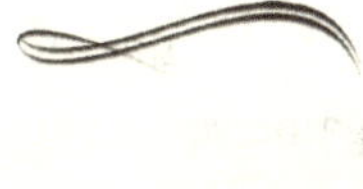

THIS MORNING I am summoned to the hotel conference rooms to have a meeting with Castellano, the entire coaching staff, and Evan Kazmeirowicz.

"Castellano got in his face and wouldn't back down. He had to be restrained by several players after he struck Cal in the face," Evan explains.

"And what did you do then?" Coach Brown asks me.

"I put him in a headlock until our captain and Lockhardt could get him off."

"Okay, well, you need to dial back the cocky attitude, Lefleur. It's not doing much for you in assimilating with this team. Work on that."

"Duly noted, Coach."

I take my lecture from coaching about being cocky, but otherwise, it's Castellano who gets the load of the beating. They suspend him for two games, which doesn't mean squat since he never plays anyway. But then they really level him by saying they won't renew his contract at the end of the season.

Castellano faces the room and announces, "This is all a load of bullshit," before storming off, the last thing out of his mouth is that he's calling his agent.

Evan breaks the pointed silence. "His agent is terrible."

"He's terrible," I reply.

"He's just disappointed."

"He should be. In himself. There's a reason he doesn't get to play and a reason the team brought me here. I can't do shit about the fact that he's not good enough. And I tried to be nice to him. I tried to tell him to work on his game so he could be ready."

"Some people want to sit around and be angry about their lots in life." Evan stands and says, "Got anything planned for your night off in the big city?"

"I'm going to a birthday party with a friend."

"Cool."

There's an awkward silence, then, and Evan looks at his phone, then his watch. "All right, mate, I've got to head out."

"Yeah, okay. See you."

IT FELT like forever until it was time to go to Billie's parents' house; the day passing slowly after the drama-charged meeting with Castellano this morning. But I've decided I'm done giving that loser another thought as I get ready to go play the role of Billie's fake boyfriend.

I choose a deep royal-blue suit with a sharp white shirt and a black tie. One thing I can say for Emily is she knows fashion and always picked out beautiful suits for me when I was in Montreal.

Billie's family lives in one of those stereotypical Malibu houses—the ones high on the rocks, overlooking the sea with vast windows that glow vibrantly in the waning light. I make my way up an incline of a driveway to the door, where someone asks my name, checks it off a list, and beckons me inside.

I wander in through a vast entryway. The house has an open floor plan, with a sunken living room on one side and a vast kitchen and dining area on the other. It's all ultra-modern and tasteful. Beautiful, though I have a hard time imagining Billie growing up here.

"Hey, you!" her familiar voice calls. I snap to attention and find her heading my way in a lacy, indigo-blue gown that shows off her luscious body.

My cock jumps. I've come to really appreciate Billie's understated style, but tonight, she looks like a celebrity. She makes me feel slightly tongue-tied.

As she approaches, she leans in and kisses me on the mouth. I'm sure it's for show but I welcome it wholeheartedly. I put my arm around her, at the small of her back, and return the affection.

She pulls away with a wicked gleam in her eyes. "What a welcome."

I huff a laugh. "You *look* amazing."

She blushes and reaches out to touch my face, where a black eye has indeed bloomed. "Nice shiner."

"Annoying."

"No, I think it's badass," she assures me. "Come on, let's go meet the parents."

She takes my arm, and we wander through a maze of people, some of whom recognize me and ask if I got the black eye during the game. I say yes because I don't want to talk with strangers about our team drama.

We near a very regal-looking couple, and I can guess that they are Billie's parents just from the family resemblance. Her father has dark, wavy hair and Billie's eyes. Her mother's hair is a lighter shade, but she has Billie's prominent nose and lips.

"You must be the boyfriend we never knew about,"

her mother says. There's a tone, for sure, and her side-eye to Billie says the rest. "I'm Ditta Hirsch."

Ditta Hirsch is a movie producer. A big name that even I recognize. I had no idea.

"I've heard of you," I say, shaking her hand. "Calum Lefleur."

"And I'm David Hirsch. The dad."

I shake David's hand. "Happy birthday, sir."

"Thanks. Nice shut-out last night."

"Oh, you saw it?"

"Watched it with my little girl. Didn't see the part where you got clocked in the eye, though."

I cringe. "Well, that was an unplanned mishap. It does happen."

"I'm sure it does in your line of work. How do you like Las Vegas?"

"I didn't want to come, quite honestly"—I look at Billie—"but I'm finding more reasons to like it every day, though."

"Good man. Well, the Crush sure have bought up all the good real estate these past couple of years. Think they're on the way to becoming a legacy team? Hockey's own Silver State Warriors?"

I shrug. "They do have a powerful first line. Second string is short, in my opinion, so the legacy really depends on everyone staying healthy and second string getting up to par."

"Kazmeirowicz going to play much longer?"

I shrug. "I don't see why not. He's still effective."

We continue with the hockey talk for a while, until a tall, Hollywood heartthrob-looking guy comes up and barrels into David for a hug.

"Kit, my boy! Nice of you to show up fashionably late."

"It's what I do," the guy says. He turns and looks at me. "And you are?"

My eyebrows shoot up into my hairline. This is Kit Hirsch, the actor. Like, the really huge and famous A-list actor. Emily drools over him every time he's on screen.

"I'm Cal."

"Your sister's hockey player boyfriend," David adds.

"You're banging my sister?" Kit levels me with a stare I'm not sure is hostile or teasing.

I cringe again. "We're just getting to know each other."

David clips Kit on the back of the head. "You're cut off until you can act like a gentleman, son."

"Sorry, I's just messing with ya," Kit says, grinning at me. "Happy birthday, Pops."

As they get into a conversation about casting for some movie, Billie and her mother move in my direction. Ditta Hirsch is eagle-eyed, looking me up and down, and not kindly.

"So, how long have you been seeing my daughter?" Her voice is heavy with the same tone she gave me before.

"Not long. We met through her work."

"Ugh," her mother groans, rolling her eyes. "Her pittance of a job in that glorified schoolhouse? Wasting her talent if you ask me."

"She is very talented," I counter. "And great with the kids."

"She's been groomed for the spotlight. That's where I want her."

"Yes, yes, Mother," Billie says. "We all know you're disappointed that only one of your children has skyrocketed into worldwide celebrity. If you'll excuse us, I want to introduce Cal to some of my friends."

Billie grabs my arm, and we head away from her family, making a beeline for the bar. While we wait, I can't help asking, "Why didn't you tell me your family was…"

"Was what?"

"Super famous?"

She shrugs. "I'm not about that life. I don't use their names or status to get things. My band hates me for it, but whatever."

We get our drinks, head outside to the stairs, and go down them to the long boardwalk that leads to the beach. There's a bench just at the sand, and we sit, sipping our drinks in silence, with only the ocean sounds filtering up from the shoreline.

"That was a lot," I say after a moment of quiet reflection.

"It's always extra like that, all the time. I'm sorry. You did great, though."

"Who were you hiding from, that you needed a fake boyfriend?"

"Oh, my mom. She's always trying to set me up with someone's actor son or singer son or producer son."

I nod. "Got it."

"My dad liked you."

"He was nice."

"The most normal of the bunch," she says wistfully. "I do love my dad."

"Not your mom?"

"It's complicated. She had me in show business before I could walk. When I decided I didn't want it, she couldn't let it go."

"I get that. My parents had other plans for me, too."

"You want to walk on the beach?"

"Sure."

We slip off our shoes and leave our glasses on the bench. She holds my hand as we walk, the sound of the waves calming in comparison to the frenetic energy of the party up the hill.

As we get to a deserted part of the beach, we stop and look out at the water. Well, Billie looks at the water. I look at her profile.

"I know this is a fake relationship, for the purposes of annoying your mother, but I do want you to know I find you genuinely attractive."

She turns, a soft and kind of shy smile on her face. "I find you genuinely attractive, too."

"There's the work at the center with the kids, you know? Like, we keep tipping over the line because there's something going on between us, but I don't know where things should go from here, Billie."

She nods, licking her bottom lip in a way that distinctly does not make things easier. "I wonder..." She sighs. "I wonder if we could have a sexual relationship and still be professional for work at the center?"

I lean in, ready to kiss her. "I can compartmentalize."

"Is that so, Mr. Lefleur?"

"Indeed, Ms. Hirsch. Compartmentalizing is my specialty," I whisper against her lips, this time fully intending to kiss her properly.

18
garage band in vegas

Cal's kiss is consuming. We had a hot, quick one when he arrived, but this one is thorough and deep, and I find myself with my hand rubbing his cock from the outside of his pants. The strap of my dress falls over my shoulder, and my breast is exposed to the warm, salty air. Cal's mouth moves to my jaw, then to my clavicle, then to lick at my hard nipple.

I gasp at the electricity it sends to my core. More. I want more from him and I want it now.

I slip out of my dress quickly, left only in my thong, which Cal pulls away before falling to his knees, parting my pussy with his fingers, and ravaging me with his mouth. I push against his face, ravenous for him, and I nearly come when he pushes two fingers inside of me, his tongue darting against my swollen clit.

"Take me," I beg. "Quickly, before someone sees us."

I turn and get on all fours as Cal loosens his suit pants and frees his cock. He's inside me in a hard, fast movement that takes my breath away. He moves quickly, his hands on my breasts as they bounce with each of his thrusts. It's wild and rough and crazy—and so good my eyes start watering.

The orgasm overtakes me hard, my pussy clenching around his cock as he roars and pulls out. I stay on the sand just breathing as the afterglow rages through me. I've had quickies before, but they've never been so...unrestrained. I definitely love when this enigmatic, reticent man lets go and becomes a little wild. From my periphery, I notice that Cal is putting himself back together. *So much easier for the men.* But then he's standing up and helping me to my feet in a welcome act of chivalry. He finds my dress, shakes off the sand, and helps me get back into it before kissing me sweetly on the mouth.

"That was...fun," he says, holding my face in his hands, his blue eyes searching mine for what, I don't know. Cal is always part mystery and part blunt honesty to me. A delicious mixture I'm getting quite attached to.

"It was," I agree. "A good stress reliever."

"Sure," he says, almost smiling. "We should go back?"

"Yes," I groan.

He laughs and offers his hand to me. "Come on, Miss Hirsch. Time to face the music again."

As we make it back to the bench to get our shoes, we find Kit waiting for us. "Paparazzi are milling around and I was checking out here to make sure they weren't on our property."

"Why would you be the one out here looking?" I ask. "You're the celebrity here. Shouldn't you have a nobody doing this job?"

My brother chuckles, rubbing his stubbled jaw. "Good point, I suppose. Still, you didn't see anyone out here, did you?"

"Nah. And they don't care about me, so I'm not worried."

Kit pulls some lingering beach detritus from my hair, a smirk on his face as he pieces together what we've been up to out here. "Well, your boyfriend is a celebrity, too, so..."

"Thanks for the warning, brother dear." I roll my eyes at him and take Cal's hand as we head back up to the party. Well, more like I take him through the party and down to the lower level, where my old drum kit sits in the middle of a recording studio.

"This is amazing," Cal says, looking around at all the equipment. "Why would you need a whole recording studio, though? I thought everyone in your family was into films?"

"My dad's a casting director but he also likes music, so he dabbles in movie sound sometimes. It's a hobby."

"And the kit?"

"My brother's. He played before I did. They don't know I still play, actually."

I sit down at the kit and start hammering out a blistering beat. Cal grabs a nearby guitar and joins in with a less complicated but still complementary guitar riff. We play together for about ten minutes before Queen Ditta stomps down the stairs, hands on her slim hips.

"What are you two doing? Acting like teenagers, that's what," she says. "We can hear all that racket from upstairs and you're ruining your father's party."

"Ruining dad's party? With music?"

"Billie," my mother warns. "What are you even doing? You were playing that drum kit?"

"Well, she is an awesome drummer in an amazing band," Cal blurts out.

I turn to him in horror and shake my head.

"Excuse me? You're in a what?" my mother screeches.

"Mom. It's just a little thing I do for fun."

"Billie Hirsch, you tell me every chance you can that you want nothing to do with the entertainment industry. You don't want to model. You don't want to act. You don't want to sing. But here I find out you're sneaking around, playing in some crummy garage band in Vegas?"

"It's not crummy," Cal insists.

I hold up a hand, my expression imploring him to shut the hell up.

My mom stares at Cal for a minute, then at me, then she makes a noise of total disgust and disappointment and turns on her very high heel to stomp back up the stairs.

As soon as she's gone, I turn on Cal. "You had no right to tell her that."

"Tell her what?"

"About the band and the drumming. I told you they didn't know I still played."

"Well, they should know. You're really good."

"I appreciate that, but it's not your story to tell. I didn't want them to know."

"Why?"

"Cal..." I sigh, exasperated.

"What?"

"I have my reasons for not telling them what I'm up to with my band. And you outed me. It's not cool."

"I'm sorry, Billie."

But he doesn't look at all sorry.

"You should be," I snap. "Seriously. My music is for *me*. It's not *for* her. She's got her own ideas what I should be, who I should be, and I just can't..."

"I always say the wrong thing at the wrong time." He says this bluntly as if he's had to say it before many, many times. "I'm sorry. Truly."

"Whatever." I blow out a biting sigh. "I'll deal with it."

Cal puts the guitar back on the stand. "I should...I guess I'll go?"

"I need to go deal with her. She's probably bitching about this to my dad as we speak."

"Okay. I'll get out of your hair, then."

Cal stands awkwardly, like he wants to lean in to kiss me goodbye, but before he can, he straightens, puts his hands in his pockets, and walks up the stairs. He looks so...dejected, but I can't deal with that at the moment.

I'd be lying if I didn't say that my mom's words stung. *"You don't want to model. You don't want to act.*

You don't want to sing. But here I find out you're sneaking around, playing in some crummy garage band in Vegas?" It was nice that Cal stood up for me, suggesting that my band isn't crummy. I'll give him that. But why is it that my mom cannot simply be happy for me that I'm happy? That I'm fulfilled? Why must she always criticize all my choices?

Because it's always about her.

And once again, as I've done so many times in my life, I've disappointed the great Ditta Hirsch. *FML.*

19
making the most of the move

Cal

"**M**r. Cal," one of the younger kids says, looking up at me with big, brown eyes, "I don't know how to make the sound you just told us to make."

"It's okay, Logan, it's a hard one. We can work on it again next week."

Logan nods once and tries again before sighing heavily and putting the guitar on his lap. I give the kids a handout of things to work on during the week, and then we all exchange our tradition of high fives before they're off to their next activity.

I work on cleaning up the space, hoping to see Billie appear in the doorway as she usually does at the end of my sessions. *Except for today.* It's fair to assume she's ghosting me since I haven't heard from her since her dad's party last weekend.

I'm not sure how to deal with the situation or what to do to make things better. I've started several texts, but honestly, the whole situation gives me anxiety. I feel like no matter what I say, it'll be wrong. I don't want to upset her more than I already have.

Still, I linger longer than normal, hopeful she might come down to see me. Finally, I pack up my guitar and shut off the light as my phone buzzes with a text message. My stomach flips, hoping it might be from Billie, but instead, I see Emily's name, and hope turns to instant dread.

> Emily: When were you going to tell me you were cheating on me?

> Cal: What are you talking about?

Em responds instantly with a screenshot, a grainy photo from a Montreal-based tabloid. The headline reads: MAKING THE MOST OF THE MOVE.

I peer at the photo, trying to drag the screen to increase the size. When I realize what I'm looking at, I lean back against the wall, breathless and sick. It's hard to make out, for sure, but I know that it's a photo of Billie and me on the beach. I'm behind her, hands on her hips. *Fucking her.*

My phone rings, and I answer it quickly, looking around to make sure no one is within earshot. Emily's already yelling into my ear the instant I accept her call.

"There is no excuse you can give me that will make me believe that you weren't screwing some bimbo on that beach in that picture."

"I'm not making an excuse."

"So, you admit you were screwing some bimbo on the beach?"

"We agreed to a break. At your request, Em."

"Taking a break doesn't mean you can just go out and have sex with whoever, wherever, Cal."

I pinch my nose between my thumb and forefinger. "I think it does mean that, actually. We're not together, remember?"

"We also didn't discuss seeing other people."

"So that guy *Nick*, from your office that you were messaging when you were here to visit? I'm pretty sure you're *seeing* him even if you won't admit it. Can you truthfully tell me you haven't fucked him?"

To my surprise, Emily is quiet for a long moment. I hear her take a deep breath before she says, "I think I'm in love with him."

A bitter laugh escapes the back of my throat. It's not like I didn't know, down deep in my heart, that this was happening. That we were ending. *That you're in love with someone else yet rang me in anger.* It's completely illogical.

"What's so damn funny?" she asks sharply.

"Nothing's funny. It's pathetic that you would come raging at me like this when you've been seeing someone else since, when, like the minute after I left?"

"I didn't realize what was happening, what I was feeling."

"Oh, you didn't *realize* what you were feeling. Okay, Em. So, when you said you wanted to make this work? What was that?"

"Cal, you said the same, but here we are. Who is she?"

"None of your business. She's a friend."

"Well, I don't do that with *my* friends." The sound

of her voice is giving me a headache. Why have I never noticed how annoying her voice is before this?

"Don't you." It's not a question.

An awkward, heated silence stretches between us for several moments, and then she starts talking.

"It was exciting, at first...being with you. You're one of the hottest players in hockey. You make a ton of money so being with you means financial stability. It felt like a dream come true but then..."

"Then what?" I'm gritting my teeth so hard it's almost painful.

"Well, you're you."

The words hang between us. *I am me.* Whatever that means.

"But you were willing to stay with me because of who I am in hockey? Because of my money? Neither of those things have changed, so why walk away from it?"

"I could ask you the same thing. You talk about wanting to be with me, but you don't know me. You don't care about the things I care about. You're not interested in the things I'm interested in. You just like the stability of your routine. You want things to stay the same."

She's not wrong. I can't argue, so I ask, "But why didn't you even try?"

Emily huffs at me through the phone. "Why didn't *you*? It's *your* photo in the newspaper. God, this is so embarrassing."

"Why are you embarrassed?"

"*Because*, Calum, you're my boyfriend. You're in another city, with another woman."

"Wait, you just told me you were in love with someone else. Weeks ago, you told me we were on pause. But it's *you* who's embarrassed?"

"People here don't know we were on pause."

"Oh, well, that's convenient. You get to look like a victim when it was, in fact, *you,* who actually cheated with *Nick.*"

Emily laughs. "Whatever, Cal. What is she to you?"

"Why does it matter, Em? You just told me you think you're in love with someone else—who you've been seeing, and probably fucking—*while we were on a pause.* The pause that you demanded. So, I had sex with someone. Why does it even matter to you?"

I look up at the sound of footsteps and find Billie, a look of hurt or shock or something on her face. I wonder how much of this conversation she's heard. I know she's not happy as she holds up a hand, shakes her head, and turns away, walking back down the hallway.

"Fuck," I growl, forgetting for the moment that Emily is still on the other end of the line.

"I know you don't like talking about emotions, Cal, but there's no reason to curse at me."

I can't take it anymore. Her voice. The tone in it. The ridiculous, hypocritical nature of this whole conversation. "Hanging up now." As I hit the button to end the call, cutting her protests off gives me a small measure of satisfaction. As opposed to not caring at all. Which is far more typical for me. I don't have these kinds of messy conversations. Ever. I don't get upset or feel glad because others are. *Except right now because Emily deserves it.*

I follow Billie's retreating form all the way up a set of stairs toward the hallway that leads to her office.

Lingering at the doorway, I watch as she studiously ignores me, logging into her computer. She types furiously, lips pursed. When she finally stops, she looks up at me with an expression of forced ambivalence.

"You never told me you had a girlfriend."

My jaw clenches. "We were on a break. We haven't been together—it hasn't been the same since I came here."

"That didn't sound like a conversation between people on a break. It sounded like a conversation between two people who are trying to hurt each other."

"That's not it at all," I say firmly.

"Well, I thought we were friends, Cal."

"We are."

"I feel like friends would tell each other important tidbits of their lives, like, say, if they had significant others. Especially if said friends were, you know, kind of intimately involved."

"It's just sex, Billie. There are things you don't tell me, like why you didn't want your parents to know you're in a band."

"That is not the same and you know it."

"I just don't get why this is such a big deal to you, when you were the one to ask if we could forget about the sex and put it behind us afterward."

"It's not," she snaps, turning back to her computer and typing again. "It's fine. I just wouldn't have slept with someone else's boyfriend if I'd known."

"And I wouldn't have slept with you if Em and I weren't on a break." Billie cringes, so I know I must not be saying the right thing, again. I shove my hands in my pockets and add, "I like you a lot. You make it bearable to be here."

"Wow, Calum." Billie laughs bitterly. "Such a ringing endorsement of our relationship."

"Look, things feel mixed up, and I'm not good with mixed up. I don't really know what to say."

"Well, I'll let you off the hook. We were supposed to keep it professional, and we didn't. You were my fake boyfriend for the span of, like, three hours. You played your part, and we can just forget about it now. Okay?"

Every muscle in my body is tense. I feel so uncomfortable. *I hate this.* I don't know what to say or how to feel. All I do know is that this thing with Billie confuses me. It confuses me in a way I never felt with Emily. *Is that good or bad?*

"I don't really know what to say to make this right," I admit. "I like you. I find you attractive. I enjoy spending time with you. And Em and I haven't been right since I moved here. She says she's in love with someone else, but she seemed jealous when she saw the picture in the paper."

"Wait, what picture in the paper?" Billie's gaze snapping back up to meet mine.

"There was a grainy picture of us on the beach in a sleazy Montreal tabloid. No one would know it was you."

"Picture of us doing what?" she asks slowly.

"Um…"

"Oh, holy hell, Cal! You didn't think to *tell* me?"

"I just found out about it a minute ago. That's why Em called."

"My mother will flip her lid," Billie mutters, rubbing her eyes with the palms of her hands.

"It's not a big deal. It's only me that can really be identified, and I'm not worried about it."

"Oh, good, well, if you're not worried about it..." Billie rolls her eyes at me. "Cal, your priorities could be readjusted, you know that?"

I frown, not having any idea what she means.

She waves me off. "I've had enough of this. Go call your girlfriend and fix things."

"What does that mean?"

"It means you're obviously just getting your rocks off with me to piss off your girlfriend or make her jealous or whatever. I'm not interested in being your bait, and I'm not interested in getting in the middle of whatever routine thing it is that will make you feel normal."

"That's not—I'm not with her just because it makes me feel normal."

"You're not with her at all, is what you tried to tell me a minute ago. So, which is it? You either have a girlfriend or you don't."

"I don't. She put us on a break. We were on a break. *Are* on a break."

"You don't seem so sure, Cal. And what do you want? Do you want to be on a break?"

"Yeah...I do now. I didn't at first, but now I know it was for the best. It's complicated, Billie. We were together for a couple of years. Em knows me."

"She knows you." Billie's voice is flat.

"She put up with my quirks."

"Well, that's the picture of romance, now, isn't it?"

"It's not about romance."

"Of course, it's not. For you, it's all about avoiding change. It's about staying in your comfort zone." Billie's feeling hurt and annoyed with me, but she's also one hundred percent correct. I *do* avoid change at all costs.

"I don't see what's so wrong with that."

Billie makes a bitter noise and faces back to her computer again. "I have to work, Cal."

"Okay," I say with a sigh. "Look, I'm sorry for hurting your feelings, for what it's worth."

Billie doesn't answer.

20
relationships are messy

Billie

I'm sweating after a blistering band practice. As I'm taking a swig from my water bottle, my phone rings. It's Kit, who hardly ever calls me.

"Yo, brother, what's up?"

"Hey, little sister, how's it going?"

I lift a shoulder, even though he can't see me. "It's okay. You?"

"Good. I'm working in post-production on my new movie, and we were talking about trying to bring in some new sound to the soundtrack."

"Yeah?"

"Yeah, I maybe might have mentioned that my sister is in a band…"

"Kit! What the hell, dude?"

"Look, Mom's in a tizzy ever since your boyfriend outed you. Dad looked you guys up and you're really good, Billie. People should hear what you're doing."

It saddens me that Dad has taken the time to listen to our band but not reach out and tell me what he thinks. But it's also not surprising. He gets so absorbed in himself...kind of like his son. What *they* don't get is that we are getting heard. "People do hear our music, Kit," I answer glumly. "Every time we play live, which is two weeks out of four. Sometimes more."

"In bars."

"Yeah, in bars. Though we've got a music festival lined up soon, too."

Kit laughs. "Well, I'm just thinking you don't have to do that whole struggling artist thing. You're not some garage band of nobodies. You have the connections to help get yourselves heard."

"I don't want it to happen that way, though. You know that."

"You're being a total brat about this," Kit insists. "People would kill to have your connections. Family who can literally open any door to help you. Instead, you want to struggle and act like these opportunities don't exist for you. Tell me something, Billie, what do your bandmates think? Are they happy doing the local scene and toughing it out like some group of teenagers waiting for their big break? Or would they maybe like to walk willingly through an open and potentially lucrative door?"

I look over my shoulder at Sven and Nikki, who are thankfully engrossed in an argument about a lyric Nikki doesn't like in one of our newer songs.

"What is it you're thinking of for us?" I ask, resigned to hear his pitch.

"Come in. Watch the rough cut. Spend a few days in the studio making songs to go with the storyline.

See what happens. We'd pay you, even if we don't use the work."

I sigh and look at my bandmates again. I know they would want to do this. And it's with Kit, rather than my parents, which makes me feel point-five percent better about taking the handout.

"Let me think about it and talk to the band."

"That's all I can ask. But don't fuck around too long. We're on a timeline here, Bill."

We hang up, and I decide I need to get comfortable with this before I bring it up with Nikki and Sven. They will say yes automatically, and I need to be on board before it happens.

I call Stuart and tell him I need to talk. We agree to meet up for dinner at one of our favorite bars, and when I get there, he's already in a booth. His face lights up when he sees me.

"Hey, you." I smile at him as I slip into the booth.

"Hey, *yourself*, sweaty McGee. Been at the cross-fit gym?"

"I was at practice and don't be mean."

"Aw, I'm sorry," he says, sticking his bottom lip out in a mock pout. "How's the music biz?"

I shrug as the server comes over, putting our favorite drinks in front of us automatically and taking our food orders. As she walks away, I tell Stuart about my brother's call. His eyebrows raise high on his head as I tell him we have a chance to make music for one of Kit's films.

"That is huge. Holy shit, Billie. You're going to do it, right?"

"Kit wasn't even supposed to know."

"Well, how did he find out?"

"Calum Lefleur," I grind out, as if his name is a dirty word.

"A hockey player has what to do with this?" Stuart asks, picking at the label on his beer bottle.

"Cal, as you know, has been volunteering guitar lessons at the club."

"And?"

"And we became...friends."

The word hangs there between us. Stuart won't look at me when he repeats, flatly, "Friends."

"For the most part, though we slept together a couple of times. It's nothing serious." I shrug for effect.

Stuart tips his bottle back, taking a long drink before setting the drink back down hard enough to give away his feelings.

"It's nothing serious," I repeat. "It started out kind of random. Scratching an itch. He's awkward but cute, and I had him pretend to be my boyfriend for my dad's party, just to get my mom off my back."

I'm talking too much. Also, it's a dead giveaway for the mixed bag of feelings I'm toting around now that I know Cal has (had?)—but who really knows—a long-time girlfriend. Is he that clueless about women? Can he not see how deceived I feel? *Hurt even?* I've tried not to overthink things and to put Cal back on the work-only shelf, but it's not been easy. I really liked him too. Enjoyed his company. Gah!

Stuart continues to stare at his beer bottle. "Scratching an itch." His tone is dead.

"Stu—"

"I'm in love with you," he blurts.

A heartbeat passes, and then I answer quietly, "I know."

"You know? And you sit here telling me about your random hookup with a dumbass hockey player? You chose to take him to your parents' instead of me?"

"First off, he's *not* a dumbass. And second, if I'd taken you, you'd have thought it was a big thing. I needed someone who knew it wasn't real."

His mouth opens, and he sits back as if he's been slapped. "That was not fair."

"I'm sorry," I say quickly, realizing how much that must've hurt him. "I just mean—"

"I know what you mean, Billie. You mean that I'm the sad puppy dog following you around since high school, hoping you'll pay attention to me. And picking me, even for something as stupid as a family gathering, means paying enough attention to get my hopes up."

"That's not true," I insist. "I care about you, Stu, you're my best friend."

"Friend zone. Gotcha."

"Well…"

"What I don't get, though," he says, shaking his head, "is why you can't see me that way. How come?"

"I don't want to jeopardize our friendship." I give him the only answer there is.

"That's fine," he says, clearly unconvinced.

"We've known each other for a long time, and I don't want to lose what we have."

"By trying to make it something it isn't?"

"Relationships are messy. I like having you in my life this way."

"Billie."

I lift my brows and give him a *What?* look.

"I didn't just magically wake up feeling this way, you know. I think, maybe if you opened your eyes, you could grow into feeling the same way about me."

I have to resist the urge to cringe. It's not that I find Stuart unattractive. Not at all. He's a good-looking man. He's successful and caring and funny and loyal. He's a good person, worth loving. But I hate seeing him like this, on the verge of begging.

Our food comes and we eat in near silence as the house band starts tuning up for the first set of the night. I'm thankful for the mic checks and guitar riffs, which fill the space between us in between awkward sentences about how our jobs are going.

When we finish our meals, Stuart insists on paying and asks if he can give me a ride home. I nod and he leads me to his car. My place isn't far, and when we stop at the curb, I resist the urge to jump out and run straight to the safety of my apartment.

"Stuart, you know I care about you a lot, right?"

"I know."

"I think you're great. I really do. You are really important to me."

"I know all that, Billie. We've been friends for too long for me to think otherwise. But my feelings are different. And I've waited to tell you, but I can't stomach the idea of you handing yourself out to some guy who couldn't care less about you when there's someone here who really loves you."

My heart melts a little, even as my thoughts go to Cal, to the way I feel when I'm with him. Stuart is good and pure. Cal is an unknown. He's strange and cocky and blunt and very stuck in his ways. But he's also talented and brilliant and sexy and sweet and very generous in bed. We connect in many ways, surprising for someone so different from me.

Stuart must mistake my silence for an invitation because he leans over, places a hand on my cheek, and goes in for a kiss. It's soft and searching. With Cal on my mind, I lean into it, but pull away quickly, feeling guilty.

"I'm just asking for a chance," he says pleadingly.

I nod, and he runs his thumb over my cheekbone before kissing me again. This time, I push feelings about Cal aside and focus on the moment, the feeling of my lips on Stuart's.

And I don't feel a single thing.

21
numbers and science

Cal

Tonight is our home opener. We've been asked to do twenty minutes of press before the game, and I'm talking to some blond woman (Kassy or Kacey??) doing her best to be pro-sports media sexy but looking more like an overgrown Barbie to me.

"So, Cal," she asks, pushing in a little closer, "tell me about your approach to your position. You stop more goals than anyone on the ice right now and are on track to top the leaderboard in career saves if you continue on this trajectory."

"Well, for one, I'd have to play for decades to take that record. But for me, it's all about science. It's geometry and physics translated into body awareness."

"Really?" the reporter asks, leaning in so deep her tits threaten to spill out of her top. "Tell me more."

"Ahh...it's not that difficult to understand. There are laws to the way things move and stay in motion." *Like, what force is defying the laws of gravity preventing your tits from poking me in the eyes right now.* "In my mind, I see the way the puck moves, the angle of it, and I adjust to meet it. Easy."

She laughs and says, "Well, good luck out there tonight."

I thank her and head toward the locker room, Evan meeting me on the way.

"You really think like that? See things like that?" he asks incredulously.

"It's just science and math, yeah."

Evan chuckles. "I think you might be a bloody savant, you know that?"

I lift a shoulder in response. "I could have gone to MIT. I've always been scientifically observant."

"MIT? Seriously?"

"My parents are both academics. They expected me to go the same route, but wanted me to be well-rounded, so they started me in hockey when I was young like every other kid in Quebec. I was awkward and didn't get along well with my teammates, so coaches never knew what to do with me."

"Shocking," Evan says, repressing a grin. "And when you're young, goalie is like code-language for not good enough."

"Right. No kid wants to play goal because they all want to be forwards, right? But I liked it, and I applied the same skills to the sport as I did in my schoolwork and became very effective quite quickly."

"So, you gave up MIT to play the game?"

"My parents were really disappointed, but I figured college is something I can do anytime. It's not just reserved for eighteen-year-olds."

Evan laughs and shakes his head, patting me on the back once. "Dude, you are blowing my mind right now."

He wanders into the locker room, making a gesture to indicate that his mind is, in fact, blown. By what, I have no idea. Lots of guys play in college. I just chose to forego college and go pro early. What's the big deal?

We suit up and go through the pre-game rigmarole. Earlier, the Crush PR showcased a short video segment about my goalie mask custom-painted with brand-new artwork for my new team. I saw it playing on the Jumbotron a few minutes ago. The artwork on my mask looks spank, I've gotta admit. It's a graphic desert landscape featuring blooming cactus flowers in a bright purply red, a guitar and music notes with classic Vegas iconography, and FLOWER in the DESERT, my new Vegas nickname lettered across the top. I enjoyed planning out the designs we decided to use. Media relations interviewed me, of course, and I explained the meaning behind the different imagery I chose. My gig at the Crush Foundation Music Workshop came up, and after I talked a little about what I do there, I gave a shout-out to each of the music class kids by first name: Will, Logan, Brayden, Andre, Keegan, LeAnne, Samantha, Jeanna, Charley, Jon, Zach, Alec, and Reilly. Yep, I memorized the list. I'm going to play a recording of it for them at the next class since I'm pretty sure none of them can afford to be here.

Home openers are nuts, with live music, fireworks, and all kinds of craziness, and Las Vegas does it up more than any other team I've seen. It is quite the spectacle, and even though I thought I wouldn't care for all the showbiz glam that comes with playing NHL hockey in Vegas, it's starting to grow on me. Typically, I want to get out on the ice and play the game, but I can see how this home arena crowd feeds the energy of the players and gets them going.

There are pre-game videos for the guys to watch on their way out on the ice. Some are from their wives or parents or kids or whatever. I start to race by, feeling certain I won't have one, but Scarlett from the social media team grabs my arm. She points to the screen, where the kids from my class at CFMW play the tune I've been teaching them before yelling, "Good luck, Mister Cal!"

It makes me smile, this video message they made. Those kids are awesome little people. Scarlett grins, and I nod in thanks before skating out at the sound of my name and the roar of a welcoming home crowd. That is one thing about this crazy town—they love their team, and every member on that team is welcomed with open arms.

The game is a barn burner, an intense battle that has Tyler and Viktor both in the penalty box for several minutes each period. I lose count of the shots on goal, but they come fast and furious with second-string defenders in place by midway through the second period. I stay focused, though, and even send a puck far enough down the ice for winger Evan to grab it and score.

In the end, I've managed a shut-out for the first game of the season, and Evan's single goal leaves us victorious, the crowd erupting to eardrum-busting volume.

Back in the locker room, the guys all talk about their after-game plans, and a few even ask me if I want to grab a drink or go to a club. I thank them but decline, showering and dressing quickly before heading for the door.

In the hallway, I'm shocked to see Emily wearing a Crush jersey with my number on it paired with dark jeans. Definitely not her usual styling.

"Hey, Cal," she says, giving me a strange, sad smile. "Good game."

My mouth must be hanging open. "I didn't know you were coming."

"It was a last-minute decision, and I didn't want to mess with your concentration on the ice."

I take all this information in for a moment before figuring out what to say. To say I'm surprised to see Emily here is an understatement. "Well, you're here now and I'm starving. Can we grab something to eat?"

"How about a pizza at your place, where we can talk?"

I nod, and she takes my arm as we head through the lower level and out into the balmy night.

"Nice sweater," I say, mostly to break the silence—which is atypical for me. Awkward silences don't usually spur me to fill them.

"I got it at the team shop. Had to let go of my Montreal one."

"Yeah," I say with a sigh that sounds a lot sadder than I feel. I'm beginning to accept the terms of my contract and trying to embrace it rather than try to fight against it. Calls with my mom have helped with my attitude, but also time with CFMW. *And previously...Billie.*

"And it's not so bad here after all?" She sounds hopeful asking the question.

"It's not," I admit.

We stop and grab a pizza, carrying it the two blocks to my apartment, where I flip on the lights and offer her a beer from the fridge. She accepts it, clinking my bottle with hers.

"I'm glad you're doing better here." She seems calm now, subdued. It's a very different energy than the last time she was here when she seemed so angry.

"It's been good. I like working with the kids at the music workshop, and the team dynamic is getting better, too."

"Well, when you deliver shut-outs, I imagine they have to accept you."

"Perhaps."

"And the woman in the picture? Does she have something to do with your evolving feelings about Las Vegas?"

I meet her gaze. "She has helped, yes."

"Do you want to talk about her?"

"Do you want to talk about this guy you're in love with?" It comes out sharper than I intend because, honestly, I'm not bothered by Em being in love with someone. Not anymore.

Look at me being all empathetic and shit.

"I don't want to fight, Cal. I want to talk."

"I don't want to fight either."

"Okay, then I'll go first." She takes a bite of pizza,

chews it, then takes a drink from her beer before talking. "Sometimes, being in a relationship with you is more like being your caretaker than being your girlfriend. It's exhausting, sometimes, living within the structure you need in order to feel okay or whatever. Since you came here, I've felt free. I don't know if you realize how rigid you can be about your routine, but it's really confining."

"My f-friend"—I have to clear my throat—"she's said things about me being afraid of change. And honestly? I know she's right."

"This is the same friend who's in the picture?"

"It is." I nod. "Billie is her name. She's a musician."

"Ah, so that's the connection. You've always loved live music." She takes another bite. "I'm glad you have someone here. I know the move was hard for you."

I take a bite of my pizza, but it tastes like ash in my mouth. Conversations like the one we're having make me have...*feelings*...and I don't know where to put all that emotion. It has to go somewhere, but I don't know what to do with it.

"You're a brilliant player with a brilliant mind, Cal." Emily is sounding as sad as I think I feel. "A genius, really, and so exciting to watch. And you're handsome. Gorgeous. Amazing body. You're a poster-boy for hot athletes. And to most people, that aloof, rigid thing probably plays like cockiness, but I know what it really is."

I tense up because I know what she really means. "But you stayed in it because it was fun to be on the arm of an athlete who makes a lot of money. Yeah, you told me that already."

"I'm sorry I said those things. I do care about you, Cal. But if we're being honest, have we ever had that consuming kind of love that people write about? Have we ever had much in common?"

"I guess not," I admit, my thoughts going to my time with Billie, to the way conversation was generally easy and relaxed. Fun. And I can't deny how my body responds to her, to the way my mouth feels on hers.

I haven't felt that way with anyone before, not even Emily, whom I was supposed to be in love with. I may be oblivious sometimes, but I know where this conversation is going. My heart should be broken right now and it's just...not.

"I feel like you see in black-and-white. Numbers and science. And I need someone who can see in color. Does that make sense?"

"Not really, Em."

"That's exactly the reason we should break up."

22

i felt something

Billie

"So, you told the band about Kit's offer?" Stuart asks as we walk out of the movie theater.

I agreed to a date with him, and it's almost like normal between us, apart from him holding my hand, which I'm not generally opposed to, even though I know it means something different to him than it does to me.

We saw a blow-up movie. Not high on my list, but it was entertaining, I guess. I don't go to the movies very often.

"I did, and I also told them I'm not keen on taking handouts from my family. They both rolled their eyes at me and said they understood, but I think it was just a stall tactic."

"Stalling for what?"

Just then, I get a joint text. From Nikki and Sven:

Nikki + 1: Outvoting you. We're doing the soundtrack whether you like it or not.

I roll my eyes and hold my phone up for Stuart to see. He chuckles and says, "Well, you called that one."

I text them back a thumbs-up emoji. What the hell. Might as well give my brother and my band what they all want.

Stuart nudges me with his shoulder. "This is a good thing. So much good can come from it."

I shrug. "Maybe. Sometimes working with my family isn't worth the hassle. But we'll give it a try."

"Your family just wants to help. They want you to be successful."

"You know better than that, Stu. You've known me a long time. You know why I came here to live instead of staying in that world. My mom had me in makeup, doing go-sees from like age five. She toted me around making me sing, and dance, and act, like I was an ornamental commodity. It was not about wanting what was best for me. And they still don't know me or what I really want in life. They just want me to conform to live within their idea of success or whatever. Unless they can mold me into what they want me to be, then I am nothing but an embarrassment."

"I'm sure it's not as bad as that, Billie. I mean, families are complicated, but it usually comes from love."

I take a big breath in and then let it out slowly. "I

know they love me, but they might love me more if I came into their entertainment world, you know?"

"Well, I would say you got the performance gene. It's in your blood. Maybe you should just embrace it."

"I do," I argue. "I perform with the band. We've been out there."

"But you're holding yourself back just to prove you can do it without them. That's not fair to your talent. It's just you being stubborn to prove a point."

"If you feel that way, then maybe you don't really know me at all." I say it sharply because he is starting to be obtuse to the point of annoyance. What's frustrating is that Cal, who has little in terms of empathy, totally got what I meant. My family smothered me, and I want my wins to be on my own merit.

Stuart blows out a breath and grins as he puts his arms around me. "Aw. Don't be like that, I know you better than anybody."

He leans in to kiss me, trying to soften the mood. I'm rigid, though, and angry, so I don't reciprocate right away. He laughs and tries again, and I remember that this is my best friend. This is someone who loves me. So, I loosen a bit, letting him kiss me, trying to want to kiss him back.

It just doesn't do anything for me.

I pull away and extricate myself from his arms. He frowns.

"Stuart—"

"You're not even trying."

"I am trying. I'm here. I enjoyed our evening. But this...more than friendship that you want from me...it just isn't working. I think you're meant to be in my life just where we are. Best friends. Nothing more. I'm sorry."

"You're sorry? We were having a good time, but the minute I didn't agree with you, you decided this won't work. That's not fair."

"I just don't feel that way about you. It has nothing to do with disagreeing."

"You know what? You're a narcissist," Stuart bites back at me. "You only think about what you want, what terms you want it on."

"That's not fair. Don't lash out at me because I said I don't want to kiss you."

"Well don't friend zone me just because I don't villainize your parents."

"That's a ridiculous thing to say to me, Stuart. You can't force me to have feelings I don't have." I turn to find a cab or walk in the opposite direction—anything to distance myself from him. "I'm out of here. Call me when you're not being crazy."

I start to walk away, but Stuart grabs my arm—hard. I turn on him, teeth bared. "Get your hands off of me!"

Before I know it, there's a blur. Another human, I realize slowly, still shocked by the way Stuart grabbed me. I blink, just as Cal punches Stuart in the nose with a sickening crack.

Stuart falls backward, hitting the ground, hands over his now-bleeding nose. Cal bends down and growls in his face, "Asshole, you don't *ever* put hands on her like that."

My mouth is literally hanging open as I look from Cal to Stuart and back again.

Stuart gets to his feet as Cal steps in front of me, ready to do some more damage, if necessary, but thankfully, Stuart isn't stupid enough to go another round with someone who could tear him limb from limb. Like, say, a professional hockey player. He looks at me, shakes his head, and rushes to his car. *Coward. What was he thinking?*

Cal turns to me, jawline rigid, showing more expression than I've ever seen on him, and says, "You okay? Did he hurt you?"

I rub my arm but shake my head. "I'm fine. I'm okay."

"Can I get you home?"

I nod, feeling a little shaky all of a sudden. "I'll call a ride."

Cal and I don't talk in the car. It's not a long ride, but it feels like forever with the whole situation running through my mind again and again. I've known Stuart for so long, and I've never seen him act like that, so possessive. The space on my arm where he grabbed me throbs, and I rub at it absently, stunned.

My phone rings. Stuart's name scrolls across the screen. I hit decline. A second later, he spams me with a series of apology texts:

> Stuart: I'm sorry!! So fuckin sorry…

> Stuart: I'm an asshole, Bill

> Stuart: I can't believe I did that shit just now

Stuart: I deserved the bloody nose.
PLEASE forgive me!

I turn off my phone and shove it into my bag, forcing back tears. This is exactly why I didn't want this with Stuart. I just wanted him to stay my friend, and now this ugly thing hangs between us.

"Can I walk you in?" Cal asks gently.

I jump, snapping to attention. "Oh, we're here." I look around, making sure I get everything from the car before sliding out to the curb, Cal trailing behind me. He hangs back, even as the car drives away, waiting for an invitation.

"Come on, then," I say, hurrying my pace, eager to get into my safe space.

Once inside, I tell Cal to give me a minute to change. As soon as I get into the safety of my bedroom, I sag onto the bed, head in hands, just trying to breathe. *Oh God. How did that escalate so quickly? Why do I feel like such a fool?* Get it together, Billie. Just breathe, and get it together.

When I emerge, I've scrubbed my face and pulled on a pair of baggy sweatpants and a UNLV T-shirt. I find Cal scouring the shelves in my living room, seemingly enraptured by music memorabilia I've collected over the years. I've got signed drumsticks, T-shirts, books, records. It's all arranged haphazardly, but I know where each piece is, where it came from. I have a memory for every item here.

"Does all of this stuff make you uncomfortable?" I ask after indulging in a moment of watching him study various items with rapt attention.

"Why would your things make me uncomfortable?" He looks up at me with a half-smile, curious.

"Well, your place is...well, everything is in its place. It's kind of sterile and clean. I thought maybe all this clutter might annoy you."

Cal stands up straight and runs a hand through his hair. "It's not annoying. Your collection of memorabilia isn't clutter...it's interesting. And I keep my place structured because that's the way my brain works. It organizes things. I'm not sentimental about physical things. I don't get attached so I don't keep things around unless they have function and value."

"Ahh, yes, function and value." I flop down on my couch and pull my favorite fuzzy blanket over my legs. Cal sits next to me, but he doesn't relax. He sits pitched forward, hands on his knees like he might jump up at any second, like he might get spooked.

I get it, I guess. Things have been weird between us since I found out about Emily Marshall. I googled until I found a reference to her in an article about the young goalie phenomenon. She's a young wannabe academic, blonde and perfect, from Montreal's high society set. I found a few pictures of them at events. They looked good together, but honestly, I couldn't see the connection between them. Both looked like they were going through the motions. I want to ask about her, but I can't gather the courage. I want to kiss him, but I can't do that either.

"What do you like about music?" I ask out of the blue. "I mean, music is emotional. It's an exercise in storytelling. It requires attachments and emotions in order to be effective."

Cal bites his bottom lip while he thinks. "For me, playing the guitar is scientific. It's math. Musical notes, rhythms...there's a formula, a pattern to it. It makes sense."

"You know, there is research out there connecting musical ability to hard science aptitude. True story." I smile at him and nod to help lighten the mood.

"Oof," Cal says with a laugh, leaning back finally. "You sound like an academic."

"I mean, I did graduate college." I laugh in return.

"What about you, Billie?" There's something about the sincerity in his voice, or maybe it's partly his sexy accent, but whatever the combination of ingredients, the way he says "Billie" is very, very lovely and has a rather indecent effect on my lady parts.

"I started playing, like in earnest, to de-stress. My mom was always really intense about wanting me to be in show business. She toted me around from a very early age and I hated every minute of it. The makeup and the poofy dresses and the show tunes." I roll my eyes. "You can't imagine the relief I felt when my grandmother asked me if I was happy when I was about eleven, I think. And how she simply stepped in, no questions asked, when she realized how much I hated my life. I just wanted to get away from the whole scene. It was a big family blow-up at the time. My mom has never forgiven me."

"So that's why you didn't want her to know about the drumming?"

"Yeah. Cat's out of the bag now, though."

"I am sorry about that," he says with regret. "I had no idea."

"I know. It's fine. If she wasn't mad at me for that, she'd find something else because she would not be a Jewish mother if she didn't have something to make me feel guilty about."

Cal looks confused.

"Jewish mom joke?" I grin. "No? Nothing? Man, you are a tough crowd, Cal."

"So, you started drumming to shut it all out?"

"Yep. It was loud, I had to use every muscle in my body, and when I was done, I would sleep like the dead. It was a total emotional outlet."

"Still is, I imagine," Cal observes. "You're very expressive when you play. It's what drew me to watch you."

I feel my cheeks go hot at the compliment. "I feel everything I play."

"I'm not usually good with emotions," he says, shifting his tone. "If you haven't noticed."

"I have," I say softly.

"When I saw that guy grab your arm, I felt something." He turns to face me. "I don't fight just to fight. But I—I wanted to kill him for hurting you tonight."

"Stuart," I correct. "His name is Stuart and he's been my best friend since high school."

"Has he been hurting you since high school?" His eyes go wide, and his mouth makes a hard line.

"No," I say quickly. "No. He's always been great. But he wants to be more than friends now, so he's feeling hurt that I don't see him that way. Tonight was...a fluke."

Cal looks dubious, but he doesn't argue with me. He just says, "I barely felt a thing when Emily said she was in love with someone else. Barely felt it when she broke up with me."

I sit back, eyes wide in shock. "She broke up with you?"

He nods. "After the home opener."

I try not to, but I frown. I can't decide if I'm jealous that she was here or upset she chose to break up with him on an important night in his hockey career. Cal seems to sense what I'm feeling, though, as he reaches over to take my hand.

"It was fine. I didn't know she was even in town until after the game. She didn't want to upset me before I had to play, so she came down to find me after the win. We got pizza and talked, and we agreed it was time to move on, for both of us."

"Oh," I say dumbly.

Cal lifts a shoulder. "She's not wrong when she says I'm stuck in my ways. But she also said she felt more like my caretaker than my girlfriend, which sucked. I didn't realize I was such a big baby." He laughs lightly and shakes his head.

"I don't think you're a big baby." I squeeze his hand for reassurance.

He gives me a soft smile. "Well, you haven't known me very long."

"Well, you may be rigid, but I suppose I am, as well. I'm sorry I got so mad at you for outing my drumming to my mom. I'm a grown-ass woman. I should have handled that better."

"We are who we are," Cal says. "Emily is who she is. But I think she and I were never really a good match. We just liked the comfort of being in the relationship. It offered a different kind of stability for each of us, but our goals didn't match and now...well, it's easy to see how flawed it was."

I suck up my fear and ask, "Why now? Because of the distance?"

"No, Billie." He shakes his head and pegs me with those blue, blue eyes of his. "It's because we both care for other people."

23

realism

Cal

illie hasn't shoved my hand away, so I assume she's not totally put off by what I'm saying.

"There's something I really like about being around you," I say, swallowing back the strange nervousness I'm feeling. "I've never cared that much about what people think of me. I know it sounds cocky or whatever, but self-doubt isn't a thing I deal with all that often. I know I piss people off and say the wrong things a lot of the time, or offend people without realizing it, whatever...but I'm just not wired to care about it all that much, for better or worse."

Billie lets out a strange sound, a kind of a laugh, I guess. I peer at her, wishing for the first time that I was better at reading people's emotions.

"It's not that I don't care about others," I say quickly, "I just—"

She puts up her free hand. "Don't blow a gasket, Cal. I'm not here to judge you. You said it, we are who we are, and we all have our quirks. I just wish I could have fifty percent of your lack of self-doubt."

"Most people just think I'm an asshole."

"Sometimes you can be. But I know there is a good heart under all that awkward."

"How?"

"How do I know, you mean?" Her eyes are so pretty, the way she's looking at me right now.

I nod once.

"Well, because I've seen you with those kids, for one. You are good with them. You care about them, and you're patient with them."

"But I really messed things up with your mother."

"It's fine," she says with another squeeze of my hand. "You didn't know. And honestly, it's turning out to be a good thing, maybe. My brother offered the band an opportunity to do some work on the soundtrack for his new movie."

"What? Really?"

"Yup." She flattens her lips into a line, and I can't read what it means. Is she happy about it?

"You're not happy about it?"

Billie lifts a shoulder. "I don't know. I like my job, you know? I like playing in the band around here. It's a good life, a life I chose, you know? I left LA for a reason."

"I think I understand that better than most," I say with a squeeze of her hand this time.

There's something about Billie that I can't describe. Something that draws me to her. I want to kiss her right now, but she seems so far away. She looks at me now like she's not sure what to say.

I let go of her hand and stand up, feeling awkward. "I guess I should head home."

She stands up, the blanket falling to the floor as she reaches out, grabbing my hand again. "Why do you feel like you need to leave?"

"I just…I'm not good at this, Billie."

"At what? Having a human conversation?"

I shrug.

"Look at me." Then, "Calum."

Something about the way she says my name makes me feel good. Not Cal. Calum.

Emily only ever said my full name when she was upset with me or scolding me, like my mom might have when I was young. Billie, however, says it differently. On her tongue, it sounds warm and inviting.

"I like the way you say my name," I blurt out because, for some reason, I want her to *know how much I like it*. Weirdly.

"For the record, I really like how you say my name too, but what other way is there to say it?" she asks, her head cocked curiously to one side, a flirtatious smile on her face.

"No one really says my full name. They always shorten it to Cal, which is fine and Cal is what I usually prefer to be called rather than Calum, except when you say it."

"Well, I like it. *Calum*," she purrs. "Calum. In the Hebrew faith, it means devotion."

"I'm not really religious," I explain. "My parents believed in science, not faith."

"My parents are very loosely affiliated with

organized religion, but I still studied the faith up until my bat mitzvah. Calum was described as a faithful protector of Israel."

"I'm not very political, either. This is a weird conversation."

Billie laughs, a surprised hiccup of sound. "You're right. You said you liked the way I said your name and I made it weird by talking about religion when I should have just asked you to kiss me."

This request, I understand. I pull her closer, putting my free hand on her cheek, meeting her gaze before touching my lips to hers. She sighs quietly, and I pull her closer, deepening the kiss as she opens her mouth, our tongues finding one another.

My hands roam, running the length of her spine, pushing under her shirt, touching the bare, soft skin there. She sighs again, against my mouth, the sound and feel of it more erotic than anything I've ever experienced before.

"I want you to do dirty things to me, Calum," she whispers against my lips.

My cock goes insta-hard, obviously liking that idea very much as I pick her up, hands on her ass, her legs straddling my waist. I shuffle us down the hall, kissing my way up her neck, breathing in the sweet scent of her hair. I hope I'm heading in the right direction for her bedroom because I've never been in her apartment before. But as soon as a king-sized bed comes into my vision, I make a beeline toward—

"Shower," she insists, through a kiss. So, I change course and head for the en suite. I reluctantly set her down, because I really like carrying her in my arms, but I want her naked more. We fumble with each other's clothing until the last item drops to the floor with a swish. Both of us stand completely naked before each other and look. I take in her body, lightly muscled from her years of drumming. Her hair is so long down over her shoulders and breasts, the purple ends contrasting sharply against her creamy skin in the soft lighting of her bathroom.

My mouth is dry, and my heart goes slightly crazy as I try to piece together all of the things I want to say to her. I open my mouth. Close it. Open it again. Close it again.

"What?" she asks, her cheeks turning pink.

"You're so beautiful." I barely manage to get the words out.

Her blush deepens and she turns away, suddenly bashful.

"I've seen you before." *You were beautiful then too.*

"I know," she says before taking a deep breath.

"Well then, why are you being shy?"

"This feels...different. Somehow. Am I wrong?"

The way Billie bites her bottom lip, her deep brown eyes wide and questioning...it makes my cock even harder, if that's possible. I'm not totally oblivious to what she's asking, but I'm still not sure how to articulate how I feel. How much I want her.

I step into the oversized shower and start the water, beckoning with one hand for Billie to join me. She takes my hand and steps in, the glass door enclosing us as the space fills with steam.

We're so close but not yet touching, save for our clasped hands. I look into her eyes, trying to convey...

something. She gives me a sweet, soft smile that makes my cock twitch for her touch.

I want to kiss her so badly. But I need to get this out. I blow out a big breath, biting the inside of my cheek because I know what an idiot I must look like.

"Words are hard," Billie says with a little laugh.

"They can be," I agree. "For me anyway."

"Well, let me help you, Calum," she says. "I know this isn't supposed to be happening. We're supposed to be professionals, just working on a project together. But we've crossed that line and then some, and I really like you."

"You do?"

She laughs again. "Of course, I do."

I let out the breath I didn't know I was holding. "I'm just...never sure. Of what people think of me."

"I didn't think you cared what people think."

"But I do care sometimes. I care what *you* think, Billie. Always."

"Well, be assured that I am firmly in the Calum Lefleur fan club."

"I like you, too. Very much."

She smiles widely. I pull her close, wrapping my arms around her, pulling her gorgeous naked body against mine as we embrace.

"This felt so much easier the last time," I comment with a chuckle. "I feel like such a virgin."

This makes Billie laugh out loud, a big laugh that has her in tears as she pulls me under the hot spray of water. We both laugh and sputter, and before I know it, the strange tension is erased as I lean in for a kiss. My thumbs brush back and forth over her nipples, circling the tight tips as she arches into the attention.

Her hand grips my cock, stroking slowly as our tongues intermingle. I pull away to catch my breath, moving my hands to push my wet hair from my face, then doing the same for Billie.

"You make Las Vegas…so much better." *No, that's not the right thing.* I try again. "I mean, I'm glad I saw you play that night. When I first spotted you up there…I couldn't look away, Billie. Even though I didn't know you, it gave me hope for what this could be."

She smiles slightly, but her eyes are hooded as she continues the rhythmic stroking. Back and forth, her hand on my cock is hot pleasure, but her mouth would be better.

"Keep up the sweet-talking, Shakespeare." A wry grin adding to the sexy, I-want-you-to-do-dirty-things-to-me-Calum look on her beautiful face. *Oh, I plan on it.*

"I was stupid to think things would work with Emily. Stuck in my own head about change. And all the while, you were right here. A *real* friend. A person who accepted me for *me.* And that means a lot because I think I might be a handful."

"I do accept you as you are. I can be difficult, too."

"I'm just glad I found your band that ni—"

"But now you need to *stop* talking."

"Okay."

Our mouths meet again, this time devouring. Consuming. My fingers play at her clit, two slipping down to part her and push deep up inside the tight heat. She flexes into my hand, my palm hard against her most sensitive spot, her moans spurring me to finger her harder, faster, until she's coming in my arms. *That's happening.*

She arches her back, pulling her mouth from mine, shaking her head like she can't take this friction. Falling to her knees, she takes my cock in her mouth as she looks up at me with those dark, magical eyes of hers. With her mouth and tongue, she continues a slow, sexy rhythm of sucking me.

I brace myself, my hands on the wall behind her, my hips moving to meet her lips, my eyes never leaving her face. Before I lose it completely, I pull her back up, my fingers finding her slippery clit again, my lips and teeth grazing along her nipples as she lets out a gasp of pleasure.

"I want you," she breathes. "Cal, please."

"Say Calum," I growl, giving one of her nipples a gentle bite.

"Ahhh...Calum." A sexy, low whisper. The sound of her saying my name like that with her naked and desperate in my arms makes a shudder roll through my body.

"Again."

"Calum." She says it again. Pleading and desperate now. "Please. Please, Calum."

I lift her, bracing her back against the tiles, and spread her wide. She's ready to take my cock, and I'm past ready to give it to her. When I push deep inside her on a rough slide and start to fuck, she cries out my name again, moving her hips to meet every thrust, our bodies in total sync. My mouth on her jaw, her neck, the hollow of her throat, every place my lips can reach.

Her nails digging into my back, urging me along with her.

Our bodies are slick, moving together, water sluicing over us, getting in our eyes, wetting our lips and tongues. Like a hazy, drugged dream I don't want to ever end, endorphins crash through my system, the tingle of energy rippling through my veins as my release builds. *Fuck. I don't know if it's okay for me to come—*

"Is this okay? No...condom..." I barely get the words out before Billie's moans grow intense and feral, her cunt tightening around my cock, her orgasms following one after another, a parade of ecstasy that spurs me to go faster, harder until I know I'm hurtling over the edge to join her any second.

"Yes...s'okaaaaay," she chokes out through the haze of her pleasure.

The sight of her in my arms, my cock pulsing deep inside her, our names on each other's lips, my forehead against hers, eyes closed, flips my go-switch. I start to come, the experience like nothing I've ever felt before, riding out the wave of intense feeling, of emptying myself, my soul...into hers.

It's so hard for me to express emotion, to show how I feel, and I hope that this shows her that she can feel it.

We stay connected for a long while, catching our breath, holding each other. When I pull away, it's only to grab the soap. I wash her, her soft, creamy breasts and pebbled nipples. I wash the sensitive space between her legs, and she moans sexily, leaning into me, making my cock hard again.

"How can I want you this much?" I marvel, mostly to myself.

Billie looks up to meet my gaze, her expression open and vulnerable, as if she's asking me to say it again, to assure her it's real.

"It is, Billie."

"What is, Calum?"

"What you said before. That this feels different now between us. You're right. It *is* different now. It's real. So fucking real."

She takes my face in her hands and kisses me sweetly while I bring her flush against my body. We stay like that for a long time, holding each other under the falling spray of warm water floating down around us like a cleansing rain.

Moments pass, maybe hours, who knows. But eventually, we turn off the shower. The last drops of water falling onto the tiles below sound garishly loud in the quiet of what we just did together as we pull oversized, purple towels around ourselves. *Purple must be her favorite color.* She goes to the sink to brush her long hair and I watch her in the mirror. When she turns, her cheeks and chest are flushed with pink.

I hold out my hand, and she takes it, her towel falling to the floor as she steps into me.

Together, we find her bed, and that realism I've never felt with anyone else before today...once more.

<h1 style="text-align:center">24
the beach looked
familiar</h1>

Billie

"Billie, Nikki, and Sven, meet Dan Rosenberg," my brother Kit says, his wide, movie star smile on full display as he introduces us to the executive producer of his new movie.

We're in LA to work on the soundtrack for the film. Dan has reservations about bringing an unknown band to the table for a tentpole of a summer film. It's an action film with lots of explosions and a hot romance, and normally, they'd contract with a hot, current band to tap into that band's fan base for added support.

"Kit has told me you're all going to be the next hot thing," Dan says, his teeth white and straight, his tan golden. He's in a crisp, white shirt that opens to show a gold cross necklace. He's one of those slick Hollywood types that I always hated when I was growing up. Smiling widely, ready to devour people like wolves devour prey.

I bristle at it, folding my arms over my chest, my

scowl deepening with each word of the lecture he gives us. He loves Kit. Kit's a rainmaker. He's got faith in Kit's taste, and he's willing to take a listen, but he's not giving away the farm for free. He needs something real, something that sells. He's willing to give us a chance, but he's not making any guarantees.

He stops short of acting like he's giving us some great gift by deigning to make time to listen to us play, but it's certainly there, in between the sharky smile and "pep talk."

By the time we head to the sound booth, where we'll play two full songs for his oh-so-discerning musical ear, I'm in a rage that roars in my ears and makes me want to break my sticks. I did not want to be here. I did not want this. It feels like a handout, like a nepotistic sleight of hand that puts us in the limelight in the most inauthentic way.

Still, as we start our first song, a rager of a rock song with heavy guitars and a complicated, engaging drumbeat, I can see Kit's eyes widen with surprise and awe, like he didn't expect us to sound quite as good as we do.

We play through both songs, and I know we sound good. I know Sven's gravelly voice will curl toes. I know Nikki and I present the image of two badass women who can hold it down with the best of them. And as we finish, Dan and Kit step into the booth, both smiling, and I know the deal is done. There is no going back.

Dan claps Kit on the shoulder and leaves his hand there. A sign of ownership more than pride, I think, but he says, "Kit, my man, you are a genius. Holy fucking shit, these guys are good."

My hackles raise at the "these guys." Sexism is another part of Hollywood that I hate, along with Kit picking my battles.

"Let me get the team together and we can all meet tomorrow with the contracts, but let's start you thinking about three full-length songs and a few filler cutaways. We've got a live band scene in the film, so we'll get you scene overviews and a casting contract as well. You'll need representation and we'll call in a music studio to manage the sound and mixing for us."

I hear very little as we pack up our gear and head out, Kit announcing that he's taking us all to dinner. He's all smiles as we pile into the back of a huge, black SUV, like the benevolent benefactor who's just made some significant philanthropic commitment.

I shove myself into the third row of seats and slump against the seat, pouting.

Nikki and Sven are bouncing in their seats with wide smiles that match my brother's. They love this. They're excited because this is what they've always wanted. They want fame and fortune. They wanted me to use my family to help us get noticed all along.

Well, here we are. And I should be happy because this is huge. But I'm just...not.

At the restaurant, I sit next to Kit, and he drapes his arm across the back of the booth, inclining his head toward mine. In a low voice, he asks, "Why are you being so weird about this?"

I shrug and mutter, "I didn't want it to happen this way."

"What way did you want it to happen?"

Nikki and Sven sit across from us, looking pointedly at their menus. They know why. They've heard it a million times.

"You know why," I answer through gritted teeth.

"Because you like to scrape and fight for every bit of everything you attain? You want to get it through good old-fashioned hard work and elbow grease? You don't like handouts?" Kit chuckles and shakes his head. "Ninety-eight percent of success in this business comes from having the right connections at the right time."

"This is an awesome opportunity, Billie," Sven says. "Three full songs? An agent? A record deal?"

"We're going to blow up after this," Nikki says.

I take a sip from my water glass. "What if we're not ready?"

Sven scoffs at this. "We've been ready. Sound wise, we're ready. It's you who's not ready."

Nikki softens this by adding, "Emotionally, he means. We know you've got...baggage."

"Look," Kit says. "You've got talent. The band is good. Why rage against the start of your own success?"

"It just...I didn't want all the parading around. The guys like Dan. The games. I just wanted to make good music that people would want to hear."

"We can," Nikki answers. She reaches across the table and grabs my hand, her expression fierce.

Kit adds, "Look, make a name for yourself. Write three kick-ass songs and show the studios what you can do. Get a good agent to work a good deal for you, one that gives you as much control as possible."

Control. He used that word on purpose. I know he's felt like he wasn't in control at many times during his career. He was a late bloomer though, didn't come into his looks or his talent until he was late in his teens. When his career went full tilt, he was at least old enough to understand what was happening.

"It just isn't for me, you know?" I start. "Getting dragged around like I'm on display. Having to dress up and walk the red carpet. Having to look pretty and put up with leering old men and just keep smiling and taking whatever crumbs people hand out."

Sven rolls his eyes, but Nikki gets it, squeezing my hand. "We can do this on our terms."

"You can," Kit says. "You can play the game better. It doesn't have to feel the way it did when you were younger."

"You say that because you have power. And you didn't get dragged around like I did. You got to go to school and have a normal childhood."

"Let it go, sis. I begged Mom to take me out with you. I would have done anything to get to act when I was young. I loved it, but Mom thought I was a talentless, fat oaf."

"Well, you were kind of fat..." I tease him, grinning.

"And you were more talented. I think she got it right, quite frankly, but she settled for supporting me once you said you were out of the game. Redoubled her efforts and helped me make the most of what small amount of talent I had."

"And look at you now."

I smile at my brother because I am genuinely

proud of him. He has done well. He's one of the most recognizable faces in movies today, as evidenced by the ten people who've come to our booth looking for selfies or autographs tonight. *Will that be me? Our band? Will we never be able to eat out in peace again?* Do I want *that*?

OUR MEALS COME, and we dig in, the conversation moving to the plot of the film and the tone Kit hopes we can convey through the songs we'll write. My mood lightens with the creative process this inspires, and I find myself feeling much better as we finish the night, heading back to the hotel, where Nikki and Sven head off to the bar while Kit and I decide to take a walk around the city.

"I know this is happening really fast," he says, holding my hand as we walk.

I gesture to where our hands meet and say, "The paparazzi will wonder what woman you're with now."

He gives me a half-hearted grin. "I don't give a shit. Plus, they're so creepy, they'll have it figured out pretty quickly that you're my sister."

"I know this is a good opportunity," I say on a sigh. "I know you were trying to help."

"And I know why it makes you uncomfortable. But you're so good. Seriously. I knew you'd be good, but you blew me away in there today. All three of you did, but the way you drum, Bill? It's..." He lets out a breath and shakes his head.

"Thanks," is all I can seem to come up with. It feels good to have him say it, to say I'm talented.

"Mom always saw that talent, too, you know."

"I don't want to talk about Mom." My tone is sharp.

He puts up his free hand. "Okay. Sorry." A few steps without talking, then, "How's your boyfriend? I saw some grainy pictures in the tabloids. The beach looked familiar, but I couldn't quite make out who he was doinking."

My brother gets a sharp elbow to the ribs for that. He yelps.

"So mortifying," I say, throwing a hand over my eyes.

"Whatever," he says, dismissing me. "It happens to me all the time. It's the downside of dating famous people. The press is always around the next corner, waiting to catch a flash of your ass or a fuck-up."

"Well, thankfully, no one's ass was in that picture."

Kit laughs. "Though it seemed quite obvious what was happening, even with the poor photo quality."

"Did Mom and Dad see it?" I dare to ask.

"Probably," he says with a one-shoulder shrug. "But they know how it goes. You'd have heard about it already if they were upset."

"Truth."

"So, you didn't really tell me how Calum is."

"And you know, I only brought him to keep Mom from trying to fix me up with some producer's son or whatever."

"Well, in spite of that, you two clearly have a thing for each other. I mean, I hire fake dates all the time, but I don't screw them on the beach outside my childhood home."

"Touché, brother." I let out an embarrassed laugh. "Well, we're still figuring things out to tell you the truth. I just know it's real for both of us."

"You like him?"

"I do." It comes out quietly, as images of our last night together play in my head. I think about it often, the sweet way he tried to show me how he feels. Nothing got resolved, we didn't talk about what we are to each other, but being with him felt incredibly right. More right than I've ever felt with anyone, and it scares me. A lot.

"Well, I like you two together, for whatever it's worth. He's kind of awkward, but I think he really likes you."

"Awkward is an understatement. He's probably on the spectrum but he's so brilliant. He's a genius on the ice and he has a really good heart."

"And you have chemistry," Kit adds.

"And we have chemistry." *So much. Loads of chemistry.* "What about you? Haven't seen you with a new, young starlet in a bit."

He makes a noise of disgust. "I'm so sick of it. The studios always try to make it look like I'm having some fling with whatever costar I have. Helps sell movies. Makes me look like a womanizer. It's so fucking stupid."

I've always known that most of Kit's "relationships" were not real. A few have been questionable, but he's a good team player, a good company man, and a good actor. People believe it when he looks into some young ingenue's eyes, believes he really feels what he portrays on screen. Believes that chemistry could translate to real life.

"So, no one, then?"

He swallows and pulls his hand from mine, rubbing it along his artfully stubbled chin.

"Kit?" I press.

"There is...someone." He chokes it out like he's expelling a demon. "I'm in love, I think."

"What?" I can't contain my surprise. "With whom?"

"His name is Josh," he says quietly, looking around to make sure no one is straining to hear our conversation. The street is busy with people, most who don't seem to notice the presence of an A-list celebrity in their midst. A few do double takes but likely think there's no way he could be here, wandering around like some commoner.

"Josh," I repeat quietly, taking in the implication. "So..."

"Yeah," he answers quickly.

My brother is gay, and I didn't know it! "Since when?"

"Since birth?" he says. Then, "I've always known but that's not what they want, you know? It doesn't sell movies."

A weight settles in my stomach when I think of what this means for him. He's got money and power and a career that is on fire, but he has to prance around with young actresses instead of being with the person he loves. Talk about a loss of control. And now I feel like a tool. How have I missed this?

Missed knowing that my brother is forced to lie every day?

"People would understand," I say.

"Would they? Would the people from Ohio and Mississippi and Montana all accept their golden boy leading man if they knew that, in real life, he was in love with another man? The studio understands. Josh lives in the apartment next to mine. He's my neighbor to anyone else. To me? He's everything, and I can't tell the world." The bitterness in his voice is palpable.

I take his hand again. "I'm so sorry, Kit."

"Yeah." He takes a shaky breath. "Well, it is what it is."

"I had no idea. Which is crazy because you're my brother and I thought I knew you pretty well."

"That's because I am such a brilliant actor," he says with a flourish. "But now that I've told you my secret, I need you to do me a favor."

"I won't tell anyone."

"No, it's not that, though I would appreciate it. I need you to take this ball and run with it, Bill. This is a real chance. And when you have that chance—at love, at success—you need to take it, sister-mine."

25

i have feelings

Cal

W'ere in the second period at home against New York. Game tied, it's been a violent, high-pressure battle since puck drop, with a whole lotta flared tempers, body checks, and on-ice smack talk. New York's left wing is a cocky, young kid named Bryce Barrymore. He's hockey royalty, the son of a legendary defenseman. Just eighteen, he went straight from high school to the pros and into a multi-million-dollar starting slot like me.

He's a sharpshooter but also a dirty player, from what I've seen tonight. A decade and a half younger than Evan, he's using it, moving quicker, pivoting with more grace. His taunting doesn't seem to be getting into our captain's head, but his play certainly is. Evan looks slow out there, especially after taking shot after shot against the glass from New York's aggressive defensive players.

Having had enough, Evan takes a cheap shot at one

of them, dragging his stick under the player's skates as he tries to whiz by with the puck. As the defenseman goes down, Bryce Barrymore comes barreling in, smashing Evan against the glass where they get into a punching match, Evan's helmet going first, then Bryce's. I can hear Evan call him "Little Lord Fauntleroy," to which Bryce spits in Evan's face.

The crowd is cheering this whole debacle on as the refs try to get in the middle of a growing group of players, now all fighting one another.

It takes seven whole minutes to clear out the brawl, a bunch of first-string players heading to the penalty box as the second string comes out, mad as a bunch of hornets and not showing any sign that they'll play a peaceful period.

We finish second period at a tie, Coach trying to keep his cool while lecturing everyone on playing with dignity.

We head out to the third period. First string still has time on the box, so second string lines up as the buzzer starts play. The first two minutes are back to normal play, tempers in check, but when we score, something changes. The penalties come off the board, and our first string start to sub back in, amping up the energy, grudge matches playing out in snide comments and needless checks.

Bryce Barrymore, returned to the game, comes barreling at me several times, taking several fast, sharp shots that I stop easily. After the fourth, he bares his teeth at me, hissing like some wild animal. All I can do is roll my eyes behind my mask, watching the puck as it moves across the ice.

With just under three minutes to go, we score again when Viktor rails a beauty of a snapshot top shelf into their net. The big Russian doesn't score a ton of goals as an enforcer, but when he does, like tonight, it's especially timely.

Moments later, a fight nearly breaks out to my right, Bryce Barrymore manages to get through the melee with the puck, flying down the ice at a wickedly fast speed.

Dangerous speed.

Is this fucker gonna slow it down?

He does not.

Rushing at me unchecked, wearing a shit-eating wolf's grin on his face, the ignorant fool body blasts himself into my net.

And me.

I know how to stop a puck, but a full-grown man hell-bent on beating the shit out of everyone on our team?

Not so likely.

I get shoved into the back of my net, the whole arena erupting into a chorus of boos. It's patently uncool to check or hit a goalie, of which Barrymore is fully aware. So even for a cocky rookie, it's a complete shock getting blasted in my own net. In my own fucking house.

This kid has a death wish.

Rattled and stunned down on the ice, I try to push back up to my feet, but there's no space for me to manage it before a violent scrum has formed all around me. My teammates coming for Barrymore was a given; they're gonna want to spill some blood on my behalf. I can only make out Tyler, Viktor, and hothead Mikhail raging to get at him. The rest are a blur of bodies in a melee exploding out from the blue paint and beyond.

I hold out a padded arm to block myself from the blows being thrown in the fight, but Barrymore shoots out his elbow, knocking my helmet off my head.

The last thing I see is that feral grin of his...and his fist.

I COME TO SLOWLY, first with an antiseptic smell in my nostrils. I move my fingers and they feel swollen. As I open my eyes, my vision takes a moment to clear, but only in one eye. I reach up slowly, feeling a bandage over my left eye, the eye that took a straight punch from a rookie's fist.

Sitting up too quickly, my head spins, and I lean over and vomit onto the floor. It's just a bit of water, but it still feels wretched coming up.

A nurse appears. "You've got a nice concussion," she says. "Might not want to move too quickly."

I groan in response, lying back, hands on my stomach as I will my head to stop spinning. When I feel like I can speak, I ask, "My eye? How can I play with only one eye?"

"I'm just here to check your vitals," she answers as she takes my temperature. "I'll let the doctor know you're awake. She can tell you more."

I lie back, unsatisfied and unsettled, falling in and

out of sleep for I don't know how long. The next time I come to, Billie is there, at my side, holding my hand.

"Hey, handsome," she says quietly.

"Mmm, beautiiiiful Biiiiillie."

"How you feeling?" She gives me a soft laugh, probably at my silly greeting. I know I sound out of it, even to my ears.

"Been better."

"I bet," she says. "That was a real cheap shot." *Have I ever heard such anger in Billie's voice? Is that for me?*

"Hate that kid," I say, gritting my teeth at the pain in my head.

"Don't blame you. Hope he never gets to play again."

We sit for a while. Long enough that I fall back asleep, only to wake with a jolt as she pats my leg. The doctor is here. She introduces herself and starts talking about a mild concussion and a detached retina—

What! A detached fucking retina!

My heart dropping like a stone in a pond, I start spouting off questions to the doctor—unintelligible, I'm sure—because she then asks Billie if they can speak in the hallway.

The minutes pass by like hours.

By the time Billie returns to my bedside, I'm moving into a full-blown panic state. "Hockey is my life. I can't play with one eye."

"Relax, champ," she says soothingly. "You're not going to lose your eye. Your retina is on the verge of detachment, but it's not fully detached. They did some procedure on you, and right now you really just need to lie back and not stress it for a while."

"Is she saying if I can play or not?"

"Ever? I think you can. Soon? Probably not. I'd guess you're on concussion protocol anyway, for a few weeks."

"Fuck," I howl into the room.

"Hey, could be worse."

"How could it be worse?"

"You could be told you're not able to play again. This is just a few weeks."

All I can do is growl, which makes her smile and shake her head at me.

"You're a smarty, you could go back to MIT and get a fancy college degree. Go be a scientist."

"I don't want that. I want to play."

"Well, I didn't think I wanted to have my family involved in my career but here we are and it's working out okay for now," she says as she strokes her fingers through my hair, comforting me with her touch.

"You were at the game." It's not a question because I had no idea she'd be coming tonight.

"Yep. Came to watch you play. I used the tickets you always have for me at Will-Call but it was totally last minute so there was no chance to tell you I'd be there before puck drop. I was having a fun time until you got hurt. I met some nice people to hang out with...Devon, team nutritionist, and Scarlett, Crush social media. Oh, and a UNLV student, Zoya Kolochev, Tyler's girlfriend? She's interested in an internship working with kids so maybe I can get her hooked up at the center. Such a sweetheart, I think she'd be a good fit. I need to talk to them anyway about taking a bit more time off."

Listening to her chatter about her time at the game takes my mind off the moment. I'm glad she met some of the WAGs (wives and girlfriends) and made new friends. Billie is easy like that. She can show up to a new place all alone and fit in with any group. Something tells me I should ask why she needs to take more time off from her job, but my murky, injured brain sweeps it away. I cringe, holding my head in my hands as a wave of pain nearly blinds me. Billie calls for a nurse, who comes in to give me a dose of pain meds through my IV.

As the cool medicine flows into my veins, I relax, forgetting what we were talking about. Billie returns to combing her fingers softly through my hair again, comforting me with just her gentle touch. So kind and caring. And beautiful to look at.

I realize she's asking me something, and I open my mouth to respond but quickly forget what her question was. She giggles and it sounds like bells.

"I have feelings…" I hear myself saying the words, but it feels like I'm standing outside of my body.

Billie laughs again. I like the sound of her laughing. I like being the one making her laugh. "Sometimes I think it would be nice to have a dog. Or a cat. Or a dog and a cat."

"Well, pets take a lot of…" Billie's answer fades out as I take in the sight of her pretty mouth. Her crazy, beautiful two-color hair. She's so damn gorgeous.

"I think people think I'm a robot."

"I doubt they think you're a robot, Calum."

"No, they think I don't care, but I do have emotions, and sometimes I feel things, and I *do* care about people. I care about things. I could have a pet."

"No one said you couldn't take care of a pet. You're really loopy right now, bud. Maybe you should take a breather? Take a nap?"

"Yeah, okay." I say, taking her advice and closing my eyes.

Eye.

But then I remember something important. Something I don't want to forget to tell her. I hope it comes out right when I say, "I like having you here with me. I wonder...if this is what love really feels like."

26

a really hot pirate

Billie

The Crush are losing, down by two points.

Sitting on the couch next to me, Calum's pitched forward, elbows on his knees, a grimace on his face as the backup goalie, Castellano, lets in a third goal of the game.

"Get out of your head," he mumbles at the television.

"Is that the guy you said was such a dick to you in the first weeks here—the one who gave you the black eye?"

"Yup, the very one."

"Well, he's probably jumping for joy that you got hurt."

He shrugs. "Maybe, but he's certainly not playing like his position depends on it. He really sucks."

"He probably did some bad mojo to get you hurt. This is karma paying him back for it."

Calum laughs lightly and shakes his head. "Not karma. He's just that bad, Billie. Really, that bad."

"You don't think he was like praying to the hockey gods to get a shot this season?"

"Sure, but whatever. He's messing it up. I can't wait to get back out there."

"All I want for Christmas is to put this jackhole to shame," I sing.

"Pretty much."

We watch the rest of the game, Calum making the odd comment about his teammates' play and decision-making throughout. Somehow the Crush manage to pick up two goals, thanks to Boris and left-wing Mikhail. The back line rallies around Castellano, taking the pressure off to avoid more goals from the opposition.

When the game is done, he gets up and stretches, revealing his ripped abs and making my mouth go a little dry. He's still on injured reserve, so technically, he hasn't been cleared for any strenuous activity. He's been doing some light workouts with the team trainers and physical therapists, but I'm certain sex (our sex, at least) might be too strenuous by medical standards.

As if reading my thoughts, he smirks. "What are you thinking about over there?"

"Um...just admiring my view is all."

He grins. "That's what I thought."

"Actually," I say, steeling myself for the conversation I was holding off for as long as possible, "I was thinking about when you were in the hospital."

"Oh really? That's what your face looks like when you're thinking about someone in the hospital?" He chuckles and walks into the kitchen. "You want anything?"

"No, thanks."

He comes back in with a glass of water and sits next to me, the length of our thighs touching. "So, you were saying?"

"I was thinking about some things you said while you were under the influence of some very powerful pain medication." Looking sideways at him, I can't help from biting my lip.

He uses his fingertips to turn my head so he can see me fully. He still has his right eye covered with an eye patch. "You look like a pirate," I say, trying to distract him from my comment about what he said in the hospital. I should've kept my big mouth—

"So I've heard. Hopefully not for much longer."

"A really hot pirate though." I raise an eyebrow at him.

"I doubt my pirate styling is related to what I said while drugged in the hospital with a gruesome injury."

"It wasn't that gruesome," I scold. "Don't be a baby."

"You are a terrible caregiver." A measured pause. "A really hot terrible caregiver though."

"Whoa, boy, you got jokes now?" I don't know if he's even aware he did it, so I want him to know that I noticed. So freaking adorable I can barely contain myself.

"I did, didn't I?" He cracks the merest smile and cocks his head to the side but then right back to a demanding pause. "But now I must know what I said to you in the hospital."

"You said you thought this might be what love feels like," I blurt, slapping my hand over my mouth with a nervous giggle. "Of course, you also said you wanted a cat and a dog and that you had feelings."

He laughs lightly. "That's a lot to unpack. Where shall we start?"

"Um." The ability to form sentences lost...apparently.

"Okay, I'll go. I do kind of remember something like that, now you mention it."

"You do?"

"Mmm."

We sit awkwardly as Calum takes another sip of his water before setting his cup on the coffee table. When I get his attention again, he's serious, his blue eyes studying me intently.

"It's okay if you don't want to talk about it," I say softly.

"No, no, it's fine. I just...I want to get this right." He takes a breath and blows it out in a rush. "I said I wondered if this was what love felt like?"

"Mm-hmm. Did you—did you not love Emily?" I've wanted to ask that for the longest time. It feels good to get it out, but my heart's about to beat out of my chest as I await his response.

"I know I cared about her, but I think it was more that I loved the idea of her, plus the steadiness of having someone. But if I'm honest, it was only ever lukewarm."

"Lukewarm?" I'm quiet for a moment, but then I gather my courage to ask him the next question. "Do you feel like we're lukewarm?"

"No." Zero hesitation, and I can't miss how his eyes are a little darker blue than they were a moment ago.

He shakes his head sharply. "No way. I feel like…I'd want to kill anyone who dared to try to hurt you. And I want to rip your clothes off every time I'm with you—not just to fuck but to make love to you, and make you feel good." He takes my hand in his and brings it to his lips. "Billie, you make me feel everything that's the opposite of lukewarm."

I swallow back a wide grin. "Well, I think very similarly about you."

"Say it."

"Say what?"

"My name."

"Calum."

He growls and leans in for a searing kiss. It takes my breath away and makes my toes curl into the carpet.

"I'm pretty sure sex is on the strenuous activity list."

"Fuck that list," he says against my mouth, pushing me back, positioning himself between my legs as he kisses my ear and neck and jaw.

"Do you want to make a go of this? Like, for real?"

"Be my real girlfriend you mean?" He pulls back to look at me, searching my face for answers maybe.

I chew on my bottom lip, suddenly shy. "Well yeah, but I meant more like maybe—"

"Do you think this might be love, too, Billie?"

Yes. That's my immediate answer. And it completely solidifies what I knew was missing with Stuart. I could never feel for Stuart as much as I feel for Calum, even after such a short time. *This feels so…right.*

"I might very much think that, yes."

"Well, then, I think we should. Make a go of it. Make sure it's what we both want, yeah?"

He kisses me again, this time gently, slowly, savoring. We go slowly, touching each other over the top of our clothes before stripping to our underwear, Calum looking delicious in his black boxer briefs. I thank the heavens I wore my cute pink lace bra and thong today as I watch how he takes in the sight of me, my body, the way my nipples peak against the lace, the way I'm wet between my legs against the satin of my thong.

"You are so beautiful." Not the first time he's told me, and I hope not the last. "When I look at you, I can't believe how I feel about you, about this. About how much I want you. More and more each time we're together, if that's possible."

"Touch me?"

He touches me, but only momentarily, before scooting down to kiss me from outside of my panties. It drives me crazy. I want his mouth all over me, but he teases, pushing the panties aside, dipping a finger inside, pulling it out. He licks at my clit then stops. I groan and writhe and beg, but he takes his time, driving me so, so close to the edge.

When he finally slips my panties down my legs, he spreads them wide, his big hands dominant and demanding. *Off-the-charts hot.* Then he buries his face against my sex along with long fingers, lapping and sucking, fingering, and biting. It's so good. So good. I cry out as I come, his name tumbling from my lips over and over and over.

Stopping only to ditch his boxers so he can be inside me, he aligns his cock to my center. Hard, hot flesh searches deep and fills me. Breathless as my body accepts the full length of him, I can only feel claimed and possessed and taken in the very best way. He looks into my eyes, trailing kisses over my mouth and neck and throat. He licks and kisses his way along my skin, laced with gentle nips of teeth. Moving our bodies together in a way where every thrust and retreat and caress is purposeful, no touch is wasted.

My breasts jut shamelessly as I arch into him, meeting each deep stroke he gives to me. The friction against his sculpted chest is almost enough to get me off again, not that I need any help. I build again, saying his name, inviting him to come with me.

"Fuuuck, Billie," he shouts before I see his face tighten, his neck muscles cording as he starts to come, my name a steady repeat from his lips.

When he collapses, I wrap my arms around him, holding him, stroking back and forth across his back, listening to him breathe, and feeling his heart pound wildly against mine.

This feels so good. So right.

It feels like love.

I'll leave the hard conversation that's coming for another time.

27

twelve songs

Cal

"Billie, you doing okay over there?" I'm looking over to where Billie hangs on to the rail, trying her damnedest to stay upright on the ice...on skates.

"Oh, yep!" she yells, as she tries letting go, slips, and quickly grabs the rail again.

I chuckle, watching my class from CFMW skate around, all of them equipped with more courage than actual skating ability. They're having fun though, so that's all that matters.

I make a lap around the rink and put my arm around her on approach. She yelps and says, "Don't make me fall."

"I won't, I promise. Let go. I'll keep you upright."

She trusts me enough to mostly let go, her fingertips still hovering over the rail, a security blanket. "The kids seem to be having a good time. Thanks for letting them come here to do this."

"Don't need to thank me. I just asked. The Crush PR team made it happen."

"Well, still. It's a big deal for them."

"I know." And I do. These kids come from really challenging backgrounds. The club, I've learned, is a place where they get a hot meal and homework help, where they can just be kids and not worry about whatever is going on at home. I've come to appreciate going there very much, even though I thought it was a stupid PR stunt in the beginning. *Still feel bad about that.*

"I may have to step away for a minute to take a call soon," Billie says. "Can you help me to the exit?"

I nod and skate her over. She makes her way to the bench and starts to take off her skates, relief obvious on her face. I make a face at her and shake my head slowly back and forth. "I'll get better with practice so don't judge. Grew up in Los Angeles, remember? Ice skating wasn't at the top of the activity list."

"Not judging you. And I know you will because I'm an excellent teacher, but who are you expecting to call?"

"Um, my agent. Well, the band's agent."

"Oh, okay."

We haven't talked much about the band's big break lately. Billie has gone back and forth for recording sessions and said everything is going well. She seems lighter about the whole thing these days, and I'm truly happy for her, though I don't know what it will mean for her if the band hits it big from their participation in this movie.

When her phone rings, she holds up a finger and

walks out. I turn to watch the kids and when she returns, she stands next to me, watching the kids skate for a long time. Her silence is heavy.

"So?" I finally ask because I don't think she's going to tell me without prompting.

"We got a really good offer to make a whole album. Twelve songs, none of them repeats from the movie."

"Wow." Not what I was expecting her to say.

"Yeah. I mean, it's a huge deal."

"So, how will you do that? Will you guys work here and then go to LA to record?"

"Um..."

I know that "um" from her. I know what it means, and my stomach sinks like a rock. "You can't leave me, Billie."

"We have to be there Monday to start working. They're ready for us," she says with a sigh and eyes that tell me the rest.

"You can't leave me," I say again.

"I mean, I don't know how long it will take, but it's not like I'm leaving forever. And it's not that far away..."

"Billie, you make this place bearable. You're part of my life now. This is not what I need right now."

"Well," she says, stiff beside me. "This isn't about you, Calum. It's about the band and the opportunity we have to really make something happen."

"It wasn't what you wanted just a few months ago."

"And we've talked about this. It's been going well. It is going well. This is a good thing that's happening."

"For you."

"Yes, for me. And I'd appreciate it if you'd be supportive."

I don't have anything to say. I feel sick at the thought of her being in LA for the next however many months. We're still in season, and I'll go back to play after the holiday break. The holiday break when I planned to take Billie to meet my family in Montreal. I guess that won't happen now.

"Calum," she says sharply, trying to get me out of my own head. All I can hear is roaring. "Calum," she says again more insistently. "Talk to me."

"I can't believe you're going to leave." I say it more to myself than to her. I back up, move away from where she's standing. "I'll get someone down here to help with the kids until it's time to take them back. I— I need some space."

I can feel her stare at my back as I walk away from her.

I can still feel it long after I've left the building.

It's then I recognize that broken feeling within me.

Billie has a bigger, brighter life to lead, something that doesn't need me in it. Soon, she'll press pause and eventually decide being my girlfriend is more like being a caregiver.

And I'll be alone once more.

28

indecision highway

Billie

ikki and Sven are on a Zoom call with me and our agent, and they are, to put it mildly, totally psyched about this deal.

I, however, feel totally overwhelmed. I ask a few questions, and we plan for Monday. But when our agent gets off the call, I say, "Guys, is this, maybe, going a little too fast?"

"No way," they say in unison.

"Billie, we know you struggle with this, but we did the work on the film, and it all turned out fine, right? It sounds good. We got a fat paycheck for it. This is an amazing next step. This is happening. We're really making this happen." Nikki's face is bright and open. She's truly excited, and I feel like a total schmuck for trying to ruin it for her.

"It's just...I have a job I like here. And they need me here. I can't be gone for like six months. They won't hold the job for me."

"Billie, you don't need to work your crappy

nonprofit job when you're making tons of bank doing music," Sven says.

"It's a really good deal, Billie," Nikki echoes. "Don't worry about the job."

"It's not a crappy job," I argue. "I like it. And I want to continue to do it. I love those kids."

"Ohmygod." Nikki scoffs at me and throws up her hands. "Then come back and volunteer every once in a while."

"And Cal..." I add.

"Cal is a grown-ass man who travels a ton for his own job," Sven says.

Every argument I make is met with a rational response, but finally, Sven puts an end to it. He says, "Look, Nik and I talked. We knew you'd freak out. And so we talked."

I feel my eyebrows meet as I frown. "And what was this talk you had?"

Nikki says, "We love you, Billie. You're the best drummer we've ever met. But you're not the only drummer out there."

My face opens back up in surprise. "Oh."

Sven faces off at me with crossed arms. "We don't want to, but if you truly cannot see yourself going all in with us on this project, we can find another drummer."

"My brother would be so pissed," I say.

"Your brother has nothing to do with this deal," Sven snaps back.

"My brother got us the gig that got us this deal. He didn't do it for you two. He did it for me."

"And he also works in show business. He knows

how this works. Lineups change all the time. And Nik and I want this. Only this. Your priorities are all over the place."

I take a second, breathing, to steady myself and my thoughts. Everything is going so fast. They're not wrong to give me an ultimatum. They know how long I dragged my feet on their requests to connect the band through my family. They know I'll hold them back.

I'm not even mad about it.

"We've been working hard, and we are ready," Nikki says. "You are ready. You are talented and we want you there with us."

I take a deep breath. "If I go down this rabbit hole, my life will change into something really different. I'm not sure I'm ready for that life, you know?"

"Well, think about it and call us tomorrow," Sven says.

"Okay." This is the end of the indecision highway for me. *I have to decide.* "Okay. I'll call you tomorrow."

I get off the call and try to call Calum, but as it has since he walked out of the arena earlier, it goes straight to voice mail. I try my brother, and he picks up immediately.

"Hey, sis. How's the hottest drummer LA has ever seen?"

I smile at his enthusiasm but then sigh due to the conflict raging within me. If anyone would get this, he would.

"In a word? Conflicted."

"Hmm. That's not the response I expected. What's going on?"

Being the good big brother he is, he listens to the day's whole story and talks me through each step.

"You're so talented, Billie. The band sounds so great. This is a dream. I cannot advise that you walk away from a once-in-a-lifetime opportunity. If it craps out, you can go and beg for your job back, but for now? I'd go for it."

"And what about Cal?" I ask pitifully. "We just...we just decided to get together. Like official. And I love him."

"Look, if Cal loves you back, he'll support you in pursuing your talents and passions. He plays hockey and you don't tell him not to play because it's dangerous or he has to travel too much, right?"

"Right?" It doesn't sound like a solid answer.

Kit laughs. "Josh and I...he understands the parts of my job that are undesirable. He loves me in spite of all the studio bullshit. Cal will come around."

I thank him and hang up, but I don't feel any better. I know Calum. I know how hard change is for him. I know that our relationship is a steadying factor that has helped him to be more comfortable in Vegas. And he's just getting back to play after his injury. He'll already feel unsteady. I hate what this will do to him.

I know one thing, though.

I can't go without talking to him first.

29
if you go...

Cal

When a knock sounds at my door, I know it will be Billie.

Steeling myself for the heartbreaker I know is coming, I get up from my spot on the couch and check the peephole to confirm it's her.

Oh, it's her...looking just as beautiful and confident as she always does.

I—I can't do this—

I abruptly open the door but turn away, returning to the couch without greeting her or even inviting her inside. It's shitty manners, yes, and she doesn't deserve to be treated this way, but maybe it'll be better for both of us to just rip the bandage off in one fell swoop. I had UNLV football on before she came, so I focus my attention back on the television. A few seconds later, I feel the weight of her body sit on the couch beside me.

We sit in silence for what feels like a long time. *Time that will steal away the last moments we have together. Sucks.*

I can smell the citrusy scent of the shampoo she uses in her hair. I know it now—a combination of lemon and orange with something darker, cloves maybe—I love smelling it when I'm close to her. But when she's gone and in LA to do her album, I won't have the intoxicating scent of her hair around to smell anymore. No Billie. No hair. No citrus-clove shampoo to smell when I'm kissing her neck or waking up to her hair tangled across the pillows.

And that all feels...fucking terrifying.

I love she's here right now, but I also hate the conversation we're about to have. She reaches out and puts her hand on my thigh. "Why are you shutting down on me?"

"You know why." I wish I could say more, but my words won't be right anyway.

"I need you to talk to me about this." She sounds so sad.

"What is there to say, Billie?" When I turn to look at her, she's so perfect, it takes my breath away. Her hair is in a messy bun, the purple ends flipping up in the back. She's wearing a Crush hoodie and a pair of workout leggings. I see her this way when I imagine us being together, living together, making a life together. And I know I should tell her these things. I should let her know how much having her in my life means to me. That I'm in love with her.

But those words are buried and don't come.

"Calum, I know you're upset about me having to go to LA..."

"You know I have a hard time with change. I've told you before. I'm finally happy here. I was playing well until the injury. I like—*I love* being with you. Things have been good. But if you go—"

"I worry that you just like having a person. Like, your person, you know? A person who makes you feel comfortable in an environment." She starts to rub her hand slowly back and forth on my thigh.

"Is that so wrong? I chose *you*. I care about *you*. And yes, it makes me feel steady to have someone to be close to, but it doesn't mean I don't love you. I do love you. You know that."

"We can love each other and be in different places for a while. Being apart doesn't mean we can't still be together. You travel a lot anyway and we talk all the time when you're on the road now."

"I know, but if you go to LA, who says you won't find someone else who's a better fit for you?"

"A better *fit* for me? Like, you think I'm going to accept résumés for the role of boyfriend? Really. Like I'm going to hire someone who better fits the skill set I'm looking for?" Billie laughs bitterly, shaking her head. "It doesn't work that way, Calum. I'm in love with you. With *you*. I'm not looking for someone else because I want to be with *you*."

"Emily found someone the minute I left Montreal."

"Well, I'm *not* Emily." A scowl crosses her face.

"I know, you're nothing like her."

"Do you? Because all I can see is someone who's scared and using his lame ex to shut down on his awesome new rock star girlfriend."

I look at her, and I hope she can see how this makes me feel, how much I want her to stay.

"I'm not Emily," she says again, with a shake of her

head. "I care about you so much and I know this is hard for you, but I'm not her. And our relationship isn't even close to what you had with her. But I need to do this and if you love me, you will understand and support that, even if it makes you uncomfortable. It's just for a couple of months."

"And then what? After you make your album? You go on tour? You leave me behind again?"

"While you continue to travel for hockey? While you're never home for longer than a five-day span before you're back on the road again? While you get to do what you love? You followed your passion even when your parents wanted otherwise. Why is it wrong for me to do the same?"

She's right, of course, but it doesn't change what I know about myself.

"I need stability." I stare down at my hands. "It's not that I don't care about your life and your dreams, Billie. I do. I see how amazing you are at the club helping those kids. The band is awesome, but who knows where it will take you. I'm happy for you, *I am*, but I'm also a realist. I know myself, but more importantly, what I *cannot* do. I know that I cannot do what you're asking of me. The not knowing will fuck me up and I can't go to that place in my head again…*twice* in the same season. I'm the goalkeeper for an elite NHL team. My job is to stop pucks. I won't be able to do that job very well if my head is all fucked from another long-distance relationship breaking down because we're in two different places." I pause. *Fuck, I hate this. I hate this so much. Like a limb is being torn from my body.* "If you go…"

I dare to find her eyes again. One last time of just looking at her and soaking in her image because it will have to be enough. There won't be more. Her dark, soulful eyes fill with tears, cutting me deep for knowing I'm hurting her. *I'm so sorry.* "I just can't go there again."

"What were you about to say before, Calum? If I go?" she asks so softly I almost didn't hear her from the blowing vortex roaring between my ears.

I say the words that'll be the death blow. There'll be no *us* after I say them.

"Then you go, Billie. But we're done."

30
i won't tell if you won't

Billie

The band is in the studio. We've been on a roll, writing some real good stuff that the producers seem happy with. They've been arguing back and forth about our name. "Love Scrum is so pretentious," I hear one of them say in the booth. Sven rolls his eyes as Nikki and I snicker.

As Sven and Nikki play around with a bass line on one of the songs, I sit in the corner with a notebook, writing out some random lyrics that have been swimming in my head lately. Well, ever since I walked out of Calum's apartment with my heart broken fifteen days ago. *God, I miss him.* I have no idea how he became my someone so quickly. Stuart and I were friends for over a decade, but his absence has barely touched me. But losing Calum? Losing him has brought so much sorrow to my heart.

I start humming a tune, then add the words to the song. Before long, I'm singing, feeling all the feelings. My fingers tap out the drumbeat on my thighs.

I look up as I trail off, only to find Nikki and Sven staring at me. The production booth is silent, too, all gaping at me.

"What?"

"Holy hell, girl," Sven says. "You can sing?"

I shrug. "I was just messing around with an idea."

"Well, it was good, for something you were just playing around with," he says.

"Had no idea you had those pipes," Nikki adds. "Want to give it a try with bass and guitar?"

I nod. "I'm game. Sven, you want the lyrics?"

He shakes his head. "Nope. This is all you, Billie."

I sit back, shocked. Sven is a peacock. He does not give up the spotlight like this. He gestures for me to go back to my kit.

"Your lead," he says as they move a mic over for me.

I play around with the drumbeat for a few minutes, and once I get a basic idea going, Nikki and Sven start playing with the bass and guitar lines, adding in some backup vocals. We run through a few ideas, tweaking until we have something that works.

We run it through three times before I'm sure we've got something good. Producers ask if we can record the next go-around just to see how it all sounds, and I give a thumbs-up.

As I sing, I think of Calum. These lyrics are about Calum. About not liking him at first. About seeing what a good heart he has. About falling in love and making love and wanting him so badly, I thought I might burst. About being disappointed. About being hurt but wanting nothing more than to hear his voice.

I'm nearly in tears as we finish it off, and when the song ends, I sit for a minute longer to get my breath under control.

Nikki appears in front of my kit, leaning down to meet my line of sight. "You okay, Billie?"

I sit up, nodding, wiping an errant tear with the back of my hand.

"I know you miss him," she says quietly. "We're glad you're here, but I know it wasn't an easy choice."

I nod. It's all I can think to do. I didn't share what Calum said to me. I didn't tell them that I was given an ultimatum that broke my heart more than I thought it could be broken. I couldn't find those words.

"Want to hear it back?" comes through from the booth. "It was intense. Really, really good."

Sven gives a thumbs-up, and the song flows back into the studio space. I close my eyes as I hear it back, raw and emotional. He's right; it *is* really, really good. Maybe one of the best we've done.

Nikki announces that she needs a lunch break, but I know she must realize I need an emotional break. I give her a nod of thanks as she drags Sven out of the studio. I wander into the booth where one of the producers, a Brit named Colin sits, fiddling with some of the production values.

"This is insanely good," he says. "You literally just made that up today?"

"I've been messing with the lyrics for a few days," I admit.

"Well, still. It's gold. I've only ever seen that come together once before. Insane."

"Thanks."

"Recent breakup?"

I shrug. "Not sure, really. I guess?"

"Ugly emotion makes the best art, luv."

I frown, Colin's comment jarring something down deep, making me think about what he just said. An idea forms...and then the dark clouds part just enough to let some sunshine in.

I know what I need to do.

"Can I...would you let me share this with someone?" I take a deep breath, a hopeful breath. "Like, can I play this for the person I was thinking of when I wrote it?"

"Will he leak it?"

"No." I shake my head. "Don't think so."

"I won't tell if you don't."

We bump fists before he airdrops the raw song file to me from the logic session. *God, I hope this works.*

31
grand gestures

Cal

My first guitar class back since the injury has left me with mixed feelings. The kids are awesome, as always. They surprised me with cupcakes and gave me a bunch of get-well cards and letters they made for me when I was laid up. They told me how much they missed coming to my class. They also told me what a douchebag Barrymore was for injuring my eye. That part felt great (the thing about Barrymore made me laugh) but it's very different now...coming here.

Without Billie.

There's a new person doing her job now. A guy named Marc. He's okay, but he's not her, so not too impressed. He also has a cringy neon-green dye job and it's not a good look. Disturbing actually. I think he scares some of the younger kids a little bit.

After my last guitarist (Keegan) does the obligatory fist bump and heads out the door, an email notification buzzes my phone.

From Children's Services Las Vegas.

It's Billie's email account.

As if she knew my schedule. Knew I'd be here today for my class. And also knew the kids had just left a few minutes ago…

I'VE BEEN SITTING in the same position for fourteen minutes reading her email.

Over and over and over because I can't look away from the words.

As soon as I finish reading to the end, I start over at the beginning and read it again.

To: Calum Lefleur
From: Billie Hirsch
Subject: Something you need to hear

Calum,
I know you're upset. Change sucks and it's hard. For all of us. I raged against it for so long. I had my little job and my little music thing, and everything was fine because I didn't have to face my baggage if I just kept going the same way. And you were the same, right? You could play in Montreal and be a superstar goalkeeper and not have to face the fact that your relationship was stale, and your feelings were only lukewarm.

And then we found each other. And I couldn't stand you at first. I thought you were cocky and strange and a real pain in my ass. But then I saw you with those kids. And I saw the way we matched up, the things we had in common. And I felt the way we fit together. It was electric between us from the start, but then I came to care about you. Eventually, to fall in love with you.

Things will always change. Slightly or a lot, but they will. Change can provide a chance to grow, to make things better, so it's not always a negative thing. And I am willing to weather those changes with you because I want you in my life. But I can't do it if you're always going to shut down on me, to push me away.

I wrote this song for you. Yes, I can sing, too. That's me singing. Listen to it because it conveys all these feelings in a way I probably couldn't in person.

Things are going well here. I hope I'll see you soon.

I love you.
Billie

At minute fifteen, I open the attached file and listen to her song.

To her amazing voice. To the steady drumbeat.

To the lyrics Billie wrote about us.

Reading them over many times, until I've memorized every word and every note of the melody, and it's cemented in my brain going nowhere.

WHEN I HEAD to practice later, it's with her song on repeat in my head.

I do my drills and go to the training room for a workout, the whole time imagining I'm playing the notes of her song on my guitar.

I learn every chord and every word of the lyrics silently in my head, going over it again and again and again.

...But then I saw
Something inside you
Something inside your beating heart
Something for keeping close...

Darin, my goalie coach, stops by to let me know I've been cleared for team training and should be able to hit the ice right after the holiday break.

He also lets me know a decision's been handed down regarding Bryce Barrymore, who'll *most definitely not* be hitting any ice after the holiday break. Not NHL ice for sure. Being hockey royalty doesn't change the fact that nobody can trust him now. Not willing to risk another incident, New York released him from his contract before the NHL Player Safety review was even complete. Given the maximum fines for "intent to injure" and "illegal check to the head" among his many sins, they dumped him down to WHL junior hockey, skipping over the AHL minors altogether. On the record? It's for the purpose of "further growth and development." Pretty sure they mean *emotional* growth and the development of some *anger-management* skills. Barrymore won't be back to the NHL for a long time, if ever. Coach said there's a rumor he's leaving North America to play somewhere in the KHL. The Russian league has a long history of welcoming players like Barrymore, who've had their asses canceled by the NHL.

Hopefully, he gets some help with his problems, but he probably won't. I guess he could write a book: *How I Blew-Up My NHL Career in One Dirty Game, by Bryce Barrymore.* I wouldn't read it though. He's dead to me and, I won't waste any more thoughts on him or time dwelling on what's over and done with. I'm just grateful the fucker didn't end *my* NHL career along with his. My eye has healed perfectly. Thank God.

What has amazed me though? The extraordinary and unmitigated support from the team, Max Terry included. I didn't exactly impress him with my loyalty on our first meet, but he surprised me with his visits and messages of support when I was in hospital and then during rehab. Impressive. I felt a part of the Crush family, something unexpected and welcome.

In the locker room, I shower and dress quickly, eager to get home to my guitar so I can start learning Billie's song for real, not just in my head—

Evan catches me before I can get out the door.

"Hey, Cal, you doing okay lately? You don't seem like yourself."

"Sorry, man." I lean against the wall of lockers with a sigh. "I'll be fine when I get back on the ice. Coach just talked to me. Said I've been cleared for right after the break."

"Not talking about your injury, my guy. You're just a little out of it."

Chewing on my bottom lip, Billie's face comes to mind. I'm not into spilling my feelings, especially not to my captain, but I've heard from Dale during one of his gossip-slash-therapy sessions how Evan and his wife, Holly, had a pretty bumpy road to what seems like a happy relationship now.

"I—I made a mistake...with someone I love." Once I start, the words do come. Evan has always been easy to talk to. "It's been hard to concentrate."

"Your girlfriend?"

"Billie, yeah. The woman I met doing that PR thing at the Crush Foundation Music Workshop. We've been...well, things were good. But she's in a band and so crazy talented. They've been in LA doing music for a movie and now an album and I'm just not comfortable with change. So, I got scared and pushed her away. Told her if she left, we were done. But I think—"

"It was a bonehead thing to do?"

"Yeah." *I know it was.*

"Yeah," he agrees. "It probably was."

"She sent me a long email and a song she wrote, and it's amazing. And I can't get her out of my head."

"That's how you know it's right, mate," he says, clapping me on the shoulder and giving it a squeeze with his big mitt. "Believe me. I have been there."

"I just don't know what I'm supposed to do next. I need to tell her how I feel, but I am not good at sharing feelings. Not at all, yeah?"

"Yeeeaaah." Evan lets out a chuckle and then a slow shake of his head. "Well, here's the thing, a lot of the guys—and that's most of them in this locker room

—who have any kind of relationship worth something has had his head up his arse at one point or another. And to add to that, there's a fun tradition around here of making sloppy, grand gestures once we get our heads right. Maybe you can think of something that would tell her, with no hesitation, that she is the one for you."

I thank him and head out, walking home with Billie's song still on constant repeat in my head.

And wracking my brain for what "grand gesture" I could possibly come up with that would be something worthy enough for the woman I love.

STUDYING the words in Billie's song more intensely, I realize these lyrics are all about me. I did get that vibe the very first time I heard the song, but I just thought the lyrics more *applied to me,* not that the song *was written specifically about me.*

She nailed it. Nailed everything. Even the title of the song.

Even the title of the fucking song.

It's all about not liking me at first. About seeing into my heart and changing her mind about me. About falling in love and making love and wanting to be with me so much, her heart might burst. It's also about being disappointed. And being terribly hurt and then having her heart broken...but still wanting nothing more than to have my eyes on her and to keep me. Her "keeper."

Wow.

THE KEEPER
Music and Lyrics by Billie Hirsch

You were always beautiful to me
Even when I didn't want you
Even when you made no sense to me
Even when you were wrong for me
A beautiful keeper...to me
To me...but so, so, so, so wrong

But then I saw
Something inside you
Something inside your beating heart
Something for keeping close
Your heart was beautiful, too
Beautiful, too...as beautiful as you

I want to live in your eyes
I want them on me...in me
I want them where you can see me
Keep you inside me
Keep your heart loving me
Loving me...until my heart breaks
  through

I'm watching you love me
I'm watching me hate you
I'm watching us battle for something
I should've told you you're worth keeping
We're something worth keeping
A love so worth keeping

You're the keeper I wanna keep
A keeper worth loving
A keeper always beautiful to me
I should've told you we're worth keeping
We're something worth keeping
Love so worth keeping

Wish you would keep me...
If I could give you anything
I'd want to live in your eyes
I want them on me...in me
I want them where you can see me
I should've told you you're the one

Because my body remembers yours
Even with my heart a hurting
I still wanna keep you
Because my body remembers yours
I still want you to be waiting for me
I should've told you you're the one

I should've told you you're my keeper...
I should've told you you're my keeper...
I should've told you you're my...
Keep-er

Five hours later.

"YOU WERE a natural at hockey from day one, Calum. But you didn't start out a superstar goalie. That took years of hard work, of finding your weaknesses and working hard to overcome them. If you can do that, there is absolutely no reason why you can't apply the same logic, the same perseverance to your emotional intelligence as well. And Billie sounds like just the person who will love you as you try. As you practice. As you learn to offer her your heart as well." My mom's soothing words settle over me as I mull them over.

"Thanks Mom, for the wise words. Appreciate you talking to me."

"I know you do, son. I love you."

"Love you too."

I hang up and flop back onto my bed, mentally exhausted but with my mind still stirring.

After spending hours going over the song and far too keyed up for sleep, I'd called my mom just to hear her steadying voice of reason.

She did not disappoint.

Her take on the situation, the lyrics to Billie's song, and remembering what Evan said to me earlier, all help to rattle things around inside my head enough to finally see clearly when I'm hit with an epiphany.

I always *think* I'm not good at sharing my feelings and emotions. That I suck at relating on an emotional level. I know I've told Billie several times, and while it's not untrue, it's also something where I've bought into the narrative over the course of my whole life. An excuse for something that's always been very challenging for me. But still, just another lame excuse for being unwilling to try.

Because sharing my feelings makes me uncomfortable.

Boo. Fuckin'. Hoo.

Just because something isn't easy, or causes discomfort, doesn't mean I can't ever be good at it. I'll have to practice, learn to share my feelings more, and I'll improve. You only get better at something if you practice doing it.

Pretty damn simple when taken down to the very basics. Pretty much like hockey.

I might've always thought I couldn't handle change, but nevertheless, change *will come* into your life. Maybe a lot or maybe a little, but change is coming...like Billie wrote in her email.

Instead of resisting change, I need to be the change.

I can *learn* to share my feelings.

I *can* learn to embrace the changes in my life.

I can learn to grow emotionally.

Learn, *I must.* To use phrasing of a certain Jedi Master.

I don't think for a minute it'll be easy, either. It's gonna be brutally, fuckin', difficult, I'm sure.

But for Billie, I can do it.

For Billie, I will.

I will do this. *Watch me.*

My hands are shaking a little, but at least I know what I need to do. I reach for my phone again and pull up my contacts, finding what I need after a minute of searching. I type out a text to a certain Hollywood celebrity I hope and pray gets back to me just as soon as his superstar ass wakes up in the morning.

32
down the beach

Billie

My mother has the house decorated for Hanukkah in the blues, whites, and silvers of my childhood. The menorah sits on the mantle in my parents' spacious living room, huge windows on either side and views of the California coast just beyond.

I'm sitting on the couch, brooding, listening to the rough cut of the full album. My job now is to listen for any production imperfections and any last changes we might want to make. When my mom wanders in, fussing with the pillows, I take the hint and leave, heading up to my bedroom to finish my work. Kit is supposed to be coming home tonight to light the third candle. It's kind of a joke, I suppose. None of us is all that religious. Still, the tradition is comforting in the way that reflecting on your best childhood memories is heartwarming. He did say he was going to introduce Josh to the fam tonight, so I'll finally be able to meet him. That's something to look forward to, at least. I'm so happy for my brother finding his person, but even thinking about his happiness in love makes the persistent ache in my chest throb a bit sharper for a moment.

My heart is quite simply broken. And I fear it will stay that way for a long, long time. It's been two long and tortuous days since I sent the email with my song to Calum. Forty-eight hours and I've heard nothing from him. I know he got it because the *read receipt* notification came through a bit later, and I know he was there teaching his guitar class the very same day. I check in regularly with my temporary replacement, Marc, who fills me in on what's happening at the center. Marc told me *all* about the welcome back surprise party the kids threw for Calum. Even though I didn't ask, and Marc merely volunteered the information, it was hard hearing about Calum being there with the kids, and me not. But even though my heart hurts dreadfully, it's gratifying to know Calum didn't give up on the kids. He's still teaching them the guitar. *Without me.* But that's good on him. The right thing to do, the decent human thing...and only makes me love him more than I already did.

I realize he's busy getting back in hockey shape after a potentially career-ending injury, but I'd hoped he'd reach out at least with a phone call or something when he heard the song. Radio silence, unfortunately. There was some good news about his eye injury though. Fully recovered with no lasting effects, he's expected to return to play after the NHL's winter pause. I read it on the Vegas Crush website a couple of days ago. *A blessing for which I am deeply grateful.*

With a heavy sigh, I go back to work on the album for another hour before my mom pokes her head in. "Still working, hon?" she asks.

Looking up, I see her inch her way into the room. She glances around, checking it out as if she hasn't been in here in years. Probably hasn't, but it doesn't deter her from coming over to sit beside me on my bed.

We listen to three songs before she pushes pause on the computer.

"Hate it that much?" I can't resist the snipe at her while jotting down notes in a composition book for the song we just heard.

"No. In fact, I think it's really good."

I can't help the look of pure shock that must be crossing my face.

"I've never wanted anything but for you to have an opportunity to show the world how talented you are," she says softly.

"Can you hear what that sounds like, Mom?"

She sighs and folds her hands in her lap. "Billie, I've always seen that light inside of you. That talent. Your dad and I make a business of finding those sparks or making something of them. And you had it. Since you were really little, you had it."

"But I didn't want that life. I didn't want to be made up and paraded around like a singing monkey. And as I got older, the way men looked at me...it was terrifying to be looked at like that as a twelve-year-old."

"I see that now." She shakes her head softly and looks...regretful. Something I don't ever recall seeing in my mother. "I pushed too hard, and I was too blind to what you needed. But I knew you had *it* and I just wanted people to see how good you were. How proud of you I was."

"So why not, like, put me in normal activities like dance classes or whatever? Come cheer on my spring recital like a normal parent?"

"I'm so sorry." Again, not a thing she says very often. It hits me like a ton of bricks that she really means it. "You are extremely talented, Billie. And I know why you left. I pushed too hard and I'm sorry for that. But I'm glad you found something you love. And I'm very proud of what you're making here."

"I'm so scared, Mom," I admit, my voice breaking.

"It can be scary to put yourself out there like this, so publicly. This is big. Your brother's movie. A whole album. It's a new world and it will be very different than the safe one you've built in Vegas."

The thought of Vegas makes me sad. I try to push it away, but I can't because the sadness is always with me now. I blurt out my pain just like I did when I was little. "I haven't heard from Cal since sending him my song. I guess he doesn't feel things after all."

"Oh, my baby." My mom pulls me into a hug and swipes away the tears now rolling down my cheek. "Well, that was the other reason I came up here. There was a 'supermodel handsome'"—she rocks her hands back and forth—"quirky young man downstairs asking for you."

"Was? Cal was here?"

She smiles for real. "Well, he said he'd be down the beach waiting for you. I told him he'd be welcome here in the house, but he said no." She gets up and brushes nonexistent lint off her perfectly pleated pants...and then she takes my face firmly in her hands. "Billie Seraphina Hirsch, no matter the mistakes I've made as a parent, as you'll find when you make plenty of them with your own children someday, nothing changes how much we love you and how much we want for you to be happy. Now dry your beautiful face and go to him."

She kisses me on the forehead before stepping out of my room, shutting the door with a soft click behind her. I stare at the closed door for a beat, indulging in one short moment of pure relief before bursting into action.

My emotions are all over the place as I race around the room, changing out of my jeans and T-shirt into a simple black dress and some silver sandals. I brush my teeth, throw on some minimal makeup, and pull my hair into a side braid.

Not wanting to wait another second, I run down the stairs and out the back door. Down the pier to another set of stairs. Once I hit the sand, my eyes search frantically. I'm looking, looking...for the shape of his body. The shape of Calum.

Finally, when my heart is about to burst right out of my chest to flop around on the sand, I see him.

Down the beach.

Sitting on a large piece of driftwood, elbows on his knees, chin resting on praying hands. Waiting for me just like my mom said he would be.

Waiting for me...

It takes every bit of control I have not to run. Still,

my pace is quick as I make my way toward him, nearly ready to cry again, taking in his sun-kissed hair and handsome face after too many aching weeks apart. I know when he spots me because I can feel his deep blue eyes on me. I can feel my Calum's eyes.

Mine? Please let it be so.

Calum stands as I approach. In khakis and a crisp white button-down, he's simply dressed, but dear God, so incredibly gorgeous. Even after all this drama between us, I still want him as much as ever. Our time apart hasn't changed how I feel. I want to strip him of that crisp white shirt and touch his defined pecs and rippling abs. I want to kiss my way up that hard jawline of his. I want to feel his strong arms holding me up—

"Bil-lie." A catch in his throat as he says my name is his only tell. Whatever this is, it's big for him. He gestures to the driftwood for me to take a seat.

I sit and look up at him, folding my hands in my lap, determined to hear him out. But I can't believe he's here—that my eyes are really seeing him right now.

I can even smell him.

Here on the beach, in the open autumn air, I can smell the glorious scent of him.

In fact, all my senses are working on super maximum overload trying to absorb every detail possible after being starved for far too long.

> *Because my body remembers yours.*
> *Even with my heart a hurting...*
> *I should've told you you're the one...*

Spicy cologne intertwined with his natural scent creates an elixir that should be bottled and sold as something like...*Man Beautiful*...comes into my sphere when he reaches behind the driftwood to pull out an acoustic guitar.

It's inevitable I'll be ugly crying all over this stunning scene in the next few seconds, so I won't even try to stop the tears.

I don't want to stop them.

I need those tears to wash away these last painful weeks without him.

From the very first chord he plays, so many emotions, so many feelings, rush in—and the tears do come...right on cue.

33
ludwig thurman

Cal

From the first strum of the strings, Billie knows what I'm playing.

The song she wrote about me.

Tears well in her brown eyes and start rolling down her cheeks, but then a slow smile spreads across her beautiful face.

I start singing the words to her song and it's truly awful. I have a terrible singing voice. So bad, in fact, that Billie starts to cry harder and maybe laughing at the same time...I think?

I start to laugh too, setting the guitar down and reaching out to offer my hand. She takes it, letting me pull her up and into a hug. I need to have my hands on her, or it feels like I might die. And I'm not even exaggerating a little bit. That's exactly how it feels since I spotted her walking toward me on the beach. It took every ounce of self-control I have not to run up to her.

"I'm an idiot," I rush to explain. "And I love you. I was so stupid. So wrong for pushing you away."

"I've missed you," she says, putting her hand up to the side of my face, caressing gently with her thumb. It's the most wonderful feeling in the world to have her touch me again.

"God, so much," I answer against her ear, feeling her shiver when my lips touch her skin. I hope that's desire making her shiver because I have plans for later that will involve a helluva lot of naked shivering for the both of us. I can't stop my fingers from playing with her braid. "I've missed this hair." I press my lips against the curled purple ends of her braid. "These lips." I take her mouth in a deep kiss that's hot and wet and intense with every bit of passion I can put into it. We've never really had a problem connecting like this though. Chemistry's always been there for us. I was captivated by Billie from the first moment I ever saw her playing those drums up on the stage. And she was *the one to kiss me first.*

I'm in a haze of feelings and emotions that are threatening to incinerate me on the spot. But as I kiss my girl, hold her body against mine, and take in the lovely scent of her shampoo, perfume or whatever it is she wears that intoxicates me, the haziness starts to clear. It all falls away like a dark curtain being pulled open. The late afternoon autumn sun warming the sand, the smell of the ocean, the sound of the waves...*everything* becomes sharply defined in contrast to the woman in my arms.

Billie is in my arms again, kissing me *and loving me* back.

My world and everything in it, rightly clicks back into place.

And then...peace.

Peace comes.

Billie

"YOU LIKED THE SONG, CALUM?" I ask once he allows us to come up for air.

"I loved it. And I hated it because it showed me how badly I'd hurt you."

"Well..." I think that one word is enough to let him know just how much, because he looks sad for a moment as he brushes his thumb down the path of my tears, first one side and then the other. So gently and reverently, he wipes them away. He mouths, *I'm so sorry* and keeps brushing away my tears.

Nodding slowly, I let him know I accept his apology. There isn't anything more to this. We were both truthful with each other at the time, and he honestly didn't feel he could go forward with the relationship. I really hope that's changed though.

"I couldn't get the song out of my head. Couldn't get you out of my head, Billie. Because this is a real thing between us. And I don't want to screw it up more than I already have."

I pull away and look him in the eyes. "Calum, this isn't going to get easier. The album is sounding really good. I think Love Scrum is really happening and that means we'll have to travel and do shows."

"I know, babe," he answers with confidence. "It's okay. I'm okay with it. I was just in my own head, as usual. I was selfish and stupid, but I'm not being selfish and stupid anymore. I'm proud of you, of what you can do. I'm proud to be with you, even if it means we have to be apart sometimes."

He kisses me again and I nearly weep. God, I've missed this. It still feels the same. The heat is still there.

When Calum falls to one knee, I throw a hand over my mouth in shock. He pulls a ring box from his pocket and opens it; a bright, white diamond ring flanked with amethysts sparkling in the late afternoon sun.

"I've never known someone who could make me feel the way you do," he says with one of those just-a-tiny-hint-of-a-smile expressions he's perfected. "I feel seen and understood. Never judged. I know I'm a handful. I know I require special care and feeding. And it's not needing those things that make me want you. It's the way you make me feel when you're near. It's your smile and your talent. It's your laugh and your intelligence. It's the way I want to be close to you, touching you, all the time. Billie, I love you. And I want to make sure you know it every second of every day."

I'm so caught up in his words, what he's telling me...I can't speak at first. Doesn't matter because my Calum isn't finished apparently.

"I was so stupid, Billie. I almost let you go but I don't want to ever let you go. And I won't stop you from pursuing what you're good at. I want you to do this and I will be there to cheer you on. We'll figure it out. It will be fine."

It will be fine.

He just said those words while offering up the most beautiful Ludwig Thurman diamond engagement ring ever created...*to me.* Calum really believes "it will be fine," or he wouldn't say it. I do know this about him.

"Are you going to take a b-breath, my l-love?" I stammer, not sure how I managed to form words to come out of my mouth at all because I'm full-on crying again. Like, a super ugly cry with what must be an absolutely dreadful look to go along with it. Gah.

But I don't care...really.

Because Calum is here, and I think he's asking me to marry him.

"Don't need to take a breath. My heart is breathing for me because you're here. Because I'm looking at *you...my* love. You are the one I choose. On you, I fix my eyes."

He says this without hesitation, without even a beat, and I know he's quoting lyrics from Phil Wickham's "Eyes Fixed." My beautiful hockey goalkeeper keeps kneeling on the soft beach sand and holding onto that open box, presenting the ring to me, forgetting to say the words, not realizing he never asked the question.

But it's perfect.

It's so much my awkward, beautiful, complicated Calum, yes, but really, it's also so very right coming from him this way.

There are no demands or ultimatums given. Just the offering of his love and his commitment to me so I will know without any doubt that for him, this means forever.

Forever.

It's him being the perfectly imperfect Calum Lefleur I love so very much.

And there is only one answer I can possibly give to the question he didn't ask me with words but rather shouted from the rooftops by his deeds.

"Well...I say yes." Then I take the stunning ring from its box and slip it onto my finger, holding my hand out to admire how well it looks sparkling against the sun now beginning its dip down the horizon. I love the band of amethysts surrounding the square diamond. A truly spectacular ring he chose for me.

Calum stands and pulls me to him, his big hockey hands cupping my face reverently before giving me one of those long-lingering-romantic-end-of-the-movie-kisses to make me swoon. He's got that certain something—a special magic that still takes my breath away when he looks at me like he is right now with his gorgeous Van Gogh iris-blue eyes.

But he is also a conundrum. In so many ways.

Sharply serious, brutally honest, deadly handsome. He is all of those, yes. But he can also be wildly romantic, madly passionate, and devastatingly swoony. I've never known anyone like him, and I'm sure it's because God broke the mold when he made Calum Lefleur.

"I think there's paparazzi taking pictures of us," he says against my lips, still holding me close.

"Oh?" I look to the side, and indeed, there are several photographers capturing our special moment, videos rolling and cameras clicking, along with the cheers and whistles from beachgoers who've caught on to a marriage proposal in progress. We've got quite the little press corps on us here. "Do you want me to ask them to stop? Or maybe we should just leave the beach?" I suggest, in case all the attention is making him uncomfortable. Though Calum doesn't seem bothered in the least by other people watching us. He did choose a public beach to do this, after all.

"No need. I think your brother was the one who alerted them."

I feel my eyes go wide. "*My brother* knew about this?"

He nods and presses a soft kiss on my forehead. "Mm-hmm. I needed a little help buying an engagement ring for a Jewish girl I'm going to marry. Didn't want to mess that up so I asked Kit to steer me in the right direction. He took it a step further and came along to Ludwig Thurman with me. Your brother really loves you a lot."

I give him a kiss on the lips. "I love *him* a lot, and he advised you well. Excellent choice in the jewelry store *and* in this ring. I love it so much. I love you so much."

"I'm glad you love your ring, but more than that, I'm just glad you love *me*, Billie Hirsch," he says, taking my hand and bringing it to his lips for a kiss.

Oh, the romance of it all.

I'm really grateful this is being captured on video because now I'll have it forever. I can never grow tired of reliving this beautiful moment—of the start of us.

"I do love you...so, so very much." Pushing up on

my toes, I reach for his lips with mine. "Did anyone ever tell you that you're a real keeper, Calum Lefleur?"

"I might've heard it a time or two, but never from anyone who mattered...until I met this insanely talented, brilliantly gifted, gorgeous drummer for an up-and-coming garage band, I found one night after I moved to Vegas. Thank *God*, I found her. She's the only person I care to hear saying it from here on out." And then he takes my chin in one hand, the other low at my back, tilts me deeply, and completely owns my lips. On the kiss scale? A verifiable ten. *Better be some pictures of this.*

But again, that's so my Calum. He can be assuredly predictable and utterly surprising at the same time. Which makes me all the more mad for him. He's simply perfect just being himself. I'd never want to change him anyway.

We remain on the beach, his strong arms holding me so close I swear I can feel his heartbeat, or more likely my own, thundering away in response to being in his arms. We turn our faces to the ocean for the impending sunset, watching together as the waning autumn sun slowly slips down over the water. Of course, it's a spectacular display of oranges and pinks and every shade of violet the color spectrum has to offer, as if fully aware this is an occasion for celebration.

Mother Nature really does know how to put on a show.

We stay until the sun has disappeared below the horizon before Calum takes his guitar in one hand and my hand firmly in his other. He's not stopped touching me once, and I don't think he will for a while.

Which is perfectly fine with me. I don't want him to stop touching me…ever.

We walk back to the house hand in hand to share the news with my crazy family and to light the Menorah.

But it's a real good guess they already know.

This whole time they've probably been glued to the living room window, taking turns at the telescope my dad has set up in there.

Sounds about right.

epilogue

Cal

Twenty months later.
Grammy Awards, Los Angeles

By some miracle of scheduling, I didn't have a game today, and I don't have one tomorrow, so I'm free to celebrate with my wife-to-be and her family after she and Love Scrum take home the lion's share of this year's Grammy Awards. Not even a question. It's happening—they're winning *big* in multiple categories. They've already won Best New Artist, and Best Soundtrack for the songs they did for Kit's film, and the show is not over yet.

But I've won big, too. Bigger, I think.

Because I'm marrying Billie in ten days, nineteen hours, and twenty-six minutes from this moment. My whole family will be there and so will hers. Also, many of my teammates (former and current) and their plus-ones will be joining in the celebration. Contrary to how I started out in Vegas, hating being there and having no friends, that's all changed in the past year. Never would I have imagined a huge celebrity wedding event with my name attached to it, but it will be that. Billie's parents' Hollywood connections will be there, along with Kit's actor celebrity crew and other big names in the film *and* in the music industry. Crazy. But that's what happens when you fall in love with a famous person. And Billie is. Her name is everywhere, and her fans are many. When Love Scrum exploded on the music scene, it blew up. Pretty much overnight. Lots and lots of attention. Which is part of the reason why we're actually having two weddings. The big celebrity event in Malibu at the exclusive Maramigos Ranch will follow a very small intimate ceremony on Billie's parents' terrace overlooking the ocean and the beach where I proposed to her.

Or, more correctly, the beach where I did everything *but* propose to her.

Like a clueless fuckin' idiot.

Yeah, she told me later I never asked her the actual question; *Billie, will you marry me?* I remedied it and asked her again the next night at sunset on the terrace.

Kind of important, don't you think? Yes, but also not a surprise I screwed up the proposal a little—or a lot—depending on who's telling the story.

Aw, hell, at least it all worked out in the end. Billie said yes to my non-question, told me she thought it was perfect the way I did it, and continues to amaze and captivate me the longer I know her. Yet I'm still learning and working on finding new ways to show her how much I love her and how proud I am of her each and every day.

I don't plan on stopping because the past year has been like nothing I ever imagined would fit into my well-ordered life. But it did. It's also been more than anything I never knew I needed in my life at the same time.

I leased a house for us in the Malibu Hills owned by a big-wig producer friend of Billie's parents who had to relocate to the UK for the foreseeable future to produce a series of franchise films. He wanted someone trustworthy living in his house. "House" not being an accurate description for the place. It's a massive complex overlooking the coast with ocean views in one direction and city lights in the other. Lots of room for Billie to work on her music with the band in its own recording studio. A state-of-the-art home fitness center and yoga studio for our use. Tons of nature trails surround the property for mountain biking and hikes in the cooler mornings, an infinity pool for when it's hot, and an outdoor fireplace area for lounging and watching sunsets together snuggled under a blanket in the evenings. We've done more than watch the sunsets out by the fireplace. What can I say, it's private and romantic, so sometimes we get carried away.

More often than not, if I'm truthful.

Pretty crazy for a Canadian lad who spent months out of every year in the frozen north for his whole life.

Not that we can use the Malibu house all that much while I'm on the road with the team, or she's doing the same with her band, but I wanted us to have our own place to be together. And to have a private place for us to decompress and recharge. The location is close enough to her parents but gives Billie her independence away from them. Which I know is important to her, and even though she just turned twenty-four, she has accomplished so much in her life.

As far as my work goes in Vegas, it's a short forty-minute flight I charter from a reputable pilot that does this for a few pro-sports clients between Vegas and LA full time. He's got the NHL, NBA, NFL, and MLB all represented on his client list, and even an F1 driver now that Vegas just built a track. Sometimes, the other clients might share a flight with me if it works out. It's a lot like having a driver—just in the air—and I've made new friends flying back and forth. Most importantly, though, Billie and I have been making it work for the last year. She comes to me in Vegas if there's a night she's free and I have to be there. We make the most of the time we have *for* each other. I'm still doing the Crush Foundation Music Workshop teaching guitar to the kids. Billie had to give up her job with CSLV, but she loves to come with me if she's in town when I go there to teach a class. She misses working with the kids directly, although she's still involved with sponsorships and volunteering in other ways to support them.

After we got engaged, I did get to take her to Montreal with me over the holiday break to meet my family. Everyone loves Billie, of course. She's easy to love. My grandpa, who played the drums in a Montreal garage band for like five minutes in the seventies, now thinks of Billie as his soul mate. I told the old man to have a look at the ring on her finger because she is taken. My mom and dad are so happy for me for finding Billie. I think they were worried I'd never find a soul mate and that I'd always be alone. I know parents hope and pray for their children to find "their person" even though they're helpless in making it happen. Nobody can make it happen for someone else.

Everyone must do it on their own—find their own happiness.

I know I'm one of the lucky few because I very much did find happiness *and* my true love.

I found her one lonely night while looking for a distraction from a bitterly disappointing trade to a strange city I didn't want to be in.

But that strange and wonderful city wanted me, and it's the reason I am sitting next to the love of my life right now, waiting for her to win the well-deserved recognition at the very pinnacle of the music industry for a song she wrote.

Thank God for that trade.

Everything happens for a reason. Destiny comes calling, and you either answer the call, or you miss it, and it may never find you again.

Thank God for destiny finding me that night.

One night when a beautiful stranger dragged me to a party I did not want to go to (and almost didn't), where she sexy-danced with me, kissed me, and pushed her way into my life with zero encouragement *from* me.

Thank God for that party, and the kiss, and just... all of—

"This is it," Kit says in my ear, interrupting my thoughts with a sharp elbow to the ribs.

Sitting to my left is Billie, clutching my hand in a

death grip as last year's winners approach the podium. I give her hand a little squeeze in return and mouth, *I love you and you're going to win.*

Feels like ages of time as each nominee is named with accompanying video and graphics up on the stage—

"The Grammy for Song of the Year goes to *The Keeper*, music and lyrics by Billie Hirsch."

YEP, yep. My fiancée just won Song of the Year.

For a song she wrote about me.

I watch her make her way up to the stage to accept her award after the celebratory kisses and hugs from me, her parents, fellow bandmates, and Kit at our seats. I know this is all being filmed live, that we're all being captured on video. Every gesture, facial expression, and probably any words I speak are being analyzed and deciphered by lip-reading experts who rabidly follow this sort of celebrity event. But I tune it all out and focus on my Billie. She's the only important thing right now.

And I do mean *only*.

Because Billie Hirsch is drop-dead gorgeous tonight. Full stop.

Well, she has always been in my eyes, even from the very first time I saw her playing the drums in a small Vegas club. She caught my eye then as she catches it now...along with the millions of others watching this the whole world over.

I think I might be jealous of them.

She's in a dark purple dress that clings to her skin like shimmering metal. Her vibrant violet-tipped hair, arranged in a single sculpted wave down her back in the vee of a very low-backed gown, is the stunning focal point as she makes her graceful approach toward the steps to the podium. This video clip of her going up to receive her award could be seen a billion times on every social platform and media format that reports the Grammys.

I know this.

Every eye in the place is on her, devouring every inch of her, admiring her talent and her beauty, falling in love with her if, by chance, they hadn't already in the past year.

She's mine, people.

Yeah, I'm definitely jealous.

My brain goes into a kind of fog as I try to process the magnitude of the moment, what this means for Billie...what this means for me...what it means for us. She's a famous celebrity from a famous family of celebrities, even though she chose not to live her life that way for many years. She might have a harder time doing that now. But that's where I come in. It's my job to be there to support her and protect her from those who might try to take advantage of her fame and talent. Billie's in good hands though. She has a family who loves her and me, of course, who'll do whatever it takes to keep her happy and safe.

My worries fade away though as she begins her acceptance speech, her words of confident but sincere thanks to the fans and to all those involved with the song, captivating the audience into a pointed silence as they hang on to her every word. "…and finally, to my *beloved* for whom this song was written. You fill my heart each day more than the day before. If not for you, I wouldn't be up here right now. My dream is realized because of you. My soon-to-be husband, my lover, my rock, my keeper. I might have to share your 'keeper' duties with the Vegas Crush, but, Calum Lefleur, you are definitely *my keeper*." She points her statuette at me and then blows me a kiss before waving to an erupting crowd as she finishes.

The audience roars their approval as I prepare to respond for all to witness. A camera operator crouches in front of me, and the crowd goes weirdly quiet.

I do not care who hears me because…well, it's totally irrelevant.

I am speaking to her and only to her.

"*I* am *your* keeper."

I think the audience just sighed a collective awww around the room…

"And you are mine, Billie Hirsch."

my thoughts about...

THE *Keeper*

afterword

Extensive creative license was applied in portraying some elements of NHL games, fan events and awards, that would **not happen in real life**. I did this intentionally to create a more enjoyable reading experience within the storyline. These stories have been carefully crafted for your reading pleasure and in no way meant to be a true and accurate representation of NHL best practices and/or official rules currently or in the past.

Hockey Romance F-I-C-T-I-O-N all the way!!!

vegas crush by trope

All books in the *VEGAS CRUSH* series are *STANDALONES* existing in a connected world centering around a Las Vegas ice-hockey team. You can read them out of order if you wish and everything will still make sense with only minor spoilers. I've made a list of tropes for you here.

CRUSHED

BOOK 1

Forbidden, Reformed "Player", Ukrainian/American Hero, Good Girl Heroine, Office Romance, Love in the Workplace, He Falls First, Sports Romance, Team Captain, Social Media Manager, Risking it All for Love, Band of Brothers

BOOK 2

Bad Boy Russian Hero, Virgin Heroine, Damaged Heroine, Forbidden, Office Romance, Hockey Defenseman, Team Physical Therapist, Love in the Workplace, Band of Brothers, Overcoming Self-Doubt and Addiction, Trust

Red ROCKET

BOOK 3

Grumpy/Sunshine, Russian Hero, Feisty Red-Haired Heroine, Forbidden, Office Romance, Hockey Defenseman, Public Relations Manager, Love in the Workplace, He Falls First, Brooding Alpha, Opposites Attract, Band of Brothers

Puck MONEY

BOOK 4

Opposites Attract, Forbidden Romance, Financial Advisor/Client Relationship, Russian/Romanian Hero, Nerdy Young Heroine, Fresh Start in Vegas, Dyslexic Hero, Gentleman Alpha, Good Guy Hero, He Falls First, Age Gap, Vegas Mafia Suspense, Savior Hero, Band of Brothers, Superstar Hockey Centerman

SMOKE SHOW

BOOK 5

Friends to Lovers, Teammates Little Sister, Young Virgin Heroine, Russian Heroine, Boston Native, Bad Boy Hero, Forbidden Romance, First Love, Age Gap, Single "Dad" Vibes, Hardscrabble Upbringing, Band of Brothers, Hockey Defenseman, New Adulting, Found Family

The KEEPER

BOOK 6

Enemies to Lovers, Forced Proximity, Love in the Workplace, Neuro-Diverse Hero, French-Canadian Hero, Rock Chick Heroine, Socially Awkward w/ No Filter, Opposites Attract, Instant Attraction, Fish Out of Water, Band of Brothers, Superstar Hockey Goalie, Rockstar Heroine, Brooding Alpha, Guitar Lessons w/ Cute Kids, Personal Growth, Sacrificing for Love

BOOK 7

Surprise Pregnancy, One Night Stand, Forbidden Romance, Love in the Workplace, Boss/Employee, Office Romance, Sneaky Dates, Instant Attraction, Age Gap, Mature Hero, Gentleman Alpha, Love After Divorce, Can't Keep Their Hands off Each Other, Career Milestones, Team General Manager, Team Nutritionist

BOOK 8

Friends With Benefits, Instant Attraction, He Falls First, Brooding Alpha, Superhero Complex, Gentleman Alpha, Damsel in Distress, Knight in Shining Armor, Living up to Father's Legacy, Vegas Mafia Suspense, Comic Book Nerd, Wedding Planner Heroine, Band of Brothers, Finding Your Voice, Parent/Child Relationships

BOOK 9

Age Gap, Secret Crush, Surprise Pregnancy, Shotgun Wedding, Opposites Attract, The Owner's Granddaughter, The Brooding Hockey Player, Forced Proximity, Only 1 Bed, Career Milestones, Forbidden, Old Family Friends, *Neanderthal* Hero, *Heiress* Heroine, Parenthood, Beliefs, Growing Up, Manning Up, Facing Your Demons, Family Legacy

BOOK 10

Christmas Marriage Proposal, No Third-Act Breakup, Proposal Problems, Brooding Hockey Player Hero, Buying a Home, Festive Holidays, Dear Santa Letter, Gentleman Alpha, Building a Legacy, Comic Book Nerd, Wedding Planner Heroine, Team Captain, Band of Brothers, Family Relationships, OTT Romantic Gifts

about the author

BRIT DEMILLE is the alter ego of *NYT* Bestselling author, Raine Miller, having an absolute blast writing books quite different from what she writes as Raine.

Stories about sexy billionaires [millionaires make the cut too] who fall in instalove with young women who may or may not be virgins, and then go on to make adorable babies together are her favorite themes. In addition to the billionaires, hot hockey players are at the top of her list of favorite heroes, along with royals and ex-military bodyguards.

Most important when she writes a story is a happily ever after. But during the actual *writing* of the story, the most important thing is a cup of hot tea with a splash of milk (and don't forget the stash of cherry Jolly Ranchers). A dog or two will likely be in between her and the chair at any given moment, which is very handy, because they are the ones who approve everything she writes.

RAINE MILLER is a #2 *New York Times*, *USA Today*, and *Wall Street Journal* bestselling author since 2012. Before that, she spent two decades teaching kiddos to read—something she's most proud of. These days, writing steamy romance books pretty much fills up the hours…for which she keeps pinching herself to make absolutely sure she's not dreaming.

#Truth

She has a handsome husband, two amazing sons, and two very bouncy Italian greyhounds to keep her busy the rest of the time. Her boys know she writes romance books but gratefully they have zero interest in reading even a single one. *Thank. God.*

When she's not writing she's likely deep into a hockey game cheering on her beloved *VEGAS GOLDEN KNIGHTS* and dreaming up a new book. The greyhounds are likely to be in her lap while she writes the books or watches hockey—both dogs at the same time of course!

She loves to hear from readers and chat about the characters she's created.

You can connect with Raine on Facebook in her reader group, **Raine Miller Romance Readers.** She pops in to visit most days because it's a super happy place where romance awesomeness abounds day in and day out with the most amazing readers on earth.

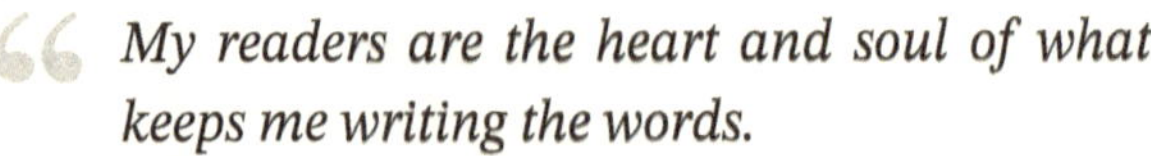 *My readers are the heart and soul of what keeps me writing the words.*

#Truth2

also by raine miller

The BLACKSTONE AFFAIR

NAKED, Part 1

ALL IN, Part 2

EYES WIDE OPEN, Part 3

RARE and PRECIOUS THINGS, Part 4

The ROTHVALE LEGACY

PRICELESS, I

MY LORD, II

BLACKSTONE DYNASTY

FILTHY RICH, I

FILTHY LIES, II

HOCKEY ROMANCE *as Brit DeMille*

CRUSHED, Vegas Crush #1

SIN SHOT, Vegas Crush #2

RED ROCKET, Vegas Crush #3

PUCK MONEY, Vegas Crush #4

SMOKESHOW, Vegas Crush #5

The KEEPER, Vegas Crush #6

LUCKY PUCK, Vegas Crush #7

Mr. HOCKEY, Vegas Crush #8

CLUSTERPUCK, Vegas Crush #9

Mr. HOCKEY's MARRY CHRISTMAS, Vegas Crush #10

CONTEMPORARY ROMANCE

CHERRY GIRL

HUSBAND MATERIAL

LOVELY PINK

HISTORICAL ROMANCE

The MUSE

The PASSION of DARIUS

The UNDOING of a LIBERTINE

Wedding Night Diaries

LORD BLACKWOOD'S VIRGIN

join raine mail

FOR MY NEWSLETTER and information on upcoming books and events, you should definitely sign up for Raine Mail. Use the QR code below.

whispers *There's so many freebies in that thing.*

subscribe to Raine Mail